continued . . .

HAPPY ARE THE POOR IN SPIRIT

Blackie Ryan investigates the attempted murder of the rich and famous Bart Cain and discovers some long-dead ghost in the Cain family closet . . .

"Greeley is a wizard at spinning a yarn."
—Associated Press

"The unflappable Blackie Ryan could definitely become habit-forming."
—*Publishers Weekly*

"Greeley writes with style."
—*Newsday*

HAPPY ARE THE PEACE MAKERS

A Blackie Ryan mystery in which the sleuthing bishop investigates a beautiful widow suspected of murder . . .

"Vintage Greeley, terrific entertainment."
—*Booklist*

"Readers will not be disappointed."
—*Minneapolis Tribune*

"Andrew Greeley just gets better and better!"
—*Dayton Daily News*

HAPPY ARE THE MERCIFUL

A Blackie Ryan novel featuring the perfect locked-room mystery—a double murder beyond belief . . .

"Spellbinding . . . appealing . . . He's a true storyteller."
—*Fort Worth Star-Telegram*

"Keeps the reader captivated!"
—*The Fresno Bee*

"Absorbing and suspenseful . . . another winner."
—*Rave Reviews*

FALL FROM GRACE

A shattering novel of sin and scandal—a woman learns the darkest secrets of politics, the Church, and her own heart . . .

"Shocking . . . Greeley's characters have plenty to confess!"
—Associated Press

"A page-turner!"
—*People*

"With unerring wit and charm . . . Greeley seems to be doing the impossible with his novels."
—*Detroit Free Press*

WAGES OF SIN

A novel about first love and last chances—a man relives the passion, guilt, and obsession of his youth . . .

"Fast-paced . . . romantic . . . emotional!"
—*Publishers Weekly*

"The mystery keeps you guessing until the last page."
—*USA Weekend*

"Entertaining and satisfying."
—Associated Press

AN OCCASION OF SIN

Greeley's boldest masterwork of passion, faith, and sinful secrets—a priest's investigation into the scandalous life of a Cardinal who may become a saint . . .

"An intriguing cliff-hanger to the very end."
—*Pittsburgh Post-Gazette*

"A surprise ending . . . engrossing, entertaining, suspenseful."
—*Publishers Weekly*

"Father Greeley's own special blend of clerical politics, sex, and salvation."
—*Kirkus Reviews*

Also by Andrew M. Greeley

THE BISHOP AT SEA

A BLACKIE RYAN MYSTERY

ANDREW M. GREELEY

B

BERKLEY BOOKS, NEW YORK

THE BISHOP AT SEA

A Berkley Book / published by arrangement with
Andrew Greeley Enterprises, Ltd.

PRINTING HISTORY
Berkley edition / November 1997

All rights reserved.
Copyright © 1997 by Andrew Greeley Enterprises, Ltd.
This book may not be reproduced in whole or in part,
by mimeograph or any other means, without permission.
For information address: The Berkley Publishing Group,
a division of Penguin Putnam Inc.,
375 Hudson Street, New York, New York 10014.

The Penguin Putnam Inc. World Wide Web site address is
http://www.penguinputnam.com

ISBN: 0-425-16080-7

BERKLEY®
Berkley Books are published by The Berkley Publishing Group,
a division of Penguin Putnam Inc.,
375 Hudson Street, New York, New York 10014.
BERKLEY and the "B" design are trademarks
belonging to Penguin Putnam Inc.

PRINTED IN THE UNITED STATES OF AMERICA

10   9   8   7   6   5   4

For Phil Depoy, the President of NORC, who arranged for my ride on a carrier, told me much about the navy, and has been a fine leader of our research center, arguably a more complex task than commanding a carrier.

He is not responsible, however, for any of the ideas and observations that Bishop Ryan, whom he has never met, may make in the course of this book.

I am grateful also to the crew of that ship, which will remain nameless, none of whom are in any way the real-life counterparts of the characters in my story. Like the bishop, I was deeply impressed by the technology of the ship and the professionalism of the men and women who staffed it. Like the bishop, I had unresolved questions, particularly about the mixing of genders on the ship—not so much questions about whether it should be but how it would work out.

And how soon.

I am also grateful for the helpful comments of Captain (Chaplain) Richard "Ace" Dempsey, U.S.N. (Rtd), pastor of the Church of the Most Holy Redeemer in Evergreen Park, Illinois.

I also am grateful to Joel Foster of Martin-Baker for providing information about the Navy Aircrew Common Ejection Seat.

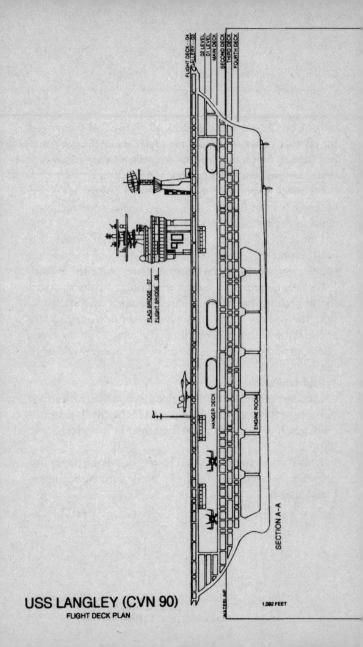

USS LANGLEY (CVN 90)
FLIGHT DECK PLAN

FLIGHT DECK - 04
GALLERY - 03
02 LEVEL
01 LEVEL
MAIN DECK
SECOND DECK
THIRD DECK
FOURTH DECK

FLAG BRIDGE - 07
FLIGHT BRIDGE - 06

HANGER DECK

ENGINE ROOM

SECTION A - A

WATERLINE

1,082 FEET

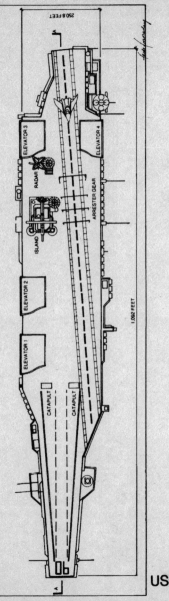

USS LANGLEY (CVN 90)
FLIGHT DECK PLAN

THE
BISHOP
AT
SEA

PRELUDE

SHE WAS TOTALLY the best pilot on the ship. Still, night traps were scary. Mary Anne had told her that it was like you're in a car without headlights going 150 miles an hour down a narrow, dark road toward a one-car garage illuminated by a single lightbulb. If you get through the garage door, your car will stop automatically. And the garage is moving around.

Tonight you had to hit the garage in a rainstorm.

Tonight her first try had better be good if she didn't want a swim in the Pacific Ocean. In her flight suit. She had only a couple of hundred pounds of fuel left—the air boss had delayed her till the end because he had confidence in her.

"N3212, Hornet," she says. She glances at the console in front of her, checks her speed, makes sure that the landing gear and flaps are in position and the arresting gear is down; "ball," she adds, indicating that she can see the glidescope indicator. "Three hundred pounds," she concludes, meaning that she hasn't much fuel left.

"Roger ball," the LSO replies.

Drat! That amadon again, the only one of them left that thinks its funny to haze a woman flyer as she's trying to land. Just her luck to get him for a night trap in foul weather.

All of them had hazed a woman officer on another ship, the first woman to fly off a carrier deck. They waved her off on what might have been good traps and let her land on dangerous ones. Finally, they waved her off seriously, and she didn't believe them and she tried for the trap and got herself killed.

Murdered would be a better word.

She adjusts the controls rapidly and skillfully to keep the amber ball on the side of the deck aligned with the row of green lights.

"A little too high," the LSO tells her.

She's not too high at all. She's never too high.

Fifteen seconds.

"Foul deck," he shouts, "wave off."

She slams the throttle forward and soars over the ship and back into the dark and rainy night.

"Want to try it again?" the air boss asks lightly.

"Was the deck really foul?"

"Will worry about that when you're down."

"Roger."

She goes through the routine again.

"Roger ball," he says with a laugh in his voice.

The garage is swaying more, the lightbulb is dimmer. She juggles the wheel a bit. The ball is right on.

"A little too low this time, Hornet."

She ignores him. Airspeed 150, any slower and the Hornet stalls.

"Still too low," the LSO shouts.

The heck if she is.

Her aircraft hits the deck with a jolt, rolls forward at 150 knots, she feels the three-wire catch the tailhook and jams the throttle forward. An invisible hand pulls the Hornet down to the deck and slams it motionless. She pulls back the throttle. The wire releases her and, like a dangerous snake, slips back into place.

Perfect trap. Naturally. Still the best pilot on the ship.

"Nice to have you back," the air boss says, relief in his voice.

"N3212, all the way up front," deck traffic control tells her, "three slot. Get it out of there."

Man with a rotten disposition.

She begins to taxi forward and away from the landing deck, though there are no planes after her.

The engine flames out.

"Thirty-two twelve, what the fuck is wrong with you?" Traffic demands, "I said get it out of there."

"You put in some fuel, and I will," she tells him. "Otherwise, send a tug."

"Roger," he backs off, knowing that they could have had a disaster on their hands if she had flamed out ten seconds before the trap.

"Air boss, are you still there?"

"That's affirmative."

"Was the deck fouled?"

Hesitation. "It didn't look that way to me."

The tug hooked on to the nose landing gear.

"Would you send a message up to the skipper for me?"

"CAG?"

"No, the big skipper, the one they call Speed."

"If it's not obscene."

"I am *never* obscene; you know that."

"What's the message?"

"Tell him I'm turning in my wings tonight unless he gets that would-be murderer off this ship."

"Roger," the air boss says.

He doesn't doubt her for a minute.

He'd better not.

CHAPTER 1

"I REALLY WOULD like to be able to make this trip, Blackwood." Cardinal Sean Cronin swept into my room like a comet with a Japanese name, a burst of energetic fuzz. "I've been counting on it."

I thought that most improbable.

"Indeed," I said, sighing loudly and permitting myself to reveal more than a little skepticism.

The archbishop of Chicago and cardinal priest of the Holy Roman Church was attired in his ordinary battle fatigues—perfectly fitted and perfectly pressed black trousers, tailor-made white shirt without collar but with cuff links on which glowed his coat of arms, and black loafers that were immune to the grime that affects the shoes of mere mortals.

He was carrying a baseball cap whose configuration he was carefully hiding.

"That idiot from Omaha called for a meeting of the administrative board in Washington and then your friend over in Rome wants to see a bunch of us about some problem they're having in Africa."

Tall, handsome, and with blond hair now mostly white and with a neatly carved face, Sean Cronin looked like a cardinal ought to look—or like the captain of an Irish mercenary band a few centuries ago who didn't care whom he fought against so long as they were either English or allies of the English. His piercing blue eyes,

behind which lingered demons known only to God, were
normally hooded—until he burst into manic laughter.

"Indeed," I sighed again. I knew what was coming, but
it is necessary that our little pas de deux be acted out so
that Milord Cronin could feel that he had not imposed
upon me and so that I could make the point that I was
being imposed upon.

He busied himself exploring the inner recesses of my
liquor cabinet. Disregarding the panel that hides the
secret cache in which my precious supply of Bushmill's
single malt resides, he removed the green-labeled bottle,
poured a generous portion for me and a small splash for
himself—as though it was his suite and his Waterford
crystal tumblers.

I had saved the file on which I was working, a study of
the work of our local story-telling theologian John Shea,
and tried to peer at the partially hidden baseball cap.

"So I'm afraid I'm not going to be able to make the
trip. My cousin Dave was really counting on it."

He glanced around my study, looking for a vacant
place on which to sit. He removed a stack of laser printer
output from my most comfortable chair and, with a
characteristic movement of exhaustion, sank into it. Above
him the three Johns of my youth—pope, president, and
quarterback—smiled blandly down upon him. I chose to
imagine that the ivory medieval Madonna, alleged to
look like my mother, God be good to her (and She'd
better or She'd hear about it) was frowning her disapproval.

Recently, these worthies had been joined by a photograph of a young woman with whom I had fallen in love,
Clare Marie Raftery, a maid of all work on Prairie
Avenue, long since gone home, who had helped me solve
a locked-room mystery a hundred years old.

"Most unfortunate," I agreed, as I tried to remember
who and what his cousin Dave was and did.

"Yeah." He leaned back in the chair, crossed his long

legs, and sipped slowly from his tumbler. "To tell the truth, I was looking forward to it."

In a pig's eye, not to put too fine an edge on the matter. He was only too happy to dump this responsibility on his always faithful auxiliary bishop, John Blackwood Ryan. What is an auxiliary bishop? Those of you who have seen the film *Pulp Fiction* will doubtless remember Harvey Keitel. He was a sweeper, a person designated by God and his betters to sweep up the mess left by higher-ups in the outfit. That's what I am, Sean Cronin's sweeper.

"Indeed?"

"Yeah," he shook his head in a poor attempt to be disconsolate. "So I guess I'll have to ask you to go out there and do the confirmation for me, if you possibly can."

The final clause, need I say, was window dressing.

"A cathedral pastor has many responsibilities," I sighed, "in the middle of Lent."

"One of the younger guys will do a good job in our absence. Maybe better."

"Arguably."

Just then I saw the legend on the cap. CVN 90. I remembered who his cousin David was and what he did. He was captain of a nuclear-powered aircraft carrier, the *Langley*, so called because it was the name of the first such craft that the Navy had used and, according to rumor, it would also be the last. My stomach knotted in protest at the thought.

"It will be an easy trip, and besides, you need a few days off. They'll pick you up in a limo at San Diego International and take you over to North Island. Then they'll fly you out to the *Langley*. You'll get the red carpet treatment—simulated rank of a rear admiral. You do the confirmation, and they send you home."

He handed me the cap, awash in gold braid as though he were passing over the archiepiscopal pallium.

"We Ryans," I said in doomed protest, "do not like to travel. Indeed, the ride from Chicago to the stadium of the Fighting Black Baptists is arguably as far as we are inclined to wander."

"Your sibs wander all over the world . . ."

"Only in the interest of facilitating marital romance, a challenge from which I have been dispensed."

He ignored me. "They won't fly you out in a high-performance jet. It'll be a courier plane they call a COD. Twin propjets. Easy landing."

"A carrier landing," I insisted, "is nothing more than a controlled crash."

He waved his hand. "Perfectly safe. A little adventure will be good for you."

I inspected my Waterford tumbler. As often happens, the leprechaun who inhabits my rooms had disposed of most of its contents.

"And they hurl you into the air with a steam catapult just as David hurled stones at Goliath."

"You're strapped in so tightly that you hardly feel it. I kind of worry about my cousin. He lost both his parents early in life. Had to fight for everything he's ever got. Now his whole career is in jeopardy. Youngest captain of a carrier in many years, too."

Now we were getting to the heart of the matter.

"So?"

He frowned and waved his empty glass, a man puzzled by mystery.

"Crew members keep disappearing. Officers, some of them. Over the side, presumably. Carrier is said to be haunted. Something about the name."

"Indeed?"

Milord Cronin considered me over the top of his tumbler, his eyes peeking from behind the hoods.

"Yeah. Something about locked-room mysteries on the ship, too. Locked hangar deck, for all I know. Haunted carrier with locked rooms."

He paused, waiting for my reaction. He knew that the mix of the occult (more likely the pseudo-occult) was irresistible to me, Lent or not.

"Fascinating," I murmured because that is my required line under such circumstances.

"A haunted carrier commanded by a cardinal's nephew." He shook his head, as though such a phenomenon might be scandalous. "That's all we need right now. Totally unacceptable."

He sprang to his feet, about to turn again into the racing ball of intergalactic ice and gravel.

"Totally unacceptable."

"Doubtless."

He pointed at me, his arm outstretched like the lance of an improbable medieval knight.

"The last thing I need is to have my name associated with a haunted aircraft carrier!"

"A most embarrassing accusation."

"See to it, Blackwood!" he ordered with his most manic laugh.

He blazed out of the room, leaving me to consider what kinds of motion sickness medicine I should procure. Arguably, every variety they made.

CHAPTER 2

"THIS IS A lot of bullshit, isn't it, Bishop?"

Vice Admiral Richard "Night Plane" Lane said with a crooked grin. Vice Admiral Lane was COMNAVAIR-PAC (Commander, Naval Air Pacific) and his remark was accurate.

"Arguably," I replied. "Though not uninteresting bullshit."

We were seated in the admiral's mahogany-paneled corner office on North Island. The office was a mini-museum of plane and ship models—everything from the old bi-wing Curtis Helldivers to the F-18, from the *Enterprise* of World War II to the current nuclear-powered ship of the same name. He was impressed that I could identify most of them. I refrained from saying why the United States Navy had interested me all my life.

Until his expletive, the said United States Navy had pretended that I was just one more very important person (*very,* very important, according to Milord Cronin). They would treat me with the same courtesy and charm, reminiscent of the Old South, as they treated all the guests who flew out to the carrier currently off San Diego. There was, they would assume, nothing at all peculiar about this barely noticeable little cleric. Certainly he could not be a specialist in such improbable events as haunted ships. There were no haunted ships in the final decade of the twentieth century, were there?

11

On the monotonous and bumpy trip from O'Hare to San Diego International, I had pondered the tidbits of information that Milord Cronin was able to provide: some sort of drug scandal, not too unusual in the services these days, since most of the enlisted persons were still in the stage of late adolescence that now persists often into the middle thirties. Officers involved. Promptly cashiered. Enlisted men sent to prison. A suicide or two. Then the suicides reappeared on the ship. More men over the side, including the XO (executive officer) who had broken the drug ring. Removed from his locked and guarded stateroom in the middle of the night.

Well, at least the hangar deck (also unaccountably called the main deck)—a cavern two stories high and running from bow to stern—wasn't the locked room.

On the basis of such information, there were a number of simple explanations for the mysteries on USS *Langley*. Unfortunately, the Naval Investigation Service people surely thought of the same explanations. Someone had leaned on Sean Cronin to send his unobtrusive little alter ego to Lala Land because the simple explanations had all failed. There was no reason of which I was aware that I wouldn't also fail. I have a very bad record in such matters, no matter what Milord Cronin thinks.

The *Langley,* I had determined from a book that reported on such matters, was a Nimitz class nuclear-powered carrier, which meant that the turbines were turned by steam generated not by diesel fuel but by heat in the nuclear reactor. It displaced some 92,000 tons. With full sea and air crew, it was manned and womaned by some 6,000 human beings, which, as I calculated, meant 18,000 meals a day. It carried eighty aircraft, all capable of one kind or another of destruction, mostly F-14 Tomcats and F-18 Hornets, but including such specialized craft as Vikings, Hawkeyes, Prowlers, and Shadows, all with mysterious electronic responsibilities. It also carried some five million gallons of jet fuel and some 2,500 tons of aviation ordinance, none of which, I was assured, was nuclear. Not on this training mission. Its flight deck was 1,092 feet long and 250.8 feet wide, more than three football fields, hardly enough, I would have thought to land airplanes on, especially an airplane with me on board. It was seventeen stories high from keel to flag bridge and rushed through the water at the speed of 31 knots, water ski speed.

It distilled 400,000 gallons of fresh water from the sea every day. Liquor was forbidden on the ship, though I had doubts about how effectively that rule was enforced.

Judging by the diagrams, it was a rabbit warren of rooms (*spaces* in the Navy term), compartments, passageways, and ladders. The printed information said that there were "3,000+" spaces, as though that were a pretty good guess. Did anyone on the ship, captain included, know who or what was supposed to be in each one of these spaces? I doubted it. What did a locked room mean on a seagoing bemouth like the *Langley*? Moreover, could not one hide on it for days or even weeks and not be found? Maybe the ghosts were merely persons who, for reasons of their own, were hiding till the ship returned to North Island.

I did not like the looks of the problem, nor did I like my role. Six thousand men and women were enough for a moderate-sized parish. My task was to explore that parish for a few days and find out what had gone wrong in it.

As is generally known by my siblings and their offspring and my friends, I have tendencies to get lost. Even in my own parish. Hence the terminal building at San Diego International presented something of a puzzle that demanded solution. Clutching my precious Compaq 5200 computer, I stumbled and bumbled around and found myself back at what seemed to be the gate where I had disembarked from the 767. Finally, deciding that it

was time to do the very unmale thing and ask directions,
I had sought help from an airport police person.

"You go straight ahead, Father. Then, at the very end
of this concourse, you turn right, then turn left, ride down
the escalator to get your baggage, and go out the glass
doors. Ground transportation is right outside."

Presumably, the clerical shirt, even sans collar, had
revealed my status.

It was fortunate that she had mentioned the baggage.
Eventually, and by dint of monumental effort and con-
centration, I found the baggage carousels, miraculously
recovered my two bags, and ascertained that I had merely
to walk out the glass doors to escape definitively from
the terminal.

If I had had trouble in a place as relatively simple as
an airport terminal, what would happen to me on a
seventeen-story ship with "3,000+" spaces?

I had been told that I would be met by the Navy at San
Diego International. I wondered how they would recognize a virtually invisible little bishop, especially in his
routine travel array of clerical shirt without collar and
Chicago Bulls windbreaker. However, the eager young
lieutenant commander in neatly pressed khakis had no
problem discovering me as I emerged from the terminal,
dragging my bishop's clothes in an oversized suitcase
and blinking against the sunlight, which we had not seen
in Chicago since early November. Possibly, my baseball
cap, which proclaimed "USS *Langley*, CVN 90" helped
him to identify me.

"Welcome to San Diego, sir," he had said with a brisk
salute. "Welcome to the North Island Naval Air Station,
sir. Let me carry those bags, sir. Seaman, take the
bishop's bag. Right this way, sir. We have our car just
across the street, sir."

I had noted that the seaman, who was also the driver of
the car, did all the bag-toting. In a nice switch, the latter
was white and the commander was African American.

"I'm Commander Dawson, sir. I'm deputy public affairs officer. This is Seaman Crane, sir."

I had sighed loudly, and, though I knew it would accomplish nothing, used my favorite opening line.

"Call me Blackie."

"Yes, sir."

Which of course meant, "No way, sir."

We had driven along the bay toward downtown San Diego, inched over to the freeway, and crossed the Coronado Bridge. I had noted that, as advertised, San Diego was the prettiest city in our republic, especially after the typical Chicago winter. However, I had told myself, it lacked the interesting culture and social structure of the City that Works. Richard M. Daley, Mayor.

Nonetheless, the pervasive blooming flowers exercised a certain hypnotic effect on me. It was not essential to the nature of things that one endure snow and cold four months of the year. Nonetheless, I told myself as we sped over the bridge to Coronado Island, which looked like it might be on loan from Disney World, this subtropical paradise lacked fifty aldermen, Lake Michigan, and Michael Jordan—and Dennis Rodman, as far as that goes.

We encountered little opposition at the entrance to the North Island Naval Air Station, arguably because of the blue flag with the three stars that flew from the prow of our Ford Victoria.

"Bishop Ryan for the admiral," Seaman Crane informed the Marine who glanced in our car.

"Yes, *sir!*"

The Marine saluted like he was a Swiss Guard and I was the pope (at least).

I warned myself that, jet lagged or not, I must respect the mores and the folkways of this institution. All human groups have such customs. Once the church emphasized courtesy and respect as much as the navy did. We had abandoned all such mummery and had not thereby improved the efficiency of our service or our charge to reveal God's love to all whom we encountered.

"Thank you, Sergeant," I said to the marine.

"He was only a lance corporal, sir," Commander Dawson advised me.

"Any enlisted man who salutes like that deserves to be called sergeant." I responded with my West-of-Ireland sigh.

The commander chuckled at my wisdom.

"Yes, *sir*."

Privately, I wondered when the last time was that the lance corporal had actually seen a lance.

"Admiral Lane's nickname, sir," the Commander had continued (actually he was a lieutenant commander, his oak leaf being gold instead of silver, but since he always called himself "commander," I went along), "is Night Plane. It refers to his success as a night pilot in the western Pacific. Some call him Night Train; but patently that is inaccurate."

"Patently," in fact was one of my words.

"Possibly a reference to the storied Night Train Lane, a defensive back who now rests securely in the NFL hall of fame."

"Possibly," the commander agreed.

Despite two massive and foreboding aircraft carriers parked at the dock across from the Naval air station, it looked like a peaceful, sun-drenched enclave designed in the New Deal modern architecture of the 1930s. The headquarters of COMNAVAIRPAC, with its plain and efficient facade, was the kind of place from which one might expect a very young John Wayne in dress whites to emerge without the knowledge that we possessed that the Japanese would attack Pearl Harbor in twenty-four hours.

However, the man in rumpled khakis and a wind-breaker who was in fact standing on the curb as we had pulled up was not a John Wayne type. Rather, I thought he might be star softball player on the North Island team (should they be so wise as to play sixteen-inch softball, patently the only kind). He had curly blond hair, an open and intelligent face, and a warm grin.

"Dick Lane, Bishop Blackie," he informed me as he opened the limo door, his blue eyes twinkling, "Welcome to North Island. It's good to have you aboard."

"It's good to be aboard," I lied, bemused by his charm.

"Sir!" said my two companions.

Only then did I note the three gold stars lurking on the lapel of his jacket. This was not the kind of admiral that one would have expected from the John Wayne films.

"Thank you, men," he said to my companions. "We'll talk for about an hour and then take the bishop over to Halsey Field. Guard his luggage carefully. They'll take care of the computer, Bishop. I promise you it will be as safe for the next several days as if you had left it in a convent, if things are still safe in a convent. Did you have a nice trip? We have a cup of tea and sweet rolls waiting in my office. Sorry we haven't anything stronger, but technically, this Navy is dry."

He had put his arm around my shoulder and led me into the building. Arguably, Milord Cronin had been correct. I was a *very,* very important person.

I had concluded that Night Plane Lane was very bright, very affable, very articulate, and a very tough man, patently much to be preferred to my stereotype of a Navy admiral.

As he had led me through the building, pointing out the famous pictures and memorabilia and later in his office, he made the case for his command.

The navy had twelve carriers, eight in the Pacific, four in the Atlantic. The eight "worked for him." They rotated between interludes of refitting at shore stations, training exercises off the coasts, and sea duty in the western Pacific and the Indian Ocean. He didn't claim to know what global strategy the United States wanted to follow.

He continued, "Carriers, however, are highly sophisticated masterpieces of technology. The eighty planes that each one of them carries could do more damage and do it more quickly than all the carriers in the fleet put together during the Second World War and indeed during the Vietnam mess, too. In an era of limited wars, any war lord would think twice about messing with the United States if one or two of these were sitting off his coast. We are five generations ahead of the Russians in technology and moving even farther ahead. When we finally let them on our ships, their eyes watered. If they'd seen what we had twenty years before, they might have ended the Cold War then. You'll be enormously impressed by the technology out there on the *Langley*. You'll be even more impressed by the young men and women, most of them under twenty-five, who operate the technology. They're skilled, responsible professionals, immensely proud of what they do and eager to explain it to you. They're the best thing the navy has ever done. A year ago, you wouldn't have lent any of them the keys to your car."

We spent some time tracing the location and movement of his ships in the Indian Ocean on live satellite. He can pinpoint them every hour of the day or night.

"More tea, Bishop? Just a sec, I'll have one of my aides get us some more Danish. Sweet rolls to you Middle Westerners.

"Race? Every color imaginable: white, black, brown, Asian, and everything in between. They might not get along all the time off duty, though we haven't had any serious problems in several years. But on duty, they work together like competent colleagues. It's the work that shapes the culture on ship.

"Women?"

Slight pause while he moved his feet on his office desk.

"We have an informal goal of at least twenty percent. That's not for political reasons, though I suppose we're not unaware of that aspect of things. We need them. To keep a complex and intricate ship like the *Langley* running, you need intelligent people. If we exclude women, we are simply not going to have a large enough pool to choose from. They are at least as competent as the men, maybe more so. We don't tolerate either fraternization or sexual harassment—and sometimes it's hard to tell the difference. The Navy has learned its lesson, though heaven knows, it took us long enough."

Another pause while he ran his hand through his curly hair.

"OK. You got men and women at sea for six months. They're young, and their blood is teeming with hormones. So you're going to have fraternization. We just don't want it to be obvious. Women on board, women as shipmates, change the whole atmosphere of the ship. Not necessarily a bad thing. I think it's good in many ways. They learn a lot about each other. But different, oh, is it different. Tensions, lots of tensions. Sexual fantasies all over the place. Sex pervades the ship. On everyone's mind. But it would be, even if there weren't women on board. Maybe they make it more realistic. I don't know. On the whole, I don't think it's any worse than a big coed dorm at a university. And if some people fall in love and decide to spend their lives together, hey, isn't that what life is about?

"Exploitation by officers? Not twice, you can bet on that. Officers' wives are very uneasy about the whole business. I'm kind of glad that I'm not a captain of a ship any more. Still, the guys who are say it is an interesting life."

Then, the routine sales pitch having been made—and maybe more candidly to me—he had dismissed it as all bullshit.

"Do you believe in this ghost stuff, Bishop?"

He moved his feet off his desk, leaned forward on his chair, and studied me intently.

"In principle, I think we have an open universe where wonderful things happen. Quarks, quanta, chaos, etc. I don't believe in putting constraints on the marvelous. In practice . . . I have rarely encountered any phenomena for which I can exclude the possibility of a purely natural explanation. The trick, of course, is defining the outer borders of the natural."

Admiral Lane nodded thoughtfully. "Yeah. I know what you mean. Me, I don't believe in ghosts, either. Still . . ."

"Still?"

"You've never been at sea for a long period of time, have you, Bishop Blackie?"

"Not even for a short period of time."

"At night . . ." he paused, as if searching for words. "At night, when you're out there alone, just a few ships in the middle of an empty ocean, and there's no moon or its obscured by the clouds, you sometimes get a sense of the uncanny. Like you're a tiny blob of protein floating around in a huge and mysterious cosmos and that there are forces and energies all around you that you can't comprehend and that we mere humans will never comprehend."

I listened quietly. The human mind, I had come to believe, is quite incapable of finding The Answer, however well it may come up with partial answers like general relativity and the double helix. We finally will not be able by methods of science to comprehend the incomprehensible, no matter how hard we try; someone's idea of a joke. Or, arguably, Someone's.

"I don't know . . ." he began again. "Well, I'm not sure. . . . See, one night I was leading four planes back from a raid in Nam, supporting some marines that had got themselves in trouble. The weather was bad enough when we took off. It got a lot worse than our meteorology guys thought it would. That's your chaos for you. Our instruments were acting weird. I had no idea where the ship was or how to get there. Our fuel was marginal, at best. Then the captain that had been our CAG—that's Commander Air Group—showed up just off my wing. He led us back to the ship. If he hadn't been there, we would have ditched in the China Sea with a typhoon brewing."

"A fortunate appearance."

"Yeah . . . especially since he'd been dead for four months. Two of the other guys saw his plane. Fourth pilot denied it, but I think he was too scared to admit it. We never told anyone on the ship. I don't talk much about it, even today."

"Understandably."

"What do you make of it?"

"I don't."

"Neither do I. . . . Then, later on, before I was sent to the Pentagon, I was skipper of the *Lexington*. You know, it was named after the carrier we lost during the war. . . ."

"Battle of the Coral Sea. She and her sister ship, the *Saratoga,* were laid down as battle cruisers and converted to carriers."

Night Plane Lane's eyes widened.

"I never knew the battle cruiser thing. I won't argue with you." He grinned, waiting for an explanation. I might tell him sometime, but not today.

"Well, there apparently was some mystery about how the ship was sunk. . . ."

"Poor decisions by an admiral. They could have saved it."

This time, he didn't even pause to wonder about my knowledge.

"The captain didn't die on the ship, did he?"

"Not to my knowledge."

"That's the way I understood it, too. Yet . . . somehow . . ."

I waited.

"Somehow, they say he got my ship confused with his. He used to walk the decks at night, get lost sometimes, because the configuration was so different, even appear briefly on the bridge. Harmless ghost, more confused than anything else."

"You saw him, of course?"

"A couple of times. Always at night. Once on the bridge. Once walking down a deck with his back to me. Turned a corner and was gone by the time I got there. Once in my stateroom when we were about to get hit by a storm. Very quick each time, blink of an eye. I thought it might just be my imagination. Maybe that's all it was."

I was shivering by now, despite the San Diego warmth.

A lieutenant (woman) brought in another pot of tea and a half dozen more sweet rolls.

"I don't want to spoil your lunch out on the *Langley*," he said with a laugh.

"Small risk of that."

He waited till the aide was out of the office.

"So, you see, when people say to me that there are ghosts out there on the ship, I act like an admiral who is responsible for eight aircraft carriers and say it's nonsense. There's human evil and nothing more. But I think to myself that maybe I'm not so sure."

"Indeed. . . . Experiences like yours off Vietnam were, I presume, not uncommon?"

"You whisper about them after a couple of drinks or tell them as tall tales that happened to someone else. . . . Anyway, something weird is happening out there on the *Langley*. Here's the report the navy investigators put together. Tells exactly nothing, which is not their fault. So I guess that's why you're here."

"An exorcist I am not," I insisted firmly as he passed over a thick file.

He grinned. "Just a damned smart guy with a flair for the weird is the way I heard it."

"Possibly," I said, secretly very pleased, especially with the second half of the compliment. "Why don't you summarize the problem for me?"

"Speed Cronin is one of our best. Fine pilot, great leader, next step up will be to rear admiral. Certainly three star material, maybe even four. Maybe even CNO someday. Especially good on safety. You see, we used to lose as much as ten percent of our air crews. When Speed was CAG of Air Wing Nine, he began a kind of personal crusade to upgrade our safety procedures. He lost only one air crew during his last year as CAG—that's the old name, commander air group. We still use it, even though we've changed the name to air wing."

"I see," I said.

"Don't get me wrong, Bishop. There's more at stake than Speed's career, which is in deep trouble, by the way. But he's the focus of this whole weird business."

"Indeed."

"So he's sent to Washington for two years to develop a program for all the air wings. It involves a whole set of procedures: elaborate, detailed, almost compulsive. But it works. We're not losing air crews anymore. Some ships go through two or even three years without a loss. People stopped griping about Speed's system when they looked at his rates. He comes back here to be captain of the *Langley*. While they're refitting here in the yard, everything goes fine. He's an even-tempered gentleman who would rather charm you than browbeat you. Mind you, there's plenty of steel beneath the sweetness."

"Doubtless."

"Well, then they send him a new XO, Commander E. Rogers Hoy. As soon as the news is out, we all know that someone in the navy department is out to get Speed."

"Ah."

"Maybe even someone in the secretary's office."

"So."

"Hoy is a son of a bitch, if you'll excuse my language,

Bishop. The XO has a lot of power on a ship. He oversees personnel and administration, and he has custody of all enlisted personnel records, he oversees career management programs, he has a staff of career counselors, he runs the print shop, public affairs, equal opportunity, and substance abuse. He can make a hell of a lot of trouble on the ship."

"Patently."

"Normally, he doesn't, because the captain writes his fitness report. But E. Rogers doesn't care. He's finishing up twenty years. He's not going to make captain; he can do whatever he wants."

"Ah."

"He's lucky he's made commander. It helps that his uncle is a senator from a Southern state with a lot of seniority. It also helps that his last assignment is as an aide to an assistant secretary. So he's spending his last year mucking up the *Langley*."

"Unfortunately, he gets himself killed."

"More precisely, Bishop, he disappears. From his stateroom in front of which two marine guards have been placed because of threats against his life."

"One trusts the marines in this role?"

Night Plane Lane hesitated. "Normally, you trust the sea marines completely when they're acting as guards. That report," he gestured at the mass of papers I was clutching, "believes them. Even gave them lie detector tests."

"I see."

The admiral shifted in his chair and made a dyspeptic face. Clearly, Commander Hoy was what the teenage staff at my rectory would call vomit material.

"E. Rogers—called Digby because they say he has rocks in his head—disrupts every assignment he gets. He's very good at it. He divides his subordinates into his favorites and his whipping dogs. He nitpicks, he hassles, he complains, he files charges—all of it within the letter of the law, but beyond all common sense."

"We are not without such personnel in the church."

"Speed Cronin doesn't know what to do with him. He's never had a guy like that working for him before. Most of it's petty and annoying, but it wrecks morale. Accidents start happening on the ship, nothing in the air crew, not yet, anyway, but people get hurt because of carelessness. You're flying out today with a petty officer we had to bring ashore because he bumped into a pipe that he had ducked under for eighteen months. Really bad concussion. That sort of thing."

"Commander Hoy was out to destroy Captain Cronin?"

"Digby was out to do what he does naturally, muck things up and make trouble for everyone. It's his vocation in life. He probably resents Speed, too. Digby is Annapolis, Speed is Notre Dame. Their commissions are the same year."

"Indeed."

"He has this interesting effect on those who work for him. He comes in, stirs up a devil's brew of trouble. Then he is nice to them and wins a lot of them over. They are on his side against everyone else."

"Coconspirators?"

"That's what they become. A psychologist tried to explain it to me. A reaction formation neurosis, she said. A collective neurosis that is impermeable. So he now has loyal allies spying on everyone else on the ship."

"And Captain Cronin?"

"Like every other good guy whom Digby has driven off the wall, he tries to be reasonable and persuasive."

"That is like pouring fuel on the fire, I assume."

"Precisely. He and his friends start a reign of terror on the ship. It gets to me, of course. I ask Speed if he wants me to relieve Digby. He says that he can handle it. Damn fool I think, but I let him have his way."

"Tragic misreading," I said with another loud sigh.

The situation, I thought to myself, may already be beyond redemption.

"He and his spies are all over the ship looking for trouble: drinking, smoking pot, sexual harassment, fraternizing . . ."

"Which means?"

"Strictly speaking, it means shipmates engaging in sexual intercourse. No one pretends it doesn't happen. Hell, they're young men and women at that age in life. They fall in love or they simply get the hots. We don't look for it. If they're careful enough, no one is going to catch them. Digby goes looking."

"Nice man."

"He also messes with the air wing, which is technically beyond his jurisdiction, but if someone from the air wing is caught fraternizing with a member of the crew, he can presume jurisdiction. This drives the CAG, Captain Frank Gill, up the wall. Bad enough that he's got more women then ever before in the wing, most of them not air crew; now he has to contend with someone who sees fraternization every time a young man and a young woman speak to one another on the flight deck."

I sighed loudly.

"The number of people up before captain's mast, that's a kind of informal hearing the captain does periodically for minor charges, doubles in the first month after Digby lands on the ship. No one can be certain that Digby isn't going to cite them. Usually, there's no evidence, and Speed dismisses the charges, but he knows that Digby is saving them up for when he goes after Speed himself."

A mean-spirited vicar general, imposed on a bishop, who tries to do the bishop in by denouncing him behind his back. The church and the navy were not all that different.

"Finally, he charges Speed and Lieutenant Mary Keane, the assistant public affairs officer, with fraternization. That's a charge that's brought to the admiral's mast, the Rear Admiral Crawford, the commander of the task force who is on the ship."

"And his reaction?"

"He dismisses it for lack of evidence. All Digby has is incidents in which he has seen them talking together intimately. By which he means intensely."

"So Captain Cronin is cleared."

"More or less. Nothing goes in his jacket, the folder with his record. Everyone in the navy knows about the charges, of course."

"I see. . . ."

"Neither one of them are married. Speed's wife couldn't live with the navy wife role. Got one of those things you people give out. . . . you know, Catholic divorces."

"Annulments."

"Right. . . . If you ask me, they'd make a good pair. I don't know what they do or don't do ashore. Probably not much. They're both straight arrows. But ashore, it's none of anyone's business. On the ship? Personally, I can't see it. Neither could Admiral Crawford, though he's no great friend of Speed."

"Ah, so the captain has resentment above and below him."

"Bishop, he's a young man, not forty yet, of enormous ability, a superb record, and great promise. Possible CNO. Ideal officer. The admiral and the XO were men at the end of their careers. The admiral, who by the way, is not one of my favorite subordinates, is at least a fair man. He wouldn't mind shooting Speed down. But there's no grounds to do so. He tells me that maybe Speed and Mary Anne are in love, but there's nothing in regulations to prevent that. Unless someone finds them in bed with one another, he's not going to take the charge seriously. Neither, by the way, do the navy investigators, though you can imagine what it does to Speed to be asked those questions."

"And to the woman."

"Sure. . . . So then Digby hits pay dirt."

"Drugs?"

"Yeah. Again, you can't keep a ship completely free of pot. Six thousand people on it. Most of them young. There's going to be some of the stuff around. We try to keep it to a minimum. If we find people doing it, we throw the book at them. There's too many lives at stake and too much valuable equipment to trust it to personnel who are stoned. Those who are messing around are careful not to get caught. Their enlisted superiors, petty officers and chiefs, take a tough, informal line with those they catch and that saves us a lot of trouble."

"Patently."

"Well, as bad luck would have it, Commander Hoy stumbles on a ring—an ensign and lieutenant junior grade, both academy graduates, who are selling it to enlisted personnel."

"Mortal sin."

"You betcha. The whole crowd is sent ashore. Their cases are pending. But with Digby dead, they'll get off pretty easy. The enlisted types will get general discharges and the officers, a man and a woman incidentally, will get reprimands in their jackets. All the evidence, you see, disappeared when Digby went overboard."

"You think he went overboard?"

The admiral frowned, pondering the question. "Hell, I don't know Bishop. No one has ever found his body. The assumption seems to be that he went overboard in the middle of the night."

"I see."

In fact, I didn't see anything.

"Finally," the admiral said as he picked up a rather grotesque model from his desk and played idly with it, "he went after Megan."

He spoke the sentence as though Commander Hoy had gone after St. Therese of the Infant Jesus.

"Megan?"

"Megan Monahan, First Lieutenant, United States Marine Corps, pilot in the marine squadron on board, VFMA 914, the Flying Cougars. He charged her with insubordination. Apparently she didn't call him sir when he asked her a question. He called this lapse to her attention, and she laughed at him. He told her that she was being insubordinate, and she laughed a second time."

"Indeed!"

"Megan has been insubordinate in that sense to the CAG, the captain, the admiral, and even to me. I'm sure she will laugh at you, Bishop. Given a chance, Megan would laugh at the CNO, the secretary, and the president, none of whom would mind Megan's laughter. Only a creep like E. Rogers Hoy would mind."

"Megans," I observed, "are everywhere these days."

There were, in fact, four of them who acted as porter persons at the Holy Name Cathedral rectory, an African American Megan, a Korean American Megan, a Mexican American Megan, and an Irish American Megan. The last named was, naturally, a Megan Anne.

"We've had our troubles with women pilots," the admiral continued. "We washed out a woman helicopter pilot who failed the test four times and the four star type who approved the decision was retired two years early. So we approved a woman F-18 pilot who had failed to qualify on the land and she crashed while attempting a carrier trap, which is what we call a landing. She didn't survive. More trouble."

"And Megan?"

"Technically, she's qualifying for carrier landings. In fact, she's a top gun. Best pilot on the ship. And knows it. Gorgeous redhead. Tough as they come and yet still very . . . well . . . womanly, I guess you'd say. Great sense of humor. Everyone's always laughing at her. We're all proud of her."

"Sounds like the sweetheart of the ship."

"We don't have those, Bishop," he said with a grin. "But yeah. Everyone holds their breath every time she breaks for a trap. We can't lose her."

Absently, he tapped the strange craft on his desk.

"Surely not. . . . What came of Commander Hoy's charges against this fabled Megan Monahan?"

"Nothing. The CAG called him every foul word that an officer in the United States Navy might have learned. Hoy charged him with disrespect. Megan had to drag him away. That night, Digby disappeared."

"Did the navy investigators suspect this virtuous young woman of doing away with the XO?"

"Sure they did. She laughed at them, too. Naturally, there was no evidence against her. But then there's no evidence against anyone."

"She is not unaware, I presume, that everyone up to and including the chief of naval operations is holding their breath until she qualifies?"

"Sure she knows. She laughs at that, too. Says that if they throw her out of the navy, the president will be impeached."

A not untypical future Irish matriarch. "Lamentable attitude . . . And is she thought to be in danger?"

The admiral put down the strange model and rubbed his hand across his face.

"I worry about her like I'd worry about my own daughter. No, there's no reason to think she's in any special danger. Except, if anyone wants to absolutely destroy Speed, he'd try to arrange it so Megan dies in a crash."

I felt a cold chill run through my body. This was a bad business, a very bad business indeed. I doubted that there was much chance of turning it around.

"Others have died?"

"Two of Digby's spies have disappeared. An enlisted

man—a JG—and a full lieutenant. They simply were not in their bunks in the morning."

"Three rather, ah, creepy individuals?"

"You got it, Bishop. Like Digby, only not so smart in his own perverted way."

"One might say diabolic."

It was Admiral Lane's time to sigh. "I've thought about that word, myself."

"And they're all seen wandering the ship at night?"

"No, only Commander Hoy. He—or his ghost— seems to be especially fond of the women's quarters. There's a lot of pure terror among the women on the ship. . . . Are you sure you want to go out there, Bishop?"

"It is imperative that I do so. . . . Tell me, does the admirable and virtuous Megan encounter this, ah, ghost?"

"I don't know. I get no reports on that. I'm sure she'd laugh at him just as she did when he was alive."

"Might he be alive and hiding somewhere on the ship?"

A few fluffy white clouds slipped by the window, blighting momentarily the clear blue sky—a strangely harmless background to a grim tale of evil.

Night Plane Lane waved his hands in frustration. "Sure, it's a big ship. The handout we give visitors says there are three thousand plus spaces on the ship. They add the plus because no one is sure exactly how many spaces there are. The *Langley* is a fifth of a mile long and has six thousand people on board. In principle, a man could hide. The marines and the navy investigators and the ship's crew have searched it from bow to fantail and didn't find anything, but if he has allies that are hiding him, he might have been able to hide for awhile. It's been almost three weeks since he disappeared. The question, of course, is why he would bother."

I could think of a number of excellent reasons why a

man who was on the thin edge of madness but not yet across it would want to try such a game.

"You should forgive my asking, but could there be secret, uh, compartments on the ship?"

"The official answer is certainly that there could not be. Yet everyone knows that there often are. When they were refitting the *Constellation* a couple of years ago, they found a sealed-up compartment. Nothing in it. Probably a mistake the contractors made when they were building the ship back in the fifties. The XO on the *Enterprise* became curious about a bulkhead that was longer on one side than on the other. He persuaded the captain to open it up with a blowtorch. They found a completely fitted machine shop that apparently had been walled in during construction."

"No one in either of them?"

"They joked about some of the admirals they would like to have locked up, but no, besides some old newspapers on the Big E, there was no sign of anyone."

"And those searching the *Langley* are aware of those stories and would have hunted for such sealed, ah, spaces while searching the ship?"

"In case they had forgotten, I reminded them of the stories."

There was danger on that ship. The evil that had been unleashed was still prowling it, though perhaps not as a ghost haunting the crew's women at night. I had no choice. Quite apart from Milord Cronin's orders, I must go out there at once.

"Why do you fear that the exemplary Megan would be a target?"

"No reason, Blackie, except that if you wanted to do the worst possible thing to the *Langley*, its crew, and its captain, you'd go after her. . . . Do you think she is in danger?"

"Oh, yes, I'm sure she is. Perhaps she can take care of herself. That, however, remains to be seen."

"When I talked to Cardinal Cronin . . ." the admiral stood up and wandered over to the window behind his desk, still carrying the bizarre model. "He said you had a knack for cleaning up these messes. You're kind of our last hope."

"No money-back guarantees."

"Has the worst happened out there that's likely to happen?"

"Arguably not. I suspect the worst is yet to come."

"I was afraid of that."

I stood up, too, the strange conversation over.

"I've told you all that I know, Bishop," he said, putting the model of what looked like a sawed-off tanker on his desk.

"I'm sure you have. . . . Incidentally, is that one of the arsenal that is supposed to replace the carriers in the next millennium?"

"This thing? Yeah, semisubmersible, as long as a tanker. Five hundred missiles that can be fired in a half hour. Programmed from the States by satellite. Forty knots. Virtually unsinkable. Crew of eighteen. It could take out the infrastructure of a whole country with the flick of a few switches."

He looked at the model ruefully. "They wouldn't need people like me or Speed Cronin on one of these things. We'd be obsolete."

"But alive."

"Yes, Bishop," the admiral smiled wanly. "We'd be alive. . . . Come on, I'll ride over to Halsey Field with you."

"Excellent," I said, wishing they would drive me back to San Diego International.

CHAPTER 3

HALSEY FIELD WAS named after the Admiral William "Bull" Halsey, an alleged hero of the Second World War. My old fella had little regard for him. He went so far as to always refer to him as "Bullshit" Halsey. The old fella did not tell many war stories, not as many as his grandchildren wanted to hear, but he always referred to the admiral by that name, even in the presence of small ones. As far as I could figure, the admiral was off on some wild-goose chase during the incident at Samar Island.

"If he had been in command at Midway," the old fella would occasionally continue, "instead of Frank Fletcher and Ray Spruance, we would have lost that battle, and you'd all be studying Japanese now."

Two of his grandchildren announced that they were in fact studying Japanese.

"I don't want anything happening to you out there," Admiral Lane had enjoined me as we rode in the limo from his headquarters down the broad streets toward the airfield.

"Most improbable," I had said. "I'm so inconspicuous that I will not be noticed as I wander about the ship. At most, I am merely an auxiliary bishop come aboard to do a few confirmations."

Night Plane Lane's frown was dangerous. He was not a commanding officer to be taken lightly.

"If whoever is responsible for the mess out there has any intelligence, he'll smell that one."

"If he had any intelligence, he would not have unleashed these demons in the first place."

"Maybe," the admiral said grimly.

The VIP lounge at Halsey Field looked like pictures of the lounge at Chicago Municipal Airport in 1935. The admiral and Commander Dawson, the public affairs officer, assisted me into a life jacket, cranials to protect my skull, a visor to protect my eyes, and ear muffs to protect my ears.

"That's the COD out there on the apron," he informed me. "It means carrier on board delivery. It's also called a CA-2 and sometimes a Greyhound. It's a twin propjet we use for delivering personnel, guests, mail, and supplies out to the carrier. Not very pretty compared to the high-performance jets, but she's solid and reliable."

"Admirable."

"She's pressurized but not insulated, so the engines are pretty loud. That's the reason for ear protectors."

I considered the ungainly craft and decided that no way did it remind me of a greyhound.

"Only a few windows."

"And none of them in the passenger area. You don't want to see the ship when you're landing. You'll think you're going to crash into the island for sure."

"Ah."

"And one more thing, Bishop Blackie, I don't want you on any of those high-performance jets. Megan Mary Monahan, good Catholic that she is, would love to take you for a spin. Fortunately, she flies a Hornet, which has room for only the pilot and not much room at that. But there's still a squadron of F-14s out there that carry a radar officer. Frank Gill, the CAG, is just crazy enough to want to brag that he took a bishop for a ride."

"Most improbable."

"Yeah, well, if I were still a CAG, I might just try something like that, too, maybe on a bet."

"You'd lose."

Commander Dawson carried my luggage out to the plane. An African American chief petty officer, the crew chief of the plane, lectured me on the COD. I would be strapped in, facing backward, and should not remove the straps until told to do so. Moreover, I should leave the visor, cranials, and ear protectors in place until I had entered the island of the carrier. I was also instructed about how to release the dye and activate the radio signal on my jacket should we have to ditch. Her somber presentation was marred by only the slightest twinkle in her brown eyes.

"We'll take good care of the bishop, won't we, Chief?" the admiral said, trying perhaps to reassure me.

"Yes, sir, Admiral sir. Best VIP treatment. Lord won't let anything happen to him."

That was a theological observation that, under the circumstances, I was not prepared to dispute.

"We never have any trouble with these things," Admiral Lane said, continuing his campaign of reassurance as we walked out to the COD. "They're the easiest aircraft to land on a carrier that we've ever developed."

Actually and in truth, I was looking forward to the trip. It would give me countless stories to tell to the captive audiences at the cathedral dinner table and family reunions. How Uncle Punk (as I am called in the family) became top gun and kept alive the family naval heritage. I was less sanguine about solving the mystery and saving the career of the cardinal's relative, but it would be an interesting puzzle. Moreover, I had wrestled with similar evil before.

Nonetheless, the requirements of the role ordained that I appear dubious about the trip, so I pursued the game.

"Is it true, Admiral Lane, that a carrier, uh, trap is nothing more than a controlled crash?"

"Well . . . it's often called that. But it's a highly refined control and much better than trying to stop a high-performance jet with brakes and reverse thrusters. In your plane, it's no more dangerous than a DC-9 landing at O'Hare. Maybe a little more exciting . . ."

"Ah."

The crew chief and the admiral helped me to climb into the maw at the rear of the plane.

"Keep in touch with me," he said as he shook hands with me. "We've programmed my office and home numbers into that phone we gave you. Cardinal Cronin's number is there, too."

"Admirable."

I was seated in the plane, which also carried a half dozen crew members who were flying back after spending time ashore for one reason or another. I did my best to attach the seat, chest, and shoulder belts on which, I had been told, my safety depended but managed only to tangle them up and myself in them.

"It's all right, Bishop," the chief assured me. "No one gets it right the first time."

"And if it's not right the first time, there might not be a second time?"

She thought that was very funny.

The crew loaded luggage, mail packs, and supply cartons into the back of the plane and climbed in. There was a whirring sound as reluctant-seeming machinery closed the door.

I was acutely uncomfortable. Neither the cranials nor the visor nor ear protectors nor the seat belt were appropriate to my frame. Why did I let Cronin get me into these messes?

After what seemed a semi-eternal delay, first one engine then the other cranked up, again it seemed reluctantly, and we inched away from the terminal and along the runways. Or so I presumed. There being no windows, I could not see what we were actually doing.

We reached the end of the runway. The pilot revved up the engines as is apparently the rule with propjets. Then he throttled back. After a pause, we began moving again. But not with the speed that one might expect on a takeoff.

We were, I was convinced, taxiing back to the terminal.

"We've got a red light on up here," the pilot informed us. "It's probably only a short in the electrical system, but we're not going to take off until we're sure. We're returning to the terminal. You will deplane while we check the engines."

Just like O'Hare.

Except that the CEO of the airline would not be waiting at the O'Hare terminal to shout at the crew.

Had the plane been checked earlier in the morning? Yes it had, sir. Was there a red light then? No, sir, there was not. Had they followed all the maintenance regulations? Yes, sir. Then what was wrong? We'll try to find out, sir.

"Tell them to get the backup plane over here immediately."

"Yes, sir."

I eliminate from this dialogue all Navy language.

"I said immediately."

"Yes, *sir*."

Immediately meant another half hour, during which time Admiral Lane fretted and stewed and complained. Doubtless, I reasoned, because he wanted to reassure himself that it was some maintenance foul-up instead of the work of the haunt out on the *Langley*.

I thought either explanation was possible. But if the haunts had sabotaged the COD, then they weren't real ghosts but rather humans with skill in their hands and malice in their hearts.

Moreover, it was most unlikely that they were well enough informed to want to keep me off the *Langley*.

Finally the backup plane appeared. They helped me on board again and trussed me up securely.

"They're sure in a hurry to get you out there, Bishop," the crew chief told me. "They're holding lunch for you."

"Admirable," I replied, realizing for the first time that I was hungry.

Our taxi and takeoff was routine this time around and, with only minor difficulty, the plane was forced to leave the ground behind and to trudge nosily through the sky.

I offered up the discomfort of the short trip as Lenten penance.

Then I apologized to Herself for seeming to be petty and asked Her to bless and protect my mission.

"I have a hunch," I informed Her discreetly, "that I am going to need more than the usual amount of your guidance this time around."

That would prove to be an understatement.

About fifteen minutes after takeoff, the pilot announced, "We have the ship in sight and are vectoring for a landing. The ship is to the left of us and we are flying parallel to it, though, in the opposite direction in the regular landing rotation. In a moment, we will make the carrier break and make our landing. We expect to be arrested by cable three."

Wondrous, I thought to myself. *Eight ball in the corner pocket.*

Then catastrophe struck. The plane heeled over and stood on its wing. In fact, it tilted over beyond its wingtip. I told myself that I had seen both John Wayne and Tom Cruise do this in the movies. This is what you did when you dove down to bomb the Japanese ship or chase off the intruding MIG.

Alas, my stomach wasn't listening. Rather, to be more precise, the result of this maneuver, which I later learned was the so-called carrier break, was instant and overwhelming motion sickness. The issue of whether we crashed on to the deck of the *Langley* became academic.

Life and death no longer mattered. Indeed, there was little to choose between them. Death indeed might be a more effective cure of the nausea that had invaded me.

I must not, I told myself, stumble off the plane vomiting. That would disgrace the church, the archdiocese, the hierarchy, and my family. Moreover, such a humiliation could not be kept secret.

Just then, the plane slammed into the deck. Or as they would say, it made its trap. In that tiny corner of myself where I was not sick, I was somehow disappointed. The bump was no worse than a sudden stop in rush-hour traffic on the Dan Ryan Expressway—a sudden stop on a snowy night.

Clearly, we were not going over the edge of the flight deck and into the Pacific Ocean.

The plane and the arresting cable gave up their fight. We taxied slowly. Surely there was not this much room on a carrier deck to taxi, even if it were a fifth of a mile long.

Then the plane stopped. The pilot turned off the engines. The same reluctant machinery cranked down the ramp and revealed a wall, which had to be the ship's island, and a group of four navy types—three men and a woman—in khaki, waiting with wide smiles painted on their faces. The good crew chief unbuckled me and helped me off the ramp.

"Welcome aboard, Bishop Ryan." An officer with a silver eagle on his lapel shook my hand. "I'm Captain Cronin. I hope you had a pleasant flight."

"It's good to be aboard, Captain," I lied.

Then I added a second lie, "The flight was excellent, and the trap was—I believe the proper term for excellent in this matter—OK."

They laughed, impressed by the smoothness of Bishop Blackie's arrival and not seeing it for the utter fraud that it was.

I was introduced around and conducted through the

door and down steep stairs to the captain's in-port cabin on what I was to learn was 03 deck. The woman, wearing two silver bars carried in my luggage. Naturally, I toted my own laptop computer. The ship was heaving dangerously.

I placed the laptop reverently on what seemed to be a dining room table. Commander Jay O'Malley, the senior chaplain (Catholic), removed my cranials, sun visor, life jacket, and ear muffs.

"You won't need these anymore, your excellency," he said respectfully.

"Call me Blackie," I said as I rescued my USS *Langley* cap and put it on my head, peak forward, of course, since I am over twenty-five.

The priest's face was pale, intense, and youthful, but his hair was snow white. He looked like an anchorite from the desert of Egypt, a man whose energy was devoted to prayer and fasting.

Actually, the ship wasn't swaying at all. I was doing the swaying. Or, rather, my furious inner ear was doing so.

"This will be your cabin while you're aboard," Captain Cronin informed me. "We ask only that you don't go out on the flight deck through the door you entered unless you're with one of your escorts—either Commander O'Malley or Lieutenant Keane."

Captain David "Speed" Cronin was a vest-pocket edition of Milord Cardinal, without the hooded eyelids: medium height, carefully trimmed blond hair, sharply sculpted face, high forehead, dimpled chin. Movie star good looks combined with charm and quick intelligence. Yeah, he'd make a good CNO someday if we could exorcise the demon from this ship—which was, incidentally, swaying too much. Again. No, it was my inner ear. Still.

The in-port cabin was worthy of a foreign minister from an Arab republic: a large parlor joined to an equally large dining room with a bedroom (king size) and a bathroom (with shower) attached, all done in tasteful Four Seasons modern. Arguably, I would be lost in it, should I wake up in the middle of the night. As I would soon discover, it had the added disadvantage that the flight deck was immediately above it and rattled every time there was a trap.

"Too neat," I murmured.

"I beg pardon?" Lieutenant Mary Anne Keane asked.

She was, I had been informed in the first round of introductions, the acting public affairs officer. If she was truly the captain's paramour, he showed decided good taste. At first glance, she did not seem spectacularly attractive: slim figure with mostly discreet curves, elegant breasts pressed against her perfectly pressed shirt, a little over thirty, short brown hair, lively eyes, a pert nose on a pretty face graced by a handful of appealing freckles. Only when she smiled—and lit up the whole state-room—did one realize that she was a lovely and intensely sexual young woman. Then you were caught by her eyes, which could only be called lilac in color. From those eyes there was no escape. You watched them for the constant play of emotions that radiated from them like beacon lights. You tried to look away, and then you found yourself glancing back to see what was happening in them now. Her every move was somehow an erotic invitation, discreet of course and modest at all times, and surely unintentional, but nonetheless subtly and perva-sively powerful. She had, I suspected, only recently become aware of her sexuality and was reveling in it, even if she did not begin to understand it or realize its impact on men. And perhaps on other women, too.

As a male member of the species, I find all the varieties of women attractive, reflections indeed of Herself. But I confess I am especially partial to those like Mary Anne Keane whose beauty is subtle, ultimately devastating, and, as these things go, permanent.

A long tour on an aircraft carrier with her aboard would not be dull. Everyone on the ship would know who she was and be aware that in some fashion she was the captain's lady. There would be speculations, different in the different genders, about what would happen between the two of them in bed. Men would, I suspected, be clinical and candidly envious. It would be a factor that would impact on the cruise of the United States Ship *Langley*. For weal or woe or perhaps a mixture of both. As the Navy increasingly was a mix of both genders, relationships like theirs would emerge. The Navy had better get used to it and be as open as Admiral Night Plane Lane.

If there were any sexual chemistry between her and the captain, however, it was not immediately obvious. But then it wouldn't be.

"These quarters are far too neat and spacious," I continued. "It will take me some time to mess them up."

The welcome committee laughed uneasily. Some of them were doubtless dubious about a bishop who was alleged to be a master of locked-room mysteries. Now the alleged bishop appears and turns out to be innocuous and unpromising. This was, needless to say, the way I wanted matters to appear.

"Moreover," I added, "I fail to see the minibar."

They laughed again.

"Ours is a dry navy," Admiral John Crawford explained with a touch of disdain in his voice. "Unlike the British Navy."

"So I understand."

The admiral was a big man, half a foot taller than I and perhaps a hundred pounds heavier. I wondered that he had passed the navy's rigorous tests for physical fitness. Well, every organization has its ways. His round, heavy face, thick lips, and thin hair suggested that he was a bit of an oaf though perhaps a harmless oaf.

A large television set, mounted on one of the walls,

displayed pictures of the flight deck. As I struggled to orient myself and size up the reception committee, it depicted planes landing on the flight deck, and each landing was accompanied by a loud crashing noise just above the cabin. Not a place to catch a nap. Periodically, a bored voice announced, "Roger ball."

"Your COD is about to depart, Bishop," Lieutenant Keane informed me.

Sure enough, the TV monitor revealed my CA-2 at the front of the ship, facing the ocean with steam drifting from a slot in the deck. Two screens rose up behind it.

"How did you like the trap, Bishop?" Captain Cronin asked me.

"Rather like braking on the Dan Ryan Expressway on a slippery night," I replied.

Then, with a whooshing noise and a burst of steam, the COD hurtled down the short space between it and the Pacific and leaped into the air. I expected it to plunge into the ocean. Instead, it poked its nose toward the sky and climbed like a Fourth of July skyrocket.

My stomach turned over again.

A trail of wisps of steam rose from the deck and slowly faded in the wind.

"A cat launch," the captain said dryly, "might be a little more exciting."

"Arguably."

"Roger ball," said the voice.

"That's the landing signal officer," Lieutenant Keane explained to me. "He's responding to a request from a pilot prepared to land for a signal from a filene lens, which provides a beam of light that guides the plane in. The beam, which looks like a ball, makes it easier to land but not easy by any means. The pilots out there can see the ball in the center of the screen. The pilots out there today are from our marine squadron. They are in the final stages of qualifying for carrier landings."

"Not a very impressive bunch," Admiral Crawford sneered, "if you ask me."

"Too high," Speed Cronin murmured as if praying. "Wave off!"

As if in answer to his prayer, the plane soared over the ship.

"They're all edgy today," the captain said with a sigh.

"They're edgy every day," the admiral observed.

"Small wonder," Father O'Malley whispered.

"The next one is Megan, sir," Lieutenant Keane said softly.

"That young woman is riding for a fall," the admiral complained, "and if she kills herself, it will be our fault."

"Roger ball," the voice didn't sound bored this time.

The F-18 appeared to approach the flight deck with authority and confidence. Everyone seemed to hold their breath.

The plane touched the flight deck almost gently, there was a modest bang outside the cabin, then the monitor showed the plane taxiing forward and off the landing deck.

"Perfect." Captain Cronin breathed a sigh of relief.

"She's good, all right," the admiral conceded grudgingly. "Might be the best damn pilot on the ship."

"The LSOs will give her a fair, she'll scream bloody murder, and they'll upgrade her after a loud shouting match that everyone will enjoy," Lieutenant Keane explained to me. "LSO stands for landing signal officer."

"The folks that used to wave the flags in days of yore?" I asked.

"That's right." Captain Cronin glanced away from the monitor at me. "Is there any navy in your family, sir?"

"Bishop" had become "sir."

"One of my nephews has served notice of his intent to marry a Coast Guard ensign person named Cindasue McCloud from a place called Stinking Creek, West Virginia."

"Really?"

"And my old fella was a reservist during the war, 1941 to 1945, that is."

"Did he see any action?" the admiral asked.

"A little."

String it out, I figured.

"Where?"

"Pearl. Samar Island."

"*Ned* Ryan?" The captain asked respectfully.

"His real name was Ned, but a lot of people called him Edward."

"We studied about him at the academy," Lieutenant Keane said in awe.

"An institution whose grounds he never entered, not even for a Notre Dame navy game."

There was a moment of reverential silence. The old fella was still a legend.

"What would he think of you being out here?" Father O'Malley asked.

"I'm sure that he and the deity are having a great laugh over it."

That the old fella had driven off two Japanese battle-ships and saved Douglas MacArthur and an Illinois National Guard division said nothing at all about my ability to exorcise ghosts from the *Langley*. But in an organization in which tradition and memory were impor-tant, his feats provided me with a touch of extra aura that could prove useful.

"Johnny," he had once said to me, "the rest of the family are all proud of their reputation of being the Crazy Ryans. You and I are taken to be the only sane ones of the bunch, the white sheep of the clan. But we know better, don't we? We're the odd ones, the kind that charge battleships for the pure hell of it."

Oh, yes.

There were, however, a lot of Democratic votes on those transports in Leyte Gulf.

"We'll organize things this way, sir, if you don't mind," Lieutenant Keane was once more the efficient, if profoundly disturbing, public affairs officer. "Because of the delay in the arrival of your aircraft, the captain will not be able to eat lunch with you in the wardroom. Commander Richard Dempsey, our acting XO, will preside over lunch in fifteen minutes. Chaplain O'Malley will escort you to the wardroom when you are ready. After lunch, with your permission, I will take you on a tour of the ship. Before supper, you and the captain will have time for a chat. Is that satisfactory, sir?"

She was, I decided, intolerably attractive, all the more so when she played the role of the efficient naval officer. Her fellow officers would glance around the wardroom when they entered to see if there was a chance of sitting at the same table. Young enlisted men, driven by hormones and not malice, would undress her in their imaginations when they saw her in the passageways of the ship. A woman like the acting public affairs officer would all by herself transform the ambience of a ship at sea.

"Grand."

The admiral took his leave with the air of someone who did not expect to be bothered with me again. I signaled the chaplain to stay behind; as the skipper and the public affairs officer drifted out, he stepping aside in courtesy to her.

"Jay, is there a medical officer on the ship?"

"Six, sir. . . . Carrier break?"

"Indeed."

"Sick bay is right next to the chapel. We'll go down and get you some medication. Are you sure you want to try lunch, sir?"

"Oh, yes."

We entered a passageway lined with pipes and wires, and then descended two stairways (which he called ladders). Only with effort did I heed his warning about not banging my knees against bulkhead doors.

"You get used to them after about a year."

"Indeed."

"They really didn't have to send you out here for the confirmation, sir," he said. "There's only a half dozen."

"Your skipper is a cousin of my cardinal."

"So I hear."

This was a strange priest. Was his nose out of joint because I had replaced him as the senior priest on the *Langley*? Clerical resentment had taken stranger forms.

"You'll say the Mass at seventeen hundred? If you're feeling better?"

"I don't want to interfere with your parish, Jay."

"No problem," he said somewhat grimly. "They'll get a kick out of it."

A very tall African American nurse (male) gave me three pills and a patch behind my ear and warned me sternly that I should take only one pill unless my condition became worse.

"This is a terrible ship," Jay O'Malley confided to me as we left sick bay.

"Some people missing, I'm told," I said cautiously.

"It was terrible before that, Bishop. This business of women on ships is a bad idea. I support the ordination of women, I think women belong in the navy. But you put a thousand women on a ship with five thousand guys, most of them under twenty-five and horny all the time, and you turn the place into a brothel."

"Indeed!"

"On a ship, the guys are starved for sex, nothing new about that. But you put women on the ship with them, they go crazy. The women love it because they can have their pick of guys. They flaunt it, especially the ones that are good looking or think they're good looking. The ship turns into a cesspool. It's out of control. Five percent of the women get themselves pregnant every year."

"Disturbing," I said to him.

Only five percent? I said to myself.

"Watch out for that bimbo Keane. She's on the make all the time. She and the captain are shacking up, and everyone on the ship knows it. You can imagine what that does for morale. They both receive communion every Sunday, too. Hell, I can't deny them the sacraments, but it makes me feel unclean."

He spoke in a soft, unemotional voice, someone telling me what everyone on the ship knew to be an undisputed fact.

"Understandably."

"And this hotshot marine pilot, Margaret Mary Monahan, she flaunts it every second. Drives the guys mad. She could get killed any minute. Flying one of those things is no job for a woman. I've thought of warning her, but it wouldn't do any good."

We were climbing another set of "ladders," I puffing several steps behind him.

"Arguably."

"You'll hear a lot at lunch about our XO, the man we lost overboard. Don't believe a thing they say about him. Commander Hoy was a decent Christian gentleman. He realized what was happening on this ship and tried to clean it up. So they killed him."

"Astonishing."

Father O'Malley's account was a different version of the story Night Plane Lane had told me at North Island. Even if he seemed a little unbalanced, it did not follow that his emphasis was entirely wrong.

"When the story of the *Langley* makes the media, it will make the Tailhook scandal look like peanuts. I don't know how the navy will ever recover from it, especially when the news leaks about how many abortions there have been on this ship."

"A grim prospect."

"Yeah. . . . You feeling better, Bishop? This ship is

pretty stable most of the time, but if you start off with a touch of motion sickness from the carrier break, it's a little hard to shake it."

"I'm doing fine." A patent lie.

"You might want to lie down for a half hour after lunch. I'll tell Lieutenant Keane if you want."

The young man, if indeed he were young, was certainly solicitous about my welfare. Moreover, his concern seemed sincere.

"You're kind of a philosopher, aren't you?"

"Mostly a pastor of a big parish."

"Yeah. . . . You ever read anything by Blessed Angela of Foligno?"

That worthy woman was a thirteenth-century mystic. In a time of many women mystics who used intense erotic imagery of their bridal relationship with Jesus (usually the suffering Jesus), she was the most erotic of the lot, perhaps because she had been married for seventeen years before her husband and children died.

"Oh, yes."

Strange reading for a navy chaplain who thought women turned an aircraft carrier into a brothel.

"You think God really loves us that way?"

"Allowing for certain uses of language that were unique to her cultural situation, I would think so, only perhaps even more."

"That's what I figure, too."

Indeed.

CHAPTER 4

"YOU DON'T REALLY think your Bulls are going to win seventy games this year, do you Bishop, sir? Why my Knicks are going to stop that all by themselves, sir. The Bulls are a bunch of old men."

Commander Richard Dempsey, the former ordnance officer and acting XO of the *Langley*, was a smooth, handsome, articulate African American with an Annapolis class ring. He presided over a table of officers of both genders and every hue under heaven with an éclat and a charm that suggested the Old South, though his accent was unmistakably New York. Our conversation was devoted entirely to where we were from, our education, our previous assignments, and our favorite sports teams. My ever-present Bulls jacket was a handy starting point for his table talk and a subject to which to return when momentary anxious silence descended on the table.

"The Knicks," I said with the usual cautious reserve I exercise when discussing sports, "are a crew of psychopaths made only slightly less dangerous by the departure of the chief thug to Miami."

General laughter from the table, which enjoyed seeing the smooth-talking XO rocked back on his heels.

All in all, however, his performance was a tour de force. He succeeded, however temporarily, in driving the anxiety from the eyes of his fellow officers—everyone, that is, except Commander O'Malley.

The only allusion to the crisis that the ship was enduring

53

was a brief remark that Lieutenant Commander Alison Reed—a blond from the deepest part of Georgia—was acting ordnance due to Dempsey's promotion to acting XO.

"A lot of acting officers aboard this ship," I commented.

Next to me, Lieutenant Keane stiffened.

"Better than those that don't act," the XO said easily, "or act too much."

At that remark, the chaplain, on the other side, stiffened.

Realizing that he might have gone a little too far, Commander Dempsey changed the subject.

"The admiral's staff has its own mess, Bishop, sir, so you won't see any of them around here. The air wing officers tend to eat by themselves in the aft mess, called the dirty mess because they don't have to dress up to eat there but can wander around in their flight suits. They also like to hang out in their own squadron ready rooms. Just as well that they do because, to tell the truth, Bishop, sir, they tend to gobble down their food without much refinement. That's just the way they are. Always in a rush."

More laughter.

The well-lighted and cheerful wardroom was divided into two parts: a long "high table" as I thought of it at which the principal officers of the ship were eating off fine china on a gleaming white tablecloth, and a comfortable cafeteria where other officers were eating at circular tables. They had picked up their lunches at the food line just outside the wardroom. We were being served by stewards (of both genders) in maroon mess jackets.

Patently, this was a special meal in honor of the visiting dignitary.

"Did you enjoy watching the traps this morning, Bishop, sir?" Commander Reed asked me.

"Yes," I replied. "I resolved I would never land on an aircraft carrier. It's a dangerous business."

More laughter.

"Not if you fly the way Megan does," a young Mexican American officer (male) observed.

Patently, Margaret Mary Monahan was a favorite subject of conversation on the ship. I guess they needed a conversational subject that was not filled with dread.

If I were plotting to devastate the morale of the USS *Langley*, or rather, to finish that devastation, I would be conspiring to eliminate this fabled marine pilot. I shivered at the thought.

"Why?" I asked in all innocence. "Is this legendary young woman such a good pilot?"

"Instinct," someone said. "All the great pilots fly on instinct. They just know what to do the instant before they do it. Everything turns into slow motion, like a quarterback who reads a defensive alignment leisurely in the three seconds before he has to throw a pass. They never panic. I'm sure that the ship's favorite redhead is not particularly scared when she comes in for a trap. She just knows that she'll do it right."

"Do the instincts of such pilots ever fail them?"

The men and women around the table shifted in collective unease.

"Of course they do, Bishop, sir." Commander Dempsey filled the edgy silence. "Those that live long enough learn to be a little less confident. They follow their instincts but with a warning light in the back of their heads. They fly until their eyes give out. Everyone worries about Megan because she is so good and because we're not sure there are any warning lights beneath that flaming Irish hair of hers—or ever will be."

"She'd be insubordinate to the secretary of the navy and get away with it," said Commander Hilda Jensen, a towering woman with short, pale blond hair and an alert, attractive face. "Our Megan is a genius at human relations, too. Not bad for a cheesehead."

Commander Jensen, I had learned, was the navigation officer.

"From Wisconsin?" I asked in some dismay. "Surely not from Green Bay."

"Exactly from Green Bay, Bishop, sir," Commander Dempsey said with a wide grin. "And I give you fair warning. She's, uh, intensely committed to the Packers."

"I understand," I commented glumly, "that they are still in the league."

"She has a picture of Bret Favre in her quarters," Commander Reed noted. "She has strong feelings on the subject of that team."

"I am duly warned," I said.

"She won't be afraid to argue with a Bishop. She's not afraid of anyone or anything."

"Not even God," Father O'Malley murmured.

"This young woman I have to meet."

"Oh, you'll meet her, Bishop, sir," Commander Dempsey assured me. "Once she finds out there's a bishop on board, she'll hunt you down. Our Meg is a good Catholic."

"She thinks so," the chaplain whispered.

"Don't expect to be treated with any respect, Bishop, sir," Commander Reed said with a laugh. "Megan doesn't know how to be respectful."

"In my real life, I rarely encounter that quality. . . . But tell me, does she not often find herself in trouble for being, ah, disrespectful?"

An instant pall descended on the table, as I had intended it should. Even the mess steward (woman, or perhaps I should say girl child since she could not have been over fifteen), who was passing me my second helping of roast beef, froze in place.

"Sometimes, Bishop, sir . . ." Commander Dempsey filled the silence again. "She does encounter a superior officer without a sense of humor. Fortunately for all of us, that is rare. The officers in the air wing dote on her, as well they might."

The men and women around the table relaxed, the mess steward gave me my roast beef with a pleasant smile, and the easy conversation began again.

It had been the day of his run-in with Lieutenant Monahan that Commander Hoy had disappeared from the ship, save for his nightly wanderings.

"Nice probe, Bishop," Mary Anne Keane whispered out of the side of her mouth.

That it was.

If the ghost of Digby Hoy was haunting the ship for revenge, this marine top gun was patently a favorite target. No wonder everyone was concerned about her traps.

And her instincts.

CHAPTER 5

"FATHER RYAN," I said, stirring from my sleep, not sure where I was, but instantly on the alert for a small-hours trip to Northwestern University Hospital.

"What the hell's going on out there, Blackwood?"

Before my tour of the ship, I had been permitted a half-hour nap after lunch to recover from the motion sickness. The tour was deemed necessary because I was still in principle just another VIP who would administer confirmation tomorrow night. Besides, it was necessary to get an impression of the ship before I devoted myself to solving the mystery of the death of E. Rogers "Digby" Hoy.

"Out where?"

"On that dumb aircraft carrier? You asleep?"

"Only piously reading the fathers."

It was patently Sean Cronin.

"Motion sickness? From the ship? Aren't they too big?"

"From the plane. And in response to your question, murder is going on out here. Three so far and maybe more in the planning stage."

"The ghost of the XO?"

"I have not encountered him yet, and I doubt that said ghost is responsible for the present evil on the ship."

"You haven't solved it yet?"

"Alas, no."

"You're not in any danger?"

"Arguably not. The door to my suite, which incidentally, compares favorably to yours at the cathedral, is guarded by two stalwart United States Marines. From Texas, though they did not attend the University of Notre Dame."

"As I remember it, they guarded the guy who went overboard."

"If that's what happened to him."

"Are you going to solve the mystery?"

"Is the pope Catholic?"

It sometimes is necessary for the cardinal's morale that I assure him of something about which I am not certain.

"Sometimes I'm not sure. . . . Anyway, I don't want you going overboard, you hear? See to it, Blackwood!"

And that was that.

Like a doting parent, he would need several phone calls every day.

Since my napping time was over, I prepared myself for the acting public affairs officer.

"You sure you want to do this, Bishop, sir?"

"Naturally. And since you are of the household of the faith, you don't need to add sir. In fact, I am normally known as Blackie or Bishop Blackie."

Once more her smile enveloped the environment, this time one of the many passageways on the ship.

"Yes, sir, Bishop Blackie."

"Some improvement."

Our first stop was the captain's bridge where the skipper was duty bound to watch the takeoffs and landings, beneath the admiral's bridge and the flag bridge.

"Bishop's on the bridge," a naval rating announced, just as if I were the captain or the admiral.

"I don't see one."

Laughter from the masses.

"Here, Bishop," Speed Cronin said, abandoning the

elevated easy chair from which he watched the activity on the flight deck. "Pretend you're captain."

"The siege perilous."

"Tell me about it."

He remained next to me, however, his shrewd eyes noting every move down on the deck.

"How are they doing this afternoon, sir?" Lieutenant Keane asked.

"Better. The deck crews are back in sync."

It was a flawless California day and far enough off the coast that no smog interfered with the blue sky. The head wind into which the *Langley* was moving briskly was light, the water was purple fabric with occasional traces of white stitching caused by the waves. In the distance on either side, two smaller ships spun through the water in eager effort to keep up with the *Langley*, pups running alongside mama dog. They were called frigates, I was told, a class of ships that did not exist in the old fella's day.

Beneath, sailors in blue and green and red and yellow bustled around among the planes with professional ease. I noted a young man in a green shirt bantering with a young woman in red—the latter standing for munitions. She loaded the rockets and bombs on the planes.

"They talk there every day," the skipper observed. "I don't know who's chatting up whom. My bet is that it'll be a sure marriage."

"The late Commander Hoy doubtless charged them with fraternization?"

"And infuriated the hell out of Frank Gill, our CAG. Needless to say, I threw out the charge. They're both innocents."

"Indeed."

The ubiquitous photographer who had been assigned to my pilgrimage had a field day with Bishop Blackie sitting in the captain's chair.

"Marine female approaching flight deck," a voice announced from speaker on the flight bridge.

The F-18 was approaching the flight deck with total confidence. It moved neither up nor down.

"Roger ball," said the LSO.

The bridge fell into total silence. This Margaret Mary (Megan) must be some sort of Druid witch to have so enchanted the crew.

I had learned that the Hornets must land at a little above their stall speed—160 miles an hour—and that then they are brought to a halt in the space of three hundred feet, one football field length of the three that constitute the flight deck. The arresting wires, four of them, are forty feet apart and two inches above the deck. They are connected to arresting engines, large hydraulic devices that spool out tensioned wire and absorb the momentum of the aircraft. I pondered my own folly in agreeing to such a patently absurd landing.

It probably was more dangerous than a winter night on the Dan Ryan, though apparently not under Speed Cronin's regime.

Meg's aircraft landed just forward of the fantail, hooked the arresting line, and thudded to a stop. Then the plane began taxiing forward toward the catapult. Someone inside the plane slid back the canopy. A red-haired pilot, oxygen mask off her face, lifted a defiant thumbs-up sign at the bridge and laughed.

"What is offensive," observed the lieutenant who was duty officer of the day on the flag deck, "is not that she's so perfect at it but that she enjoys her perfection so much."

"You got it, Lou," the captain agreed.

"She may not have a long career in the navy," the DOD said, almost sadly.

Ah, this young man was sweet on her. Fair play to him, as the Irish say.

"What counts is that she's going to qualify on this trip.

You and the rest of her legion of courtiers seemed to have made no progress at all with her. Maybe she'll end up as a nun like she threatens."

"But only for five years," Mary Anne Keane reminded them.

I cleared my throat.

"Presumably there is a guard following that young woman around all the time."

"The wing has its own personnel guarding her round the clock," the captain replied. "I insist that two women marines be in front of her cabin every night. So that's four guards. She rooms with two navy pilots who also watch her. Women pilots, Bishop."

"Her reaction to the watch persons?"

"Pretends she doesn't see them."

"Figures. . . . It remains to be seen whether the locked rooms are really locked or that the marines, admirable young women that they doubtless are, will be able to protect her."

"You believe Meg is in serious danger, Bishop Blackie?" Lieutenant Keane asked uneasily.

"Patently. That's the only conclusion I have drawn since I came on board. If there are crazy killers on board, she's too good a target to pass up."

"You should personally guard her quarters at night, captain, taking turns with her own commanding officer. I consider this to be a matter of immediate urgency."

"They won't let us in that side of the ship, Bishop. It's off limits to men."

"A lamentable limitation on human freedom . . . Also, someone might try to sabotage a plane she will be flying."

"I'll see to it," he said grimly.

"Excellent; now, Ms. Keane, let us continue our tour."

I had warned the delectable woman that until I became "Blackie" she was "Ms. Keane."

We visited a number of spaces (I was beginning to

master the lingo) which were undoubtedly designed for Hollywood films and then adapted for aircraft carriers. The most impressive was CDC (Combat Direction Center) and I was familiar with it from many films. A darkened room was arrayed with a large number of screens, many of them transparent, on which sailors in fatigue uniforms occasionally made small markings, short-range radar monitors, long-range radar monitors, location and charts for every craft in the area. The movement and voices of the personnel were so grave and measured that I thought of the old Missarum Solemnis, the solemn pontifical liturgies of the pre–Vatican Council church.

"The skipper sits in that easy chair on the platform," Lieutenant Keane explained to me, "and can tell at a glance the position of every ship, every aircraft, every missile in the battle area, which extends for hundreds of miles. He has total control of our response to every situation."

"ComAir bearing at oh-nine-oh, ninety-five miles," one of the acolytes intoned.

"Commercial aircraft," Lieutenant Keane whispered to me.

"If anything suspicious shows up, we can respond instantly," the lieutenant continued her whispered commentary. "Obviously, we don't expect anything in these waters just off California. However, in a combat area, we'd be able to monitor a missile that was coming our way as soon as it was launched. Obviously, we would destroy it long before it got to us."

"Reassuring."

Then we went to a nearby space where the activity was much more vigorous: the Carrier Air Traffic Control Center or "Cat-see." Here the air ops officer supervised the movements of the aircraft as they landed and took off and vectored around the ship. He and the captain were in constant communication through a squawk box. Sailors with portable equipment periodically made announcements about various aircraft.

Men in dark khaki coveralls with massive insignia on their chests loitered around the room watching what was going on with what seemed casual interest. These were the pilots, the men for whom the rest of the carrier existed.

"Another wave off," the air ops officer protested, "that kid has to improve, or he's not going to make it."

"He'll make it," said the man in coveralls with an eagle on his shirt collar who stood next to him. "He just needs a little bit more confidence in himself."

"You're the original mother hen, Frank," the ops officer replied.

"Hey, Mary Anne, good to see you here," the man with the eagle—a captain though patently not *the* captain—said. He slipped out of his chair and reached out his hand to me.

"Hey, Bishop, Frank Gill. Welcome to Cat-see."

His accent was West Texas. West of the Pecos.

"Captain Gill," Mary Anne explained, "is the CAG, the commander of Air Wing Eleven. That motto on his shield, as you doubtless know, means 'To Higher Things.'"

His shield depicted a jet pointing straight up with the motto "Ad Altiora."

"That's Latin, I believe."

Frank Gill was a man no taller than five eight, with a slender face decorated by a trim mustache and perfect white teeth. His quick movements and decisive speech said top gun, albeit a genial and friendly top gun. In the church he might have been a vice chancellor or a bright young pastor in the inner city.

"Certainly had a more holy meaning before, eh, Bishop?"

"Humankind has always aspired to the heights, Captain, of whatever variety."

"Hey, Bishop, that's a good line. I'll have to use it someday. . . . Did you see the darling of the fleet do her last trap?"

"I'm not competent to judge such matters, but I gather she was close to perfection."

"And will holler like hell if any of the LSOs dare to question that. One of the many interesting things about our Meg is that she won't use marine language. She's got a whole lingo of her own. A fucking asshole, you'll excuse me, Bishop, but I'm just quoting the way marines talk, becomes a frightful amadon. Isn't that something else? I guess an amadon is a kind of goof in Irish."

"Arguably."

"Never known a qualifier to attract so much attention." He shook his head in bafflement. "Guess it's because we never had a woman marine fly a plane off this ship, much less one who is so good, eh, Mary Anne?"

"With red hair," Lieutenant Keane added, "and a very loud Irish mouth to match."

"Much of what you'll see on the ship is mechanical, Bishop. Almost automatic. We have our careful routines. They have to be routine so that we know what to do in time of crisis, and they have to be careful so that the crises don't catch us flat-footed. It's a delicate balance."

"Indeed."

"I don't mean just the crisis of someone shooting a missile at us in the Persian Gulf. I mean the kind of crisis that might occur every time a high-performance jet comes in for a trap or we launch one from a cat. We live and work on the edge between boredom and disaster. That's our daily life. Those that find it crazy get out. Maybe those of us who don't get out are crazy. It's easy to have second thoughts. I suppose the same thing is true in your work."

"Arguably. It is, however, easier for us to deceive ourselves."

Captain Gill eased us toward the door and out into the passageway.

"How much time, Mary Anne?"

"A couple of days, Frank. At the most. We can't keep it quiet much longer. There's bound to be a leak. Then we have the story about a haunted carrier and a brothel ship."

"Damn shame if it plays out that way."

She shrugged. "I'm so tired of trying to keep the lid on that I feel like we might as well face it and get it over with."

The CAG turned to me. "Good luck, Bishop. You're our last hope."

"Not entirely," I replied. "There are other positive factors at work." *Give me a couple of hours and I might be able to figure out what they are.*

Mary Anne Keane led me down several ladders—and the stairs were steep enough to earn the navy name for them—and weaved through a maze of passageways.

If I imagined that the ship was a city—a metaphor that had been used often during this long day—the passageways with their pipes and wires and bulkhead doors (with "knee knockers" that I avoided only because of Lieutenant Keane's care) were the roads, and the spaces were houses or shops. The living quarters were packed with bunks, six of them in a small area for enlisted personnel, arguably less comfortable than even a prison, though they were better than the hammocks in which the ratings slept in the old fella's day.

Langley was a densely crowded and cramped city, much of which was never touched by daylight. Many of the citizens, officers and CPOs usually in khaki (marines—the elite sea marines—in blue trousers with white belts and khaki shirts with red trim), and enlisted persons in fatigues, saw very little of daylight from one cruise to another. They lived rather in the glare of artificial light reflected on beige metal walls and blue chairs, with an occasional phony panel of wood to make the place seem more livable. After a few hours, I found the environment depressing. Six months? Thank you, no.

Still, it was better than the wooden man o'wars of Horatio Hornblower and his ilk. Yet it was not a city most of us would choose to live in.

The citizens we encountered as we picked our way down the artificially lighted streets of the city were unfailingly courteous and friendly. Navy discipline was responsible, yet there was truth in the old adage that if one acted courteously, one also began to feel courteous.

The miracle was not that nerves could become frayed in this city but that there was not constant open conflict.

"Now hear this," the public address system announced. "There will be a general quarters drill at sixteen-thirty. I repeat, it will be only a drill. All hands except those on special work will participate. We will assume fire and major casualties on the hangar deck. I repeat, it will be only a drill."

"I'm legitimately excused," Mary Anne Keane assured me.

"Excellent."

"The chaplains naturally have their general quarters tasks. That's why I'm your escort this afternoon."

"Fortunate for me. Good Father O'Malley is not the world's most cheerful fellow."

She laughed and illumined the passageway down which we had turned with her smile. "He's a good priest, but I admit kind of dour."

"Indeed."

"We are back on oh-three level, Bishop. The same level as your cabin, air ops, and traffic control. Officers' quarters are, for the most part, on this level. Enlisted personnel on oh-two level below us and every place else on the ship where we can find room for them. My office is on the deck below that, oh-one level. Below that is the hangar deck, which we call the main deck, where the aircraft are stored. The wardroom and other mess areas are on the second deck, the next deck down below the hangar. That's at the waterline. The third deck is where a lot of the machinery is stored. The fourth deck is the engine room."

"I see," I said, trying to remember what she was saying. The system seemed as irrational as are many of the systems in the church. However, we had many more years to work on irrationality.

We turned a corner, stepped over a "knee knocker," and entered a short passageway.

"This is Commander Hoy's stateroom, Bishop. No one is living in it now. Would you like to inspect it?"

"I suppose I'd better."

She inserted a key and opened the door.

The term "stateroom" was an exaggeration. The XO's quarters were larger than an old Pullman drawing room, but not by much. The lights were bright, the metal polished, the beige paint cheerful, the bunk looked comfortable, the TV in the wall was of presentable size—and our rooms in the seminary were larger and better designed for human habitation.

"This is all an XO gets?"

"It's all relative, Bishop, sir. This space above the bunk that looks like another cabinet is a second bunk. A lieutenant commander would share this room with someone else. And the bathroom"—She opened the door—"which in these quarters is shared with one person in the next stateroom would be shared with two more persons in the next room. I share a stateroom this size with five other women. Comfort, as we'd know it ashore, is available only to captains and admirals and I should add that Captain Cronin's sea quarters are not nearly as luxurious as his in-port quarters."

"Doesn't this crowding together of people make for tension?"

"The staterooms are much more pleasant than on the

older carriers, sir. And better than the homes most of our ancestors lived in, to say nothing of the quarters on the ships in which they crossed the Atlantic. But, to answer your question directly, yes, the crowding does make for tension, especially when there is already tension on the ship."

Lieutenant Keane was being careful and controlled in her comments. Yet it seemed very likely that she wanted to talk about the problems that had brought me to the ship. So I would have to give her the opportunity to talk.

"You say there is an adjoining stateroom?"

"Yes, sir. The next stateroom is occupied by the supply officer, Commander Glendenning Shorter."

"That was his room at the time of the, ah, incident?"

I looked out the door and down the passageway. I noted the faint aroma of her very discreet scent.

"And the marine guards . . ."

"Were stationed in the passageway. They could, of course, see the doors to both the staterooms."

"Why were they stationed in the passageway?"

"The XO demanded protection. He claimed that he had received threats on his life."

"Did anyone see the threats or hear them?"

"They were all oral threats, no one else heard them, and Commander Hoy claimed to have heard them from behind his back or at the door of this room and was unable to identify the voices."

"Ah . . . And how did his disappearance manifest itself?"

Making sure that the door remained partially open, I sank into the stateroom's single chair. I was overwhelmed by the sleepiness induced by the motion sickness medication and not at all sure I would be able to remove myself from the chair.

"He did not appear punctually in his office the next morning. He had always been fanatic about being there on time. Commander Shorter reported that the door to the

bathroom had been locked and that Commander Hoy
would not open it. The skipper came down here with the
chief master at arms—that's the officer in charge of
security—and knocked on the door and yelled. There
was no reaction. He summoned a machinist mate with an
acetylene torch to cut away the lock. He burst into the
stateroom and found . . ."

"Nothing?"

"And no one . . . He ordered an immediate search of
the ship. No trace of the commander. When the agents
from the NIS came over from San Diego, they did their
own search. Needless to say, they gave the marine guards
a very hard time. But they passed lie detector tests."

"The bathroom doors can be locked from either side."

"Yes, sir. Someone could theoretically lock one door
from the inside of the john and then hold the door to his
room open, lock it from the inside, and then close the
door."

"Thus locking both cabins out of the bathroom."

"Right. Sometimes that happens, especially when
we're in the berth at North Island and an officer comes
back, ah, disoriented. They have to go to the chief master
at arms to ask him to open the john door with a lock pick
he keeps."

"And the situation in the bathroom when the captain
forced entry?"

"Both doors were locked from the inside . . . as if
Commander Hoy had locked himself into the john and
then disappeared up or down the pipes."

She sat on the edge of the bunk, head bowed in
discouragement.

It seemed to me to be patent that there was a relatively
easy way to arrange the locked-room caper. The critical
question, however, was why bother with it?

"So, officially, the commander is missing?"

"And the two officers who were part of his 'team' as
he called it, Blackie. Team of spies."

"You think they went overboard, Mary Anne?"

"Probably. I suppose they could be hiding somewhere on the ship, protected by their allies, but it's hard to understand why they would bother. We've been searching for them for two weeks now. It's unlikely that they could hide this long."

"It's a big ship."

"That's true."

"Who might have had reason to kill him?"

"Most of the six thousand people on the ship. He had a reign of terror going. Everyone was afraid of him. Women, especially."

"Why?"

She sighed and shifted uneasily on the bunk.

"During the Gulf War, he had served on a command and supply ship. There were three hundred sixty women on board. When the war was over, exactly ten percent of them—thirty-six women—were pregnant."

"Indeed!"

"Some of them would have become pregnant on shore, too. Still, it was a wild ship and many of the women were as bad as the men. We discipline ourselves much more effectively now. We understand that shipboard orgies are just another form of male exploitation. Yet women still become pregnant. Digby Hoy was convinced that every woman on a navy ship was trying to become pregnant. He treated us with blatant contempt."

"But not quite so blatant that he would risk charges of sexual harassment?"

"Exactly," she said with a shiver and then went on. "It was scary the way he looked at us. His eyes would undress us, but his manner was not just lewd. He seemed to be sneering at us, almost like he was taking . . . well, sadistic delight in embarrassing us."

"Do you believe he is still alive?"

She hesitated.

"I don't think so. I think someone threw him over the

side and then those two cronies of his, Wade and Ericsson."

"Group of someones, more likely."

"I suppose so," her chin sank to her chest.

"It is said that his ghost walks the ship at night."

"Do you believe that?" she looked up at me, her face even more pale.

"The problem is that many of your shipmates seem to believe it. Do you?"

She paused, her lilac eyes troubled. "I never believed in ghosts. But I've seen him a couple of times."

"Indeed."

"He wanted me, Bishop, when he was still alive. I don't know why. He could have had any of those women who swarmed around him. Lieutenant Commander Wade especially. She was my boss and a very attractive woman. But he wanted me."

"Captain's woman?"

She took no offense at my question.

"Maybe. It was all very subtle—and very lewd without a single word being spoken."

"Lovely man."

"I saw him in my stateroom the other night."

"Ah?"

"We don't wear much at night. It's hot out here, and the spaces are stuffy. I couldn't sleep very well. I've had a hard time the last couple of months. I rolled over and opened my eyes. There he was . . . standing above me and grinning. I felt paralyzed. I couldn't move, I couldn't scream. I just lay there while he leered at me, absorbing everything with those creepy eyes of his."

"Terrifying."

"Then he reached out like he was going to touch my breasts. I felt a terrible clammy chill run through my body. He . . . he touched me. I thought I was going to die. He seemed to be laughing at my fear, torturing me. Then . . ."

"Then?"

"Then he wasn't there anymore. He didn't fade away or leave the room. He just disappeared. I felt terribly hot, but still I was quaking with the cold. It wasn't a dream. I know it wasn't. I was wide awake. The other women were all asleep. I didn't go back to sleep. I was afraid to close my eyes for fear that if I opened them, he'd be there again."

"Others have had the same experience?"

"I don't think they'd talk much about it if they did. But other women have seen him wandering along the passageways and into our shower rooms. Even in the daylight. He disappears too quickly to be a live human being."

"There must be terror in the women's quarters."

"Near hysteria, Bishop. He seems to be going after us where women are the most vulnerable. That's the way he was when he was still alive, though it was more indirect then. If we don't stop him, there's going to be some kind of explosion."

Collective neurosis? Parapsychological phenomenon? Combination thereof? Lieutenant Keane was a sensible, intelligent woman, mature enough to distinguish between a dream of sexual terror and a real apparition. She thought her experience was the latter.

I repressed my own inclination to shiver.

"He must have been a frightening man," I said cautiously.

"The navy sent him here to destroy the skipper," she burst out angrily. "That was the plan from day one. They've got away with it, too."

"How so?"

Mary Anne Keane wore no makeup or jewelry, except for her Annapolis ring. She probably had no awareness of her beauty, perhaps because she had matured into a sexually appealing woman only in her late twenties. There was, I thought, little doubt that she was in love with the skipper as she called him. Moreover, so intense and vulnerable was her attractiveness that he doubtless found her irresistible.

"The navy stinks, Bishop Blackie. I'm a third-generation Academy grad." She held up her ring to confirm it. My father and grandfather were both pilots. Grandfather died at the end of World War II in an accident. Daddy was shot down over Vietnam when I was only four years old. Once the navy was a proud group of humans with a proud tradition. Now it is corrupt, even evil. Most of the people in it are good men and women, but the system is corrupt, and the people who run the system are liars and thieves and male chauvinists. They've lied so often they don't know the truth anymore."

"The same could be said of many of my colleagues in the hierarchy."

"You've had a couple of thousand years to work on it," she said, a touch of color rising in her pale cheeks. "We've done it in less than a half century."

"No mean feat."

"For forty years and more, the navy lied to Congress and the American people about the threat of the Russian Navy. After awhile, we believed our own lies so completely that we couldn't give them up even when our intelligence people had incontrovertible evidence that the Russians' only intent was a defensive force and that most of their ships wouldn't work because of incompetence and mechanical failures. In the eighties, during the Reagan years, we babbled about expanding to a six-hundred-ship navy, provided dishonest cost estimates, built more carriers, and squandered money—all based on intelligence estimates that we knew were wrong. Then when the Gulf War came along, our carriers were useless. The marines did a fine job ashore and the Tomahawk missiles were devastating, but the F-14 is unreliable and often a flying coffin, the F-18 is fun to fly but doesn't have enough range, the A-6 is still our best plane, but it's so old that we couldn't use most of the planes that we had. Our bombs were not as advanced as those of the air force, and a lot of our stuff didn't work and one of our high-tech cruisers shot down an Iranian passenger plane by mistake. We were disgraced, despite the trillion or so dollars we had spent during the previous decade."

"That's a powerful indictment, Mary Anne."

"Oh, it's all on the public record, Bishop. Vietnam was even worse. There was no need for carriers in that war. Our planes could have operated from the ground. But we had the carriers and pilots who were able to fly off them, so we used them. We lost over eight hundred men, including my father, and even more planes in a foolish war and to foolish tactics, but we'd beaten the Japanese with carriers and we were convinced that all other wars would be the same. . . . Even today we still half believe it."

"So."

"It was during Vietnam that the pilots became drunks and womanizers, courtesy of the brothels the navy ran at Subic in the Philippines. The pilot culture has never recovered, which is why we had things like the Tailhook scandal. Which we tried to cover up, just like we try to cover up every mistake and just make things worse."

"Why?"

"Incompetence, cronyism, politics, ambition, dishonesty, favoritism, abuse of power, indifference . . . You name it, Bishop, we have it. . . . The reason why the skipper has been able to develop his safety program is that there was so much carelessness with equipment and men. . . . Sloppy maintenance, incompetent pilots, drunks."

"So ships like the *Langley* are just so much excess baggage the taxpayers are carrying?"

"Not necessarily. Properly run and with the right kind

of planes, they should scare the living daylights out of anyone who wants to make trouble. If the Gulf War were now instead of four years ago, we'd do much better, even with planes that were mistakes from the first line on the drawing board. Since 1945, we've been playing catch-up."

Bishops have been playing catch-up since we got out of Jerusalem. "Always too little and too late."

"Exactly. By the time of the Gulf War, we had the tools we could have used in the Vietnam War. This ship, manned and equipped as it is now, would be superb for the Gulf War, even with our inadequate planes. The skipper's safety program clearly works. If it had been in operation in 1972, my father would not have been cleared to land on a deck with fouled-up cables."

Her lips were drawn tight, but she was not weeping.

"So, is there hope for the navy?" Hope for the hierarchy? I didn't think so, not till we went back to the old way of the people selecting their own bishops.

She sighed and shifted again on the bunk.

"Sure, there's many bright and dedicated men in the navy. During the eighties, we had poor secretaries of the navy and CNOs—that's chief of naval operations. They spent most of their time deceiving Congress, promoting cronies, and covering up scandals. Things are a little better now, there's a little more opportunity for bright and able young men like the skipper. But the old guard would rather cling to its own power and then clean up the mess."

That sounded like bishops, too.

"They want to destroy Captain Cronin?"

"Certainly. He's so straight and so smart and so dedicated to the navy that they don't want him ever to become an admiral, much less the youngest admiral in the navy in the next batch of promotions. With all his accomplishments and excellent fitness reports, it will be hard to stop him. Even our own admiral, who doesn't like him much, has had no choice up to now to turn in excellent reports. But this mess will give Admiral Crawford all the excuse he needs."

Oh, yes, she was in love with him, all right. Not that he didn't deserve her love.

"This is a drill, repeat, this is a drill. General quarters. There is a fire on the hangar deck and casualties. General quarters. This is a drill, repeat, this is a drill."

"Don't worry, Bishop, we're excused from that. . . . This crew is first rate, too, even if they're edgy now because of Digby Hoy. . . . David, uh, the skipper believes that he'll make admiral because of competence and hard work. But he doesn't have any patrons in Congress like Hoy did and not all that many in the Pentagon."

"Ah?"

Crew members were dashing down the passageway. Impressive.

"Digby is or was some kind of distant relative to a powerful Republican senator. When the word gets out about his disappearance, there'll be a big fuss."

"But might not the captain invoke the help of Senator Cronin?"

"She's not a relative, is she?"

"Oh, yes."

Mary Anne smiled affectionately. A faint tinge of pink rose to her cheeks.

"How like Dave never to have mentioned that to anyone."

Certain kinds of innocence, I thought to myself, *were not virtuous.* There was no offense in using clout as a means of self-defense against those would use their own clout illegitimately against you. It would be necessary to take certain compensatory steps to equalize the playing field.

"So his career depends on resolution of this mystery before worse things happen?"

"I think so, Bishop. There'll be other promotion boards, but if they can label him at this one, he might just as well wait till he has twenty years in and retire."

"Which would be a great misfortune for the navy?"

"I think so. . . . Incidentally, I chose public affairs instead of air crew because right now I think public affairs is more important."

"Arguably it is."

"And we're not lovers, Bishop. I think most everyone on the ship knows that."

This I very much doubted.

"I mean we are lovers, but we're not lovers."

The blush became deeper and brighter. She smiled again and her lilac eyes glowed.

"I suppose you don't understand what I mean?"

"Might it be that you and the skipper are in love, but that you don't act out that love on the ship?"

She laughed, happy for a minute.

"Exactly! I won't say that we didn't act it out on shore, but there it's no one's business."

"Indeed."

"We didn't want to become involved. We've both had difficult relationships. His wife left him because he wouldn't quit the navy. Got one of those annulments. No children. She didn't want children. I made the mistake of believing a pilot. Both of us figured that we could do without sex. So we were easy victims for one another. I know it's hard to believe about someone like me, but I'm afraid I took the lead."

"I don't find it hard to believe."

"Is that a compliment?"

"Arguably."

"David says things like that, too. . . . Maybe I don't know myself all that well. . . . Anyway, we swore that we'd never be alone together on shipboard, and we've kept that pledge. Many of our friends think we're foolish. They think there ought to be a romance between the two of us."

"And there isn't?"

"Not really. David will be going to Washington on his next assignment, admiral's star or not. I have another year and a half on this ship. We agree that it would be a natural end to a relationship that was unwise from the beginning."

I offered no comment on this foolishness.

"You think we are both out of our minds?" she asked shyly.

"Sexual attraction," I said in my most pontifical tone, "is a trick God plays on us to break us out of our fear and loneliness and open us up to love, including most especially Her love."

"You think we should marry?"

"You've been around the Catholic church long enough, Mary Anne Keane, U.S.N., to know better than to ask a priest that question."

"So you won't comment on our abstinence on shipboard?"

"Only to say that I always admire virtue, so long as it is motivated by virtuous sentiments and not by fear."

She smiled wanly. "You know too much."

"Unlike poor Father O'Malley, who does not know much at all and that not accurately."

"He looks like he's going to die when he gives me communion at Mass."

He should, I thought to myself, *mind his own business*.

"He doesn't know swat," she added.

"I beg pardon?"

"A Megan word. When others would say 'shit,' Megan says 'swat.'"

"Secure from general quarters," the P.A. announced. "I

repeat, belay general quarters. This is the end of the drill, this is the end of the drill."

"Thank you for listening, Bishop Blackie," Lieutenant Keane said, rising from her sitting position on the edge of the bunk. "Maybe I've said too much. Only . . ."

"Only?"

"The cabal of cronies in Washington who will vote on the skipper includes a lot of adulterers. He was faithful until his wife walked out on him. It doesn't seem fair that they use our temporary relationship against him, especially since nothing has happened on shipboard."

"No, it doesn't. . . . Oh, one more thing. I need information about how the cabins are arranged. You said you shared your quarters with how many other women?"

"In fact four. But there's an empty bunk. We have two tiers of three bunks each. Junior officers, ensigns, and jaygees are in cabins with three tiers. Same size cabins as ours but more crowded. Then, when and if I become a lieutenant commander, I move into a different kind of cabin. One tier of two bunks, lap of luxury. It's like this only except that in this one, the top bunk is closed. In times of emergency or overcrowding, this top bunk can be lowered."

She reached up and slid the top bunk down. It was neatly made up, ready for an occupant.

"Bunk choice in a cabin is based strictly on seniority. For instance, if I was a lieutenant commander and was sharing this cabin with another woman, the more senior of us would have the choice of top or bottom bunk."

"And which would you choose if you were senior?"

"The top bunk, naturally. I like it up high. . . . Only the silver oak leaf rates the privacy of your own cabin. Which means they close the upper bunk. You still share a common john, but it's a lot more privacy."

"Not exactly five star."

"No, but neither are college dorms. And they're a lot

more comfortable than they used to be. You learn to think about other people's feelings."

"It would not be possible to arrange for quarters for married shipmates."

"Sure it would," she said hotly. "Admittedly, I have a vested interest in the subject. You'd have some problem with johns and showers, but that could be worked out. I tell the skipper that it's crazy not to make such arrangements."

"And he disagrees?"

"No, of course not. He always agrees with me. He says that it will take time for the navy and Congress to come to terms with sexual intercourse on its ships. They'll also say that married couples should not be on the same ships because spouses will be more concerned about one another than the good of the ship. Which is total nonsense."

"And those who are in relationships, as they are called nowadays?"

"People like us?" she laughed. "Skipper says that it will take longer to persuade the American people that fornication or possibly adultery on a naval vessel is not intolerable. He says that they'll approve alcohol first and that will take a long time."

"And your opinion."

"Women in the navy are going to demand it, Bishop. And soon, I think, as soon as they get oriented and figure out what's going on. I mean, I don't want the skipper doing my fitness report," she blushed deeply and rushed on, her voice rising in anger. "But he wouldn't be doing that anyhow. And I don't think it would hurt the ship or the navy or Congress or anyone in the country if we could be lovers, married lovers mind you, on this ship. It would probably help."

I almost said "Arguably." Instead, I substituted another word more appropriate to the context.

"Doubtless."

"It would change the whole culture of a ship like this, and that would be a distinct improvement, if you ask me. . . ."

She trailed off uncertainly, fearful perhaps that she had been too candid.

We left the stateroom. She carefully locked the door.

"Do you think, Bishop Blackie, that it's usually up to the woman to bring closure to a relationship?"

"Oh, yes. Especially when it is the case of a decision about marriage."

"I can have him if I want him?"

"I don't know either of you well enough to answer that question."

"But you suspect . . . ?"

"I generally tend to believe a woman's assessment of a situation."

"Thank you, Bishop," she said with a happy smile.

"You're welcome."

"I'll pick you up at your quarters at seventeen-fifteen to take you to the chapel for Mass."

"Eucharist," I said.

She actually laughed. I wondered how long their promise not to make love on the ship would hold up. Not that it was any of my business.

I sprawled on a most comfortable chair in the in-port cabin and picked up my portable phone.

"Cronin."

"Ryan."

"Have you solved it yet?"

"We progress. . . . However, now I have certain instructions for you."

I gave him my instructions.

"Well," he said cautiously, "I don't see anything wrong with that. I'm not sure what Senator Nora will think."

"Yes you are."

"Well, maybe I am."

"We must occasionally strike a blow for the forces of cosmos in their endless battle against the forces of chaos."

"That's one way of putting it."

"See to it!" I said, closing the phone and feeling inordinately proud of myself.

However, as I well knew, the forces of chaos had yet to play their last card, arguably, their last several cards.

CHAPTER 6

"YOU DON'T LOOK much like a bishop," a skeptical womanly voice informed me.

I was vesting for the Eucharist in the minute sacristy in the bowels of the ship, the second deck, I thought. I had little doubt as to whom the voice belonged.

"I take that as a high compliment," I said, turning around. "And I would note that you don't look much like Tom Cruise."

Wild laughter. She extended a hand.

"I'm Megan."

"Doubtless. Though I might have thought Kathleen Ni Houlihan."

"No red petticoat." She spread her hands. "Or is that Pegeen Mike?"

"It might be any and all of them."

"Yeah, we Irish troublemakers are all pretty much alike."

First Lieutenant Margaret Mary (Megan) Monahan, USMC, was a throwback to the Neolithic Age, a giant warrior woman of the sort the first Celtic invaders found dominating the west of Ireland when they arrived there. She was at least six feet tall, had long, flaming red hair, a red face to match, and dangerous eyes of the deepest and most volatile green. All she needed was a spear or pike to fit the image of Queen Maeve the Mad. She leaned casually against the bulkhead in her green flight suit with its VMFA insignia (Marine Fighter Attack

Squadron) and surveyed me with a manner and a smile I could only term respectful insolence, a matter to which I am not unaccustomed, having spent a long life coping with Irish matriarchs—though none as pure a specimen of the early days as this one.

Was Megan Monahan beautiful? Well, yes. But one noticed her full-figured beauty only after one was overwhelmed by her sheer physical presence.

One did not mess with her. No way.

"You're the bishop who solves locked-room mysteries and is going to get poor Skipper Speed off the hook?"

Despite her broad smile, she seemed skeptical about my ability to do that—or anything else.

"Who put him on the hook, Megan?"

She rolled her eyes. "A lot more than that jerk Digby Hoy, Lord have mercy on him."

"Is he dead, Megan?"

She rolled her eyes again. "Maybe."

Just then, the other local Irish matriarch, Lieutenant Mary Anne Keane, entered the sacristy.

"Nice traps this afternoon, Meg."

"Yeah, well I had to argue with those swat-head amadons for an hour to get them all rated OK."

"Both you and they would be disappointed if you didn't have to argue."

Megan grinned. "Gotta do something to have fun on this frightful ship. They're good guys, not like that amadon who tried to kill me and Skipper Speed threw off the ship."

"Meg, the bishop asked earlier in the day if the sexual harassment and hazing had diminished in the navy, and I said somewhat. Tell him what you did to the guy who tried to grope you in flight school."

"My frightful instructor." She continued to grin. "I just broke his arm. Told him that if he tried it again, I'd break the other arm. Naturally, he was afraid to bring charges.

You break a few arms, you earn some respect, right, Bishop?"

"Arguably."

I tried with difficulty to control my laughter. Megan, for all her brashness and insolence, was really a sodality prefect about whose womanliness and even vulnerability there could be no doubt.

"Father O'Malley is kind of dubious about giving me and M. A. here communion, Bishop. He thinks we're sinful women. Do you have an opinion on that subject?"

"I leave such judgments to God, and I assume that She's on your side."

Loud laughter from Megan, quiet laughter from Mary Anne.

"Well," Megan continued, "I don't know about Lieutenant Keane because she's got a crush on the skipper, which shows good taste, if you ask me. But I'm as pure as the driven snow, Bishop. I wouldn't have anything to do with any of these frightful amadons, except maybe Skipper Dave, and she's already staked her claim on him."

"Megan!" Mary Anne screamed in embarrassment.

"Yeah, I know. I should keep my big Shanty Irish mouth shut. Isn't that true, Bishop?"

"God forbid that I should try to answer that question."

The answer was that Megan's cracks might be outrageous, but they were never unconsidered.

At that point, I was rescued by Commander O'Malley, his handsome face creased by a Thomas Merton frown.

"We should keep it down to a riot, Lieutenants," he said sternly. "This is, after all, a chapel and His Excellency is preparing for the Eucharistic liturgy."

"His *Excellency!*" Megan protested. "Are you really excellent, Bishop? I thought your real name was Blackie!"

I pointed firmly at the sacristy door. Megan drifted out reluctantly, followed by a rueful Lieutenant Keane.

"I don't know how that loudmouth," Father O'Malley said with a frown, "ever got through a Catholic high school."

"She probably ran it," I said, putting on a chasuble.

"She would drive a husband crazy, Bishop."

"One way or another," I agreed.

Before the Eucharist began, I prayed for everyone on the ship, especially those whom I had met this afternoon and especially for Lieutenant Keane and the skipper, that they would learn that some things were more important than the United States Navy. And most especially for the red-haired marine, that God would protect her exuberant charm.

It was a very dangerous ship. Something would have to be done, and quickly. Only I wasn't sure what.

In addition to Father O'Malley and me, the participants in the Eucharistic assembly were eight in number, five Filipinos, one African American, and the two Irish American women—the last three serving doubtless as the parish Altar and Rosary Society.

The skipper came in after my homily about the exuberance of God, a tragic loss for him. Megan beamed, of course. An exuberant God was just fine with her. Which is why I preached on the subject.

Father O'Malley frowned his disapproval when the three Irish Americans received the Eucharist. What a strange mix of old and new he was.

After I told them to go forth in peace, I remained behind a few moments for extra prayers, sitting, needless to say, on a chair.

"You've got me into this," I told Herself. "And it's up to you to get me out of it."

I noted that Megan had also remained to pray—on her knees and gracefully upright, eyes closed, lips parted in a slight smile, face peaceful and composed.

Mystic, too? Why not?

She caught up with me in the sacristy, now dead serious. "You realize, Bishop Blackie, you gotta solve this mystery?"

"So I understand."

"I think I know what's happening."

"Ah?"

"But I want to go over it a couple of times more before I tell you, OK?"

"Certainly. Don't wait too long. And don't take any chances."

"Me take chances! Don't be silly!"

"Do you think Commander Hoy is still alive?"

"Course not. Except maybe he is."

"Do you ever see him at night?"

Her green eyes opened wide in astonishment. "Course not. The dead don't come back. You know that, Bishop."

"Some of your colleagues think they have seen him."

"Yeah, I know. . . . He was a bad man, Bishop. But not just a bad man. He kind of appealed to some women's most ambivalent fantasies, know what I mean?"

"Arguably."

She shrugged. "Torture. Bondage stuff. Ugly, but in a weird way for some of them obsessively appealing. Fantasy. Not real, you know?"

Far too sophisticated for one so young.

"They're fantasizing his ghost?"

"Something like that. . . . Well, if his ghost should intrude when I'm taking a shower, I'd break his arm. I'd break both of them. Ghosts or not."

"I'm sure you would."

"Skipper's waiting for you." She nodded toward the door. "He's really cute. Lucky Mary Anne . . . See you later."

"I thought we might have supper served to us in your quarters," Captain Cronin said politely.

"Temporary quarters."

"Of course. . . . We'll have some privacy there."

"Which I think we need."

He sighed heavily. "Indeed, we do."

CHAPTER 7

"HI, FATHER," THE skipper said as we walked by Jay O'Malley's office.

"Evening, sir," the priest replied glumly.

He was reading, I noted, *The Instructions* of Blessed Angela of Foligno. Heady stuff indeed for a troubled man.

"Not a happy camper," Dave Cronin said to me. "Never has been. But a good priest."

"Some obsession with sexual sins, is there not?"

"This ship would do it to you. . . . I don't know what you think, Bishop. But if we're going to put young men and young women on a ship together for a sustained period of time, we need something better to respond to the energies we unleash than old-fashioned American Puritanism."

"Not just young men and women," I said somberly.

"That's true. . . . I don't have any idea what the alternative is. Respect and good taste and some common sense, but you don't find that often in nineteen-year-olds, or thirty-nine-year-olds, either, as far as that goes. Morever, while I'm being a rebel, I think we'd have less trouble with drugs if we were willing to follow the example of the Brits and dole out some grog every now and then."

"Splice the main brace."

"You even know the words! We'd have to use beer

instead of rum and gin. Can you imagine how Congress would react to that?"

"Its respected members would doubtless choke on their gin martinis."

As we climbed the ladders and slipped down the corridors, Dave Cronin greeted everyone with a smile. He seemed to know the first names of everyone on the crew.

"Good evening, Jenny."

"Good evening, Skipper."

"Good evening, Mike."

"Good evening, Skipper."

"Good evening, Jean . . . no, Joan!"

"Got it right this time, Skipper, sir. . . . Good evening."

"You know all their names?"

"Not all of them. But they like it if I try. The old-fashioned ranting, raving, screaming captain doesn't work anymore. If it ever did."

"I imagine your admiral wouldn't agree."

He glanced at me sideways, decided he could trust me, and said, "He has a hard time remembering the names of everyone on his staff."

In my quarters, a linen tablecloth was spread on the dining room table. China and crystal and silver service were appropriately arranged. All we needed were wine goblets. No such luck on a ship of the United States Navy. In some respects, the church was better organized than the navy.

A pretty and extremely young steward in a maroon mess jacket and tie awaited us.

"Good evening, Martha. . . . Another perfect setting."

"Sure do beat anything you'll see in the Florida Panhandle, suh! Good evening, Bishop, suh."

"Good evening," I replied.

"I'm a Catholic, too, Bishop, suh." She smiled at me. "Never did meet a sure-nuf bishop before."

"You must not judge the whole fraternity by me."

"Go 'long with you now, Bishop."

She was wearing a very thin wedding band.

When she left the room to wheel in the cart with the first course of our supper, I whispered to Dave Cronin, "Surely she's too young to be married."

"Just barely old enough. So's her husband. He's a radar operator. On this ship. Technically, they're not supposed to fraternize. Rogers Hoy caught them making love in a storage locker and brought them up for captain's mast. It didn't matter whether they were married, he said."

"And you?"

"Threw out the charges and told them of a private space where they could sleep together every night so long as they didn't mind a single bunk. They didn't mind that at all. I'm sure Digby put it in the dossier he was keeping on me."

"He's the source of all the problems on the ship, Captain?"

We consumed the avocado with crab legs salad, the roast beef with béarnaise sauce, the stuffed potatoes, the squash, the peas and carrots, and the freshly baked rolls. I generally had two helpings, much to my young co-religionist's delight. For her part, she kept a discreet distance from our table so that we could converse without her hearing anything.

"In the short run, yes, of course. In the long run, we have so many problems in the navy today that he was only a symptom. I realize that all organizations have their share of cronyism, but no corporation in the United States would have tolerated a man like that. He used the rules to pervert the purpose of the rules. He was evil. I had made up my mind to relieve him when . . . when he disappeared. I am furious with myself that I didn't do it much earlier. Naive optimist that I am, I thought I could talk reason to him. I've never had any experience before with a man who was a walking collective neurosis. I heard about Rogers Hoy, I had been warned about him, but I couldn't believe it when I watched him play his game."

Milord Cronin's cousin was a man of reason, not only a naive optimist by his own admission, but a naive Lockian optimist. He would have to become more sophisticated if he really was going to reform the United States Navy. Yet his handsome face, his bright eyes, and his measured voice all suggested enormous inner strength. Maybe he could pull it all off. I wondered why his wife had left him, not that it was any of my business. Well, maybe it was my business.

"Do you think he was sent here to make trouble for you?"

"The navy in its present form isn't that smart. Someone was looking for a place to dump him for his last two years. They thought, *Why not the* Langley. Since I would be relieved shortly, no captain would have had to put up with him for too long. Then someone else noticed the assignment and thought that it might be a chance to finish me off, so they let it go through. That's how things usually work out."

Also in the church.

"Were they right?"

He laughed. "Right now, it looks like it, doesn't it? I wouldn't bet much on my being promoted this time around. Then they can use this time as an excuse for stalling the next time. I may still get my star, but then will be the end of my career. I'll retire with twenty five years and the appropriate pension."

"Unfortunate."

"The way the game is played, Bishop. I knew the risks I was taking when I started to push my theories."

"Which are?"

"They're not just mine. A lot of younger officers are

convinced. No one bothers even to refute them. Almost two decades ago, our intelligence people came up with proof that the Russian Navy was a farce, at most an incompetent, failure-prone crowd whose sole aim was defensive. We didn't really deny it. We ignored it and went right on building carriers and lying to Congress. It is obvious to everyone that we have to get smaller and more efficient, but we ignore that, and some of our admirals are still warning the Republican reactionaries about the threat of the Russian Navy. It's hard to believe."

"What do you want?"

"First of all, better planes. For all the money we spent, we have come up with two lemons, defense department compromises. All right, if we can't have better planes, let's be content with fewer planes, but all of them in good shape. Fewer pilots, but all of them qualified. Bishop, half these kids who are trying to qualify should never have been sent out here. They're good kids, but they haven't got it. I'd like to get rid of all the drunks and the hot dogs and the Tailhook womanizers and have a professional air crew resource again. Better maintenance. More insistence on safety. Better morale on ships."

"And the carriers?"

"Five years more, ten at the most. Then the arsenal ships will take over. That's why I don't think we're going to get better planes. We'll always need a few carriers to cover the marines and to ferry planes to their in-country airfields. Even now, we could get by with six or eight carriers at the most. I'd like to have ten, but if its a choice of six with professional air crews, quality maintenance, and rigid safety requirements, that's what I'd choose."

"Just as the church should be content with fewer priests but better ones."

He smiled wanly. "Can you sell that to Cousin Sean?"

"Without any difficulty. He sells it to me."

"He should be chief of naval operations!"

"Arguably."

"The most serious of all the problems, Bishop, is the feminization of the navy. Women are becoming a major component of our personnel, partly for political reasons, but partly because we need them. That means a deep change in attitudes that are a couple of hundred years old. Maybe a thousand years old. Respect for our women shipmates and the attitudes that the Tailhook scandal revealed are diametrically opposed. Many men bitterly oppose the change. They have persuaded themselves that it can be reversed. It's a tough fight. We had a veteran LSO who tried to kill Megan one night. Murder her. There's no other word for it. I threw him out of the navy. There's men on this ship who never forgave me."

"How would you characterize that attitude?"

He thought for a moment. "Women are objects to be used and puzzles to be feared." Dave Cronin sighed. "They'll ruin the navy."

"Will they?"

"They'll change it. For the better, I believe. But we have no idea what the changed navy will look like. In the meantime, ships like this are giant laboratories of change."

"And this feminization of the navy may be the cause of the mysteries on the ship?"

"In part, Bishop. Digby had a strange influence on women and they on him. I can't quite figure out how it worked, but I don't think he would have gone as far as he did if he didn't have an audience of women to fear him and other women to admire him. He loved it."

"I can well imagine that he did."

"Did you ever encounter anything like my problem with Rogers Hoy, Bishop?" He said, rubbing his hand over his face.

"Only once."

"Perfectly reasonable, sensible people suddenly turn mad."

"While all the while," I agreed, "wearing the veneer of reasonability and common sense. An impermeable collective neurosis focused around the most improbable of men. . . . Did it affect many on the ship?"

"Not really, only those in his immediate control, personnel, printing, public affairs, substance abuse, and mostly officers and chiefs. Fifteen, twenty people at the most. The enlisted personnel seemed to be immune. You have to understand, Bishop, that the people he won over actually believed that he could and would relieve me and assume command of the ship."

"Was that possible?"

"An XO could do that only under the most unusual circumstances with overwhelming evidence of incompetence and dereliction of duty. Never with an admiral on board and COMNAVAIRPAC only sixty miles away."

"The admiral did not support him?"

"Admiral Crawford has no love for me. He thought I should have relieved Hoy at the very beginning of his effort. He is probably right. I guess I just couldn't believe that Hoy could turn so many people into zombies."

"Zombie is not a bad word. Borderline personalities can do that to people. . . . I presume they're still zombies."

"I'm told that they think I'm responsible for Hoy's death and ought to be killed myself. But they're utterly passive: bland faces, glazed expressions, like sleepwalkers."

Yet a couple of them might be dangerous sleepwalkers.

"Most of them will leave the navy at the end of this cruise and slowly return to normal life," I observed. "At least, that seems to be the pattern."

"The pressures to conform must have been terrible. Lieutenant Keane, who was in the midst of it all and knew it was crazy, told me that she experienced grave difficulty in resisting their myth about what was happening on the ship."

"Did she?"

He nodded solemnly, not yet ready to talk about how his acting public affairs officer was both a personal and professional problem.

"I don't think," he continued, "she's over it yet."

"Arguably. . . . Would someone have attempted to do away with Commander Hoy to protect you and to save your career?"

He played uneasily with his coffee cup while I signaled to the virtuous Martha that, yes, I would have another slice of flourless chocolate cake.

"I've thought about that, naturally. It would have been mindless, to put it mildly. Mutiny talk from a disturbed XO hardly affects a man's record. Three murders on his ship are another matter."

"You think the three missing people are dead?"

"Hoy, Wade, and Ericsson? I don't think it's possible they're hiding on the ship, not for two weeks. I can't imagine enough of the crew would cooperate with such a trick."

"Their bodies were thrown overboard?"

"Maybe. Possibly while they were still alive. More likely, however, their bodies are still on board. In a few days, we might begin to smell them somewhere."

It was not an appealing thought. However, I continued to consume my chocolate cake.

"You don't think this is a plot on the part of someone in Washington to ruin your career?"

He laughed wryly and drained his coffee cup. "Another touch of the decaf, Martha, please."

Martha beamed happily as she filled the cup of her adored skipper.

"I'm not that paranoid, Bishop. I don't think they deliberately sent Rogers Hoy out here to make trouble for me, and I don't think that whoever killed him had me as a kind of secondary target."

"Your enemies will, however, make the most of these

events. And doubtless with Admiral Crawford's passive assistance."

"I'm more worried about the fact that we have a killer or more likely several killers on the ship and a crew that's seeing ghosts. The killing may not be over. I hope it is, but I can't be sure. What do you think? You're obviously worried about our irrepressible Megan. . . ."

"Oh, yes. Remarkable young woman. She must be protected. There is evil on this ship, unless I am mistaken, and she's the natural target, as you have told me she has been before."

"We will have two more women marines and my senior woman C.P.O. guarding her quarters tonight as well as the marines. I could hardly be in the women's section of the ship."

"Patently."

The perceptive reader will realize how completely wrong I was about the nature of the threat to First Lieutenant Monahan. I can plead only that the various motion sickness medications that were coursing through my bloodstream had affected my brain.

"You sense the evil, too, Bishop?"

"One can almost smell it."

He nodded. "I worry about my crew. I worry about Martha over there and her husband. I worry about Megan. I worry about the kids in the galley. I worry about our flight crews. I worry about my officers. I worry about Dick Dempsey, who inherited a real mess. I wonder when lightning is going to strike again."

We were both silent for a moment.

"Even the admiral sees Hoy's ghost."

"Admiral Crawford?"

"Scares the hell out of him."

"Do you?"

"Certainly not . . . What about the locked room, Bishop?"

"There are a number of ways that might have been

accomplished, but the question is why someone would want to do it and indeed why someone would have wanted to kill Commander Hoy and Lieutenant Commanders Wade and Ericsson."

"Maybe they're trying to terrify us, Bishop. As a prelude to something else."

"Arguably."

Dave Cronin was no fool. He had put his finger on exactly what I thought was happening. Someone was deliberately trying to spread terror in the *Langley*, for reasons of their own, which might not have anything to do with either the collective neurosis around the possibly late Commander Rogers Hoy or the career of the ship's captain.

"Thanks, shipmate," the captain said to Martha as she cleared the table. "The next time we have a bishop for dinner, we'll have to provide more chocolate cake."

A skipper calls a mess steward shipmate. Speed Cronin had the touch, all right. He would have made a great Chicago precinct captain.

"In fact, Bishop," he continued, "Mary Anne will take you through one of the galleys and the bake shop as part of the evening tour. You might find some more cake down there."

"That would be a good work," I agreed.

Martha had left the stateroom.

"You have perceived that I am in love with her. Crazy in love with her."

"Oh, yes."

He nodded. "Not on the ship, of course."

"Patently."

"She's been so wonderful through this crisis. Everyone thinks that."

"Hmm."

"When we get ashore, I'm going to ask her to marry me. I don't propose to take no for an answer."

"Improbable response," I murmured.

"We've both made mistakes before."

"Ah."

"But that doesn't mean this is a mistake."

I was supposed to validate his judgment. My approval didn't matter in the least, so there was no reason for my not giving it. I figured I'd make it solemn high to reassure the poor, troubled man. "No man who shares bed and board with that one could possibly be making a mistake."

He grinned. "Only when we get ashore."

There was a light tap on the door.

"Your tour guide, Bishop."

"Doubtless."

There was a hint of sexual embarrassment between the captain and his beloved as he transferred me to her care. *They had better get ashore quickly*, I thought to myself.

"Nice dinner?" she asked casually.

"Presentable."

"Nice man?"

"I could argue against that premise until the day before the last judgment, Lieutenant Keane, and you wouldn't believe me."

"It was kind of obvious in there, wasn't it?"

"Only because both of you trust me."

"I want him, Bishop, and I mean to have him. He's my man for the rest of his life."

"I suspect he won't run very fast."

We thereupon continued our tour of the ship, galley, bakery (a wondrous place, presided over by a marvelous cook who had prepared a mix of chocolate chip and oatmeal raisin cookies for my delectation), medical and dental headquarters, engineering center, and boiler room. The last named was as hot as purgatory was reputed to be in the old theology and filled with thick pipes that I was repeatedly told not to touch, not that I had any inclination to do so. The nuclear reactor, however, seemed remarkably prosaic, hardly an instrument of terror.

For a moment, I wondered if the terror that was slowly enveloping this ship was somehow connected with that reactor.

As I struggled up the ladders toward the main deck, now thoroughly exhausted, we encountered Jay O'Malley.

"Hi, Mary Anne," he said in a friendly enough tone. "Hi, Bishop. Good tour? You've got the best guide on the ship."

"Patently," I said, gasping for the breath that I had left several decks below.

"Better get some sleep," he added. "You've had a long day. You look tired."

"A strange priest," I observed as we struggled to the main deck.

"Moody," Mary Anne replied. "One time I'm a nice young woman, another I'm a sexual threat."

"Not incompatible roles, I should think. Indeed, how could you be the former without being the latter?"

She laughed. "In my better moments, I agree with you. This business with Hoy, both the collective neurosis and then his disappearance and the haunting, has been hard on Father. He's an extremely sensitive man."

"He was one of Hoy's converts?"

"Not really. On the fringes, maybe."

"Does he see the ghost?"

"He has never said that he does."

"He is, of course, in love with you in his own way and resents the skipper."

She turned on me, her face solemn, her eyes piercing. "You don't know that!"

"It is patent. Perhaps what you mean is that he doesn't perceive it. Arguably, he shows good taste."

Her expression softened and she smiled, lighting up the whole hangar deck, the door to which she had just opened.

"Yes, Bishop, that is what I mean. I suppose I ought to be flattered, but I'm not."

Could a devotee of Blessed Angela of Foligno fall in love with a public affairs officer—acting public affairs officer?

Had not Tom Merton fallen in love with a student nurse?

And were not these difficult times on the Langley?

"Better that then, denial."

"I suppose so. . . . This is our hangar deck. It runs the full length of the ship. You see those sets of massive doors? One of them is closed now because of the drill we had earlier. The doors split the deck into four compartments so that we can seal off fire or smoke. We can park about half the planes down here."

The hangar was a massive, badly lighted cave three decks high. It looked like three basements of the United Center in Chicago strung together, only the noise was not of the ineffable Bulls driving down the court but of jets banging down on the flight deck above us. Mechanics were working on some of the planes, drilling and scraping and polishing, it seemed to me with enormous care.

The hangar deck, for reasons that doubtless made sense to the U.S. Navy, was the main deck. The deck above it, I reminded myself, was level 03 or the gallery deck, where there were officers' cabins, the combat information center, the air ops office, the traffic control center, and the squadron offices. Between the gallery and the main deck in the space not occupied by the hangar were 01 and 02 levels (not decks) where, among other things, one could find weapon storage, the TV studio, and public affairs offices. Below the main deck was the second deck (counting down) with the wardrooms, the other messes, the galleys and the bakery, and the third and fourth decks. Counting up, the flight deck was 04 level (the gallery being 03). Since my quarters were

below the flight deck, I was on 03. I'd map it all out
before I went to bed.

As we entered the gloom of the hangar deck, I sensed
that if one were to encounter a ghost anywhere on the
Langley, it might be here. Rogers Hoy might pop around
one of the big planes and leap at you . . .

And then he did.

Mary Anne screamed and jumped back. I grabbed for
my pectoral cross which, astonishingly, still hung around
my neck, and wondered whether St. Brigid was good at
repelling haunts.

"Hey, Mary Anne, sorry to scare you!"

"Captain Gill," she stammered.

"Hey, Bishop, I'm not a ghost. Sorry to frighten you.
Everyone's edgy, I guess. Not a happy ship right now, is
it?"

His calm grin and his soothing voice had its intended
impact on Lieutenant Keane.

"I'm sorry, sir," she said nervously. "It's been a long
day."

"Long couple of weeks . . . I was down on the cat-
walk watching the night traps with the LSOs. I like to
patrol through here on the way to air ops. Make sure that
the mechanics are taking care of things."

"How are the traps?" Mary Anne Keane asked, most of
her poise recovered.

He shook his head sadly. "Don't ask. At least a quarter
of those kids should never have been sent out here. And
it's a clear night. Rain or a rough sea, and we'd lose
them. Sad . . . Can I show you my aircraft, Bishop?"

"Please do."

"This big one with the two tails is the F-14, the
Tomcat. A cantankerous aircraft at best, it was designed
to be both a fighter and a bomber and was never really
very good at either. Fortunately, we never had to use it as
a fighter against anyone. They tried to soup it up and
made it even more difficult to fly and more dangerous.

We have only one squadron of them, and I'll be happy when it's phased out."

"Understandably."

"Speed hasn't lost a single one of them on this ship, which is kind of a miracle. When you hear about a navy plane crashing, you can count on it, it's one of these. . . . Now this sleek baby," he patted a trim aircraft with a long, pointed nose, "Is the F-18 or the F/A-18 as the navy department likes to call it. The Hornet. Our friend Megan flies one of these. . . . You meet her yet, Bishop?"

"Oh, yes."

"Remarkable woman. Best thing ever happened to the air wing. Anyway, it's one of the sweetest airplanes the navy has ever owned. Fun to fly, probably the best fighter aircraft in the sky. Too bad there's no one to fight with it. It's supposed to be an attack plane, too. Do what the old A-6 Intruder and the Tomcat did and with only one crew member. Not bad at it, so long as it doesn't have to fly any more than a half hour from the ship. Otherwise, pretty useless."

"I see."

"So we have two kinds of useless planes, one of them dangerous and one of them a beauty. And we poured billions of dollars into them. . . . Anyway, these other planes are all pretty good. The prop jet with the big dome on top is our Hawkeye, a command and control aircraft. First rate. The jet with the funny tail is the Prowler, an electronic warfare plane. Those two over there that look alike are the Viking and the Shadow. The Viking is antisubmarine, the Shadow is long-range recon. No Pentagon admiral messed any of them up by trying to make them do too much. Penny wise and pound foolish, if you ask me."

"So you have great technology and poor combat aircraft."

"Best there are in the world." He jammed his hands in

the pockets of his green flight suit. "Only not very good. Too many compromises to save money. The Hornet at least is safe to fly. . . . Incidentally, we have two helicopters, angels, the pilots call them. Both are topside during flights, one in the air, just in case. Some of those kids out there might need them before the night is over."

"I wonder, Captain . . ."

"Frank, Bishop."

"Blackie."

"Fair enough."

"What I was wondering was whether there are any old planes down here in the hangar that you don't use any more."

"Like those wrecks you see at the fringes of airports? No, we clean them out pretty quickly. . . . Wait a minute, there's an old A-6 back in number three compartment. Used them in Vietnam and the Gulf. Terrible aircraft, but they did the job. Rather have one of them than a Tomcat. Had to retire them because of metal fatigue. Couldn't fly this one off the ship and didn't want to just dump it in the ocean."

"Fascinating."

"Like to see it?"

"If I may."

Captain Gill considered me intently, perhaps thinking what I was thinking.

"Come to think of it, Blackie, I'd like to have a look at it, too."

We walked rapidly down the hangar deck, our shoes clanging on the deck. Frank Gill opened a door in the mammoth compartment wall and held it for Mary Anne.

"Real Tennessee gentleman, Blackie, even though she's a couple of grades lower."

"Thank you, sir."

"You're welcome ma'am."

It is called whistling in the dark by the graveyard.

"It's that old wreck in the corner. We're going to off-load it when we get back to North Island."

An outstandingly ugly plane, the A-6 had seen much better days. It also smelled of corruption. The three of us stood silently for a moment.

"Well, I'd better climb up and have a look," the captain said. "Someone closed the canopy, I notice."

He moved a stepladder from the wall and climbed up to the wing, then reached over and slid the canopy back. He turned away quickly, his face gray with nausea.

"You were right, Blackie. He's been dead a long while. But you might want to say some prayers."

"Prayers never hurt."

He climbed down the ladder.

"Say them down here. No point in going up there."

"Ericsson?" Mary Anne asked with a shudder.

"Yep, best as I can tell. Someone shot him in the head with a forty-five. I'll go phone Speed."

"A decade of the Rosary, Mary Anne?"

"A decade of the Rosary, Bishop."

So we said several decades of the Rosary while planes thudded into the flight deck above us. I asked Herself to grant peace to all who had died in the service of their country and indeed to all the souls of the faithful departed, a prayer the answer to which was already guaranteed by our faith.

Captain Gill joined us after he had made his calls, head bowed, hands clasped in front, a Protestant joining mutely in papal murmuring.

After the XO and three of the medical officers had arrived (the captain's presence being required on the bridge during flight activities), the skipper had decided not to move the corpse until the Naval Investigative Service officers came, and a half squad of marines appeared to guard the old plane. A pale Lieutenant Keane and I climbed up the multitude of ladders to the captain's bridge.

"Bishop's on the bridge," one of the seamen announced, a young man whose challenge was to report the comings and goings to and from the bridge of the captain and the admiral. His announcement of my arrival was not required, but it brought a touch of laughter to the grim bridge.

"You two all right?" the skipper asked us.

"Of course, sir," Lieutenant Keane replied, still whistling in the dark.

I said nothing.

"It's Ericsson all right?"

"Yes, sir. Captain Gill identified him. So did Commander Dempsey."

"You figured it out, Bishop?"

"An outsider's luck."

"Do you think Hoy and Wade are aboard, too?"

"Lieutenant Commander Wade, probably."

"Any ideas?"

Our young captain's face was gray. He had to continue to watch the attempted traps outside and still make decisions about murder on the ship.

"During our tour, after I was shown the catapult mechanisms, I believe we pass a storage space for auxiliary fuel tanks."

"For the F-18s. They really need them."

"If Commander Wade was a small person . . ."

Mary Anne turned away. A ripple of repulsion crossed the skipper's face.

"She was . . . You don't think, do you . . . ?"

"A possibility."

He reached for his phone.

"Dick, Dave here. Get together some of the weapons people, even if you have to get them out of bed, and . . . and have them search the auxiliary fuel tanks on oh-one. Search for what? Another body! What else?"

"Only a guess . . ."

"I've notified NIS. They'll come out first thing in the

morning on the COD. They'll be swarming all over the place again."

"Doubtless unhappy that they didn't find the body of Lieutenant Ericsson and ready to blame you for that fact."

"That's one thing I hadn't thought of."

Outside, a plane slammed down on the flight deck. Hard. And then zoomed off again.

"Fourth bolter for that poor guy," Dave Cronin sighed. "And it's a calm night. . . . Lieutenant Keane, we'd better get ready for the media before the day is over."

"Yes, sir. I imagine that decisions about that will be made at COMNAVAIRPAC."

I didn't think that it would be a good thing for the media to be poking around the ship.

"Or the Pentagon. They'll want to cover it up if they can."

"Naturally, sir."

"I note that the admiral is not on the bridge," I observed. "Shouldn't he be here during night traps?"

"Doesn't have to be. He looked kind of pale tonight, even before he heard about poor Ericsson. By the way, he wants you to have breakfast with him in his wardroom tomorrow morning. Oh-seven hundred all right?"

"Nine o'clock, Chicago time. I'll be wide awake."

"Good. The NIS people will be here around oh-nine hundred. Routine ship operations will continue, including flight operations. Tomorrow night, too."

Another plane smacked into the deck. Apparently, the arresting gear had caught the cable.

"Thank God we finally got her in," the skipper sighed. "Three wave-offs."

"Megan!"

"Course not. Ms. Perfection never gets a wave-off."

He didn't sound happy about that, but then Captain Cronin didn't sound happy about much of anything. No reason he should.

"You've never watched flight operations at night, have you, Bishop?"

"Alas, no."

"For a really experienced pilot, a day landing, even if the weather is rough, is not a big deal. Everyone is scared of a night landing. All our safety rules are extended to their limits. From up here, it looks exciting until you realize that lives are at stake. Somehow we manage to do all right."

"I read somewhere,"[1] Mary Anne took up the point, "that it's like you're in a car without headlights, going a hundred fifty miles an hour down a narrow, dark road toward a one-car garage illuminated by a single light-bulb. If you get through the garage door, your car will stop automatically. And the garage is moving around."

Another plane slammed into the garage and boltered off.

"Better this time." The skipper sighed. ". . . Maybe we've kept you up too late, Bishop. Tomorrow could be a difficult day. Lieutenant, why don't you take the bishop down to his quarters?"

I didn't argue.

"Yes, sir."

"Oh, Bishop, one more thing. I've ordered a guard on your quarters. Tonight. Just a precaution."

"I'm not going out," I assured him. "And no one is getting in."

They both laughed softly. Not much to laugh about.

"Bishop leaving the bridge!"

The guard, in marine blue trousers and khaki shirt with red insignia, was a young woman marine who may have been almost five feet tall and was perhaps thirteen years old, hardly any bigger than the massive side arm strapped to her waist.

"Sir!" she said, saluting.

---

[1] In the May 1995 issue of the Smithsonian's *Air and Space* magazine.

"Nice to have you here, Ms. . . ."

"Dawkins, sir. Lance Corporal Dawkins."

"I will sleep soundly because you're here."

"Yes, sir."

Inside my quarters, I searched in the captain's closet and, as I expected I would, I found a bag of golf clubs. I hesitated. A three iron would be too big and a nine iron two small. I settled for a five iron.

I unpacked my bags and noted in one of them a container filled with a brown liquid. A note was attached to it with Scotch tape. "It wasn't your idea to bring this on board, but I thought you might need it. Don't let anyone else on the ship know, lest we give scandal! George."

My thoughtful associate. I poured a splash or two into a government-issue tumbler, realizing that it was almost sacrilege to do so, and sipped it thoughtfully. Only after I had disposed of all the scandalous Bushmill's Green did I realize that it probably wouldn't mix all too well with the motion sickness medicine.

Then I prayed again for the safety of the ship and its crew, for those whose lives were in danger, and for all those who go down to the sea in ships. Myself included.

With the five iron as a companion, I fell promptly to sleep.

Somewhere in the course of the night, I was awakened by a presence in the room, a sickly, half-evil, not altogether human presence.

"I am tired," I informed the presence. "I need my sleep. Get the hell out of here and leave me alone."

The presence hesitated, perhaps not used to such treatment.

"Go away!" I ordered it, gripping my bed companion firmly, just in case I had misread the phenomenon.

It seemed reluctant to take its leave.

"All you're really good at," I continued, "is frightening

anxious women and offish admirals. You don't scare me. Get out of here. Now."

It left.

But not completely. As I returned to sleep, I felt it lingering, defeated but not routed, at the fringes of my cabin.

CHAPTER 8

"THEY FOUND JESSICA Wade," Lieutenant Keane informed me at a quarter to seven (oh-six-forty-five navy time) when she met me at the door of my cabin. "Just as you suggested. Execution style. She had been stuffed into an auxiliary fuel tank. The sailors who found her are spooked. So is the whole ship."

The young woman looked even more worn and weary than yesterday.

"Indeed."

"So am I. She was my C.O. A pathetic, lazy incompetent. I had to do all the work. Still, she wasn't a bad woman."

"Nor, I daresay, was Lieutenant Ericsson a bad man."

"They were two of a kind, actually." She led me down the passageway where I was to have breakfast with the admiral. "Ineffectual, pleasant, washed up in the navy."

"Ah." As I had expected.

"They both had jobs waiting for them. They never really liked the navy. Then Rogers Hoy came along, and they were swept up in whatever magic power he had over such people."

"You felt pressures, too?"

"Affirmative. Enormous pressure. I knew they were crazy, and I love the skipper. Yet working with them all the time, I began to feel like maybe they were right. They were like cult members. Anyone who didn't see what was happening on the ship the way they did was deceiving themselves."

"Typical. True believers."

"So, two of them died for their beliefs."

"Arguably."

"Is Hoy's body somewhere on the ship?"

"That remains to be seen."

"The NIS will give me a hard time this morning."

"Not twice, unless I am much mistaken." I had resolved that I would tolerate no interference from the navy cops. None whatsoever.

"Have a nice breakfast with Admiral Crawford." She knocked on the door with its two very large stars.

"I doubt it."

"He is scared swatless, as Megan would say."

"Ah, the virtuous and skillful Megan . . . Never underestimate God's mercy or his love, Mary Anne Keane."

"Come in, Padre," the admiral said, greeting me at the door. "Good to see you. . . . Some of the best officers that have ever served under me were chaplains of your faith. Real men."

"I'm delighted to hear it." Whatever charges have been leveled against me in a checkered career in the priesthood, I have never been characterized as a "real man." More likely, as I may have noted before, as "the little man who wasn't there again today."

"You know Captain Henry, my chief of staff, Commander Klein, my aide, and Lieutenant McCarthy, my staff assistant. He's one of you Romans."

I did not know them, but I shook hands with reasonable firmness with all of them. They were, I surmised, doomed to be yes-men.

I sat at the table, covered with linen and china, a smaller and more elegant wardroom than the captain's. Despite his hardiness, the admiral was as pale as the linen.

"Terrible thing happened here, Bishop," the admiral said. "Isn't it, men?"

"Yes, sir."

They had given the appropriate answer.

"Poor Speed. None of it is his fault. Wouldn't have happened if they hadn't sent that horse's ass Digby Hoy off to this ship. My fitness report on him stands. Speed is one of the finest officers I've ever known. Isn't that true, men?"

Again they agreed unanimously.

I gave my modest breakfast order to a Hispanic (male) mess steward: grapefruit juice, raisin bran and cream, an order of bacon, well make that two orders, and an English muffin with raspberry preserves. Well, make it two.

The steward smiled appreciatively.

"I don't know what the promotion board will make of all this stuff. Probably make him wait till next year, though it wouldn't be fair, and they all know it. But Hoy had connections."

"I believe that the captain is a close relation of Senator Nora Cronin."

"Really? He never said that. I don't think anyone knows. Typical of Speed."

People would know before I was finished. The playing field would be tilted back to even. Doubtless, Admiral Crawford would contact his allies and patrons in Washington with the information.

And doubtless, too, Milord Cronin had sent me to take action to level the playing field for Dave Cronin. The cardinal could tell the senator that it was my idea. The senator had often said that she trusted my judgment more than that of her brother-in-law. A perfectly reasonable position, it always seemed to me.

The other Roman took up the conversation.

"Do you have any idea, Bishop, of where we might find Commander Hoy's body?"

"Yes," the admiral reclaimed the conversation. "Damn clever thinking on your part to figure out where the other two bodies might be."

"I'm afraid not. Perhaps those who murdered the other two did not have the time to throw them over the side of the ship."

"It wouldn't be all that easy a task," Admiral Crawford agreed. Drag them up to the flight deck, give 'em a pretty good heave. Take a couple of people to do it."

"Two pretty strong people," Captain Henry ventured to agree.

"Well, I suppose the NIS will get to the bottom of it this time," the admiral dabbed his lips with his napkin, indicating that breakfast was over. "At least they have two corpses to work with."

My breakfast, however, was by no means finished. Even though the three hollow men promptly excused themselves and left the wardroom, I continued to fulfill my daily obligation to store up energy. The admiral made no motion to leave. Doubtless, he wanted to talk to me about whatever had scared him so badly.

"I think he's still on the ship, Padre," he said as soon as the door had closed on his staff.

"Indeed."

"In some form or another."

"So?"

"I've *seen* him, Padre. A couple of times. Last night he was in my cabin. I came in and found him poring over my charts. He turned around and smiled at me and then . . . Well, he seemed to disappear. It was a hideous smile."

"Most disconcerting."

"This was before they found the bodies."

"I see."

"I've been through some rough stuff in my life, Padre. Things in Nam I don't like to talk about. But this is the damnedest thing I've ever encountered. Is Hoy alive or dead?"

I was not about to show my hand, especially since it was empty.

"Something evil, very evil, is happening on the U.S.S. *Langley*, Admiral. I'm afraid it's not over. I have reason to suspect that Commander Hoy activated it; he may have been only a minor actor in the drama."

That was pretty oracular. I didn't have any precise idea about what I meant. In fact, I had made it up on the spur of the moment. However, having said it, I felt that it was plausible, all too plausible.

The admiral tried to light a cigarette, but his fingers were shaking, and he gave it up as a bad business. How did a man with his nerves ever rise to command?

"Well, like I say, I'll be glad when the NIS boys get aboard and straighten out this mess. This is my last command, you know, Padre. None of what happened is, strictly speaking, my responsibility. But it doesn't look good. . . . Do you play golf, Padre?"

"Alas, no."

"Some of your men are the finest golfers in the fleet. Thought you might come and play with me someday. Retiring in San Diego, of course. Can't beat the climate."

I had a brief fantasy of him as a C.O. in British India saying the same thing about Simla.

"Come visit us, anyhow?"

"Surely." It was merely a conventional reply and hence not a falsehood.

"If you could have seen him, Padre." The admiral rose from the table. "He looked dead! And my cabin is still clammy." He shivered. "I almost don't want to go back there for fear he is waiting for me."

I took my leave. Neither Admiral Crawford nor I offered to shake hands. Lieutenant Keane was waiting for me.

"Is he still scared, Bishop?"

"That's affirmative. He is terrified. . . . Did he and the late Commander Hoy ever serve together?"

"I think he was XO on the *Enterprise* when Hoy was a junior officer. Do you think that explains anything?"

"Perhaps the depth of his terror . . . Would it be possible to interview some of the other officers who were involved in the Hoy neurosis?"

She hesitated. Lieutenant Keane became more appealing, the greater her worries and concerns.

"I think Chief Larsen from my office and Lieutenant Chisolm who supervises our television station both might be willing to talk. They are among the more reasonable—what should I call it—survivors of the cult. It was kind of like a cult, wasn't it, Bishop?"

"That's a useful model. . . . And how are you doing?"

"Becoming more neurotic each hour," she said with a laugh. "More worried about Dave. More in love with him, to be honest. More convinced that I don't belong in the navy."

"And he does?"

She shrugged her slim, vulnerable, and attractive shoulders.

"As long as he thinks he does, then he does."

"Let me ask you a candid question, Mary Anne. Does being in love with the captain interfere with you doing your job?"

"No," she replied promptly. "It might interfere with my life just now. But I'm a professional. I do my work regardless. Maybe being in love helps. It makes me more alert, more sensitive, more perceptive. . . . Why do you ask?"

It also made her more beautiful, but she didn't know that.

"I'm curious about the more general question of the impact on shipboard life of the presence of substantial numbers of both genders."

She laughed, almost gaily. "It makes it more complicated and more interesting. It's forcing the navy to look at people in a different way. It's distracting, especially when there's a man around with whom you want to sleep. Or a woman, I suppose. I don't think that it impedes our efficiency. Some men said it would, but they didn't understand human nature very well."

"Not quite monks and nuns?" I asked.

"Not quite, but partly, some of the time."

We had arrived back at my quarters.

"Lieutenant Colonel Williamson would like to talk to you, Bishop. And Lieutenant Commander Shorter. The colonel is the C.O. of the marine squadron and the commander is the supply officer.

"I see. I would seem suddenly to be popular."

"You solved two mysteries last night. I'm sure the NIS will want to talk to you, too."

"They will be giving the crew a hard time, I presume."

She sighed. "They're not nice men. They like to intimidate and haze."

"Indeed."

She would certainly be a prime target for their hazing. It was her superior officer whose body had been found curled up in a fuel tank. She was also the kind of lovely and vulnerable woman that some cops liked to pick on. As well as some Naval Academy midshipmen.

"You can see Colonel Williamson out on the flight deck, sir. They're doing a walk down for FOD—foreign object damage—now."

She opened the door to my quarters.

"What's a walk down?"

"The air crews and anyone else who wants to, line up across the deck and walk from the bow to the fantail looking for foreign objects that might be drawn into a jet's engine or interfere with a trap. It's a safety precaution and a bit of a social occasion, too. I can take you out on the deck, if you wish."

She escorted me across the dining room/parlor section of the captain's in-port cabin, up the steps, and opened the door to the flight deck, which I had been sternly warned against opening unless I was accompanied by one of my official escorts.

Speaking of escorts, where was the good if troubled Father O'Malley? Avoiding Lieutenant Keane?

"Josh Williamson, Bishop," the C.O. of the VMFA squadron confirmed his name and shook hands as Lieutenant Keane introduced us. "Good to meet you. Fantastic job of figuring things out. Thanks for bringing the bishop out here, Mary Anne."

"You're welcome, sir."

Colonel Williamson was a tall, sturdy man with a lean face, dark red beard, and a receding hairline. His voice was gruff, but his words were measured and thoughtful.

"The idea is that we talk while we keep our eyes on the deck."

"So I understand."

It was a hot day without a breeze. Summer weather instead of late winter off the California coast. Many of the FOD team were wearing shorts and T-shirts, including Megan, who was bounding about giving orders to everyone.

"Nice woman, Mary Anne. Nothing against the dead, but she's a lot more competent than her predecessor. And better looking, too. Skipper shows good taste."

"Just a minute," I turned around and retrieved a small bolt from the deck.

"Lemme see. Nice going, Bishop. I missed that one. It could make trouble. Skipper would be furious if it ruined a fan blade in an engine. We don't permit that kind of accident on the *Langley*."

Just then, Megan galloped up, a plastic bag in hand. "Colonel Williamson, sir. I don't think we should let Bishop Blackie participate in the FOD, sir. I'm sure that

with those Coke bottle glasses, he can't see anything on
the deck, sir."

Megan was killing two birds with one stone, mocking
me and her C.O.

"Show this pilot what you found, Bishop."

I produced from my Bulls jacket pocket the offending
bolt.

"Oooh!" Megan exclaimed. "From one of the tractors,
right, Colonel, sir? Gimme! I collect everything in this
bag and then we examine each piece carefully afterward.
Sometimes Skipper Speed wants to inspect the bag, too,
doesn't he, Colonel, sir?"

Megan snatched away my prize and bounded farther
along the slowly moving line.

"Naturally you appointed her to responsibility for the
plastic bag."

Josh Williamson chuckled. "It might be worth my life
if I took the bag away from her and gave it to someone
else. . . . She's a great morale boost for the squadron—
and the best, absolute best aviator I've ever served with."

"Ah."

"I don't suppose a bishop would notice those long,
lovely legs."

"Not the first thing," I replied.

"Good point . . . Everything's not what it seems on
this ship, Bishop. I'm sure you've noticed that."

"Indeed." Was this a change of subject or a continua-
tion?

"Speed is a great skipper. The kind of savvy, humane
guy we need these days. It isn't only safety, not even
mainly. He's searching for the best way to deal with the
problems of a ship with a thousand women on board. It
isn't easy, and not everyone likes what he's doing.
Doesn't help, I suppose, that he's in love with one of the
best. Or maybe it does help. I don't know."

"Ah."

"Some officers feel that women ought not to be on

combat ships. They know the decision has been made, but they don't accept it. A skipper that prevents hazing and harassment and insists we treat them as shipmates we respect offends a lot of guys."

"I would imagine that it does."

"Rogers Hoy made it worse, stirring up all the trouble about women and then almost hypnotizing some of them. Real nut case. Course, men get hypnotized by nutty women, too."

"I have observed that phenomenon."

"It doesn't bother me, not so long as they're good at what they do. Generally, they are better than men, too; more careful, more diligent. Then there's someone like your friend with red hair and the tight T-shirt. She can fly in my squadron any day or night."

"Patently."

"Mind you, I have a hard time with the picture of her killing someone in combat. I don't know, maybe I'm old-fashioned. Women can fly combat planes, but I don't want them killing anyone. It just doesn't seem right."

"You don't think they'd do their duty?"

"Yeah, they would. I'm not worried about that. I'm worried about afterward. Guys get cut up when they think about the people they've killed. Women would get cut up more. I don't know. Maybe I'm just making that up because of my prejudices. That's what my wife says. She says I want to think women are more tender than men."

"Do you?"

"Yeah, Padre. I do."

Josh Williamson was trying to tell me something. I wasn't picking it up.

"She's met Megan, of course. I tell my wife that Megan is more tender than all the men in VMFA put together, and my wife says that the poor thing has to be. On the face of it, those words don't mean a thing, but I've been married long enough not to say that."

"Wise man."

"But you see my point?"

We had reached the island in our detection of foreign objects. I found a quarter-inch piece of identifiable metal. Megan was summoned to take charge of it.

"You're really good at this, Bishop Blackie. . . . Do you sleep in that Bulls jacket or does it only look that way?"

"I sleep in my purple cassock."

She guffawed and dashed off.

"It's hard on the wives ashore, their men out here with a thousand women, most of them unattached. Not on my wife. She says that I can have a divorce anytime I want, but I get the three teenagers. Not all women are that secure, if you see what I mean."

"Oh, yes."

"So Speed is trying to create a situation on this ship where everyone is relaxed about something that's hard to relax about. Moreover, he's done a pretty good job, if you ask me. With some of the guys, that's a black mark against him."

"I can imagine."

"I figure it's like drinking. It's a lot of damn Protestant nonsense—and I'm a Methodist—not to let young men have a bottle of beer or two every day."

"And older men a drink or two."

"Right. So long as it doesn't interfere. I don't support public fornication, either. But I don't see how you can prevent some private stuff on a ship this size with six thousand people. You see my point?"

"Legislate against it, but you can't make it unpopular."

"Lot of guys say a brothel can't be a good fighting ship."

"Those very words?"

"Those very words. They call Speed the whoremaster."

"Is the *Langley* a brothel, Josh?"

He laughed. "Are you kidding? Most of the women realize that they're in control and intend to stay in control. Somehow the guys don't like that, either. They want it to be a brothel both so that there won't be any more ships like this and so they can get theirs while the getting is good."

He was warning me that there were other and potentially more dangerous opponents of Captain Cronin on the ship than the passive aggressive followers of Commander E. Rogers Hoy.

We reached the fantail. Megan gleefully waved her plastic bag. As I walked back to the island, she caught up with me.

"Isn't it awful about Commander Wade and Lieutenant Ericsson, Bishop Blackie? What kind of people would do that?"

The ever changeable hoyden now displayed tears in her vast green eyes.

"Bad people, Megan. Very bad people."

"They didn't deserve to die. Not that way."

"None of us deserve to die, Megan, and there are no good ways to die."

"I'll die someday," she said, an act of faith in what seemed to her presently an unlikely event.

"Most people your age are not willing to admit that."

"Oh, we know it, all right. We just don't want to think about it."

"God's love is totally implacable, Megan. She never turns away from any of us. Human lovers, even the best of them, have their bad moments. God never does."

"I certainly give Her a run for her money," she said with a sigh. "I mean, I go whole days without thinking of Her once."

"I'm sure She enjoys you, Megan, more than anyone else does."

"I hope so. She'll take care of the commander and the lieutenant, won't she, Bishop? Even if we couldn't?"

"You can count on that. . . . Still, pray for them both."

"Oh, I will, Bishop, I will," she said fervently.

"And for the rest of the ship."

"For everyone."

Then she bounced away and bounced back again.

"I'll see you at the confirmation this evening. Air ops will be over by then. CAG promised."

"You are involved in the confirmation?"

"Sure. I'm a sponsor. Can you imagine that! Was I ever flattered when Tina asked me!"

Patently, we could not have a confirmation on the ship without Margaret Mary Monahan being involved. No way.

Mary Anne Keane appeared outside the island, her lips tight, her eyes tense, her shoulders slumped.

"NIS wants to see you now, Bishop. They're in the lounge next to the wardroom."

"I don't have to ask how your session with them went?"

"Somehow I am responsible for the death of my superior officer. They're horrible men."

"Doubtless."

"They want to see you right now."

No one, but no one, talks to Kate Collins Ryan's son that way. "Tell them I'll drop by in an hour or so."

CHAPTER 9

I SPENT THE next hour and a half straightening out the time line for the problem of United States Ship *Langley*—something I would have done the day before if scopolamine had not dimmed what is left of my gray cells.

December 10, Commander E. Rogers Hoy reports for duty on *Langley*, just before it sails for cruise off California coast.

December 14, Commander Hoy tightens up on all personnel immediately responsible to him. They must salute at all times. Anger among personnel. Appeal to captain, who rescinds the order.

December 16, Hoy accuses two enlisted personnel on his staff of fraternization because he alleges that they were holding hands. Charge dropped at captain's mast hearing.

December 18, Hoy accuses his staff of general incompetence, promises unfavorable fitness reports for all of them.

December 20, Hoy begins patrols of ship, looking for evidence of drugs, alcohol, and fraternization. Ericsson and Wade accompany him.

December 21, Hoy and team break small drug ring run by two jaygees, one an Academy graduate. Men arrested and turned over to authorities on shore for court martial the next day when the ship docks for Christmas break.

December 22, immediate staff sponsors large Christmas party for Commander Hoy.

It had taken exactly twelve days for him to spin the magic of his neurosis. I had seen this marvelous game played once before and had read the sparse literature on it as provided by my sister Mary Kate, who is a shrink of some renown. I had been deputed to investigate the behavior of a new chancellor in a diocese not too far from Chicago who had won over the entire staff of the chancery against the bishop, a kind, gentle man who had appointed the priest chancellor because he couldn't get along with people in his parish. Within a month, he and his entire staff were petitioning Rome for the bishop's removal.

The dynamics are simple, Mary Kate informed me. You come in and are vicious to everyone. So all those with father hang-ups hate you instantly. Then you convert that hatred to another and higher father figure and ally yourself with your subordinates against him. You then become the good father. They adore you and link their destiny to yours, even though your plots don't have a chance of being successful.

"He's sleeping with at least one of the women, Punk (an affectionate family diminutive that has come to convey, at least on rare occasions, respect). Count on it. Probably more. It ties them even more closely to him. Sleeping with the good father figure is great fun for that kind of woman."

In fact, the man, who hardly seemed a prime sex object, was sleeping with the bishop's secretary and the director of religious education, though not, it would seem, at the same time.

Was Rogers Hoy, the firm crusader against fraternization, sleeping in some safe, hidden space with Lieutenant Commander Wade?

Probably. And with others, too.

I returned to my chart.

January 5, Hoy brought charges before the admiral of fraternization between the captain and Lieutenant Keane. He charged that he and others had seen them "talk intimately" and that the captain had spent the Christmas weekend in the lieutenant's San Diego apartment. The admiral had dismissed the charges as vague and unsubstantiated and informally reprimanded Commander Hoy for spying on the captain when he was ashore. There was no rule against fraternization ashore.

Doubtless, but Hoy had made his point to his by now intensely loyal followers.

I checked the records. Mary Anne Keane had assumed her assignment as deputy in the public affairs office in late October. It had been a quick love affair with the skipper. Two tired and lonely people seeking joy at Christmas.

God, I had to presume, understood.

Hoy devoted the rest of January and February to stepping up his campaign. Every week there were a new batch of charges brought to captain's mast. Increasingly, other officers on the *Langley* protested the harassment of their subordinates. When Hoy accused Megan Monahan of insubordination, both Captain Gill and Colonel Williamson howled in protest. Other members of the wing may have made threatening remarks to Hoy. Naturally, he loved it because it tightened the net of supporters around him.

The six weeks between the middle of January and the end of February brought more than forty charges, some of them trivial, some of them serious. Fifteen of them alleged fraternization, as hunted out by Hoy's people.

The captain had asked his XO to stop the witch hunt. Hoy had replied that the ship was out of control and someone had to do something about it. Admiral Crawford had urged the captain to relieve the XO, but Captain Cronin said he would give him one more chance. He ordered Hoy to cease the frivolous charges. Even the

NIS, which had no aversion to the truth unless they were told to cover it up, agreed that most of the charges were frivolous.

The XO laughed at Captain Cronin and reminded him that he was the one who had discovered the drug ring.

Lieutenant Keane was charged with something every other week: disrespect to Commander Wade, chronic failure to finish her work, habitual tardiness. All the charges were supported by Hoy's crowd. Each time, the captain had dismissed the charges as either groundless or fatuous.

On February 27, Commander Wade had recommended to the XO that Lieutenant Keane be relieved of duty. Hoy promptly relieved her and appointed a young ensign, just out of Annapolis and not part of his team, as acting deputy public affairs officer.

The captain countermanded the order.

No wonder Mary Anne Keane looked so thin and pale.

On March 1, the captain, under pressure from the other senior officers of the ship, including the admiral and CAG, ordered the XO to cease all further harassment of the ship's personnel or be relieved of his command. The XO replied that if anyone was to be relieved, it was not him.

Like the chancellor of the diocese where I had to clean up the mess, E. Rogers "Digby" Hoy had been lucky. The bishop in the diocese was an intelligent, humane, and liberal man, loved by his priests and people. Rational gentleman that he was, he could not believe what was happening. He saw the sickness spreading all around him and thought that he could reason the sickness away. In fact, he should have fired the chancellor on the spot and suspended him if he refused to leave his office. By that time, there would have been a public fight, but the bishop would have won it.

So, too, Dave Cronin should have dismissed his XO and recommended psychiatric treatment for him. By this time, as the NIS report had observed, the XO and his supporters were actively discussing behavior that could be construed as mutiny.

It wouldn't have worked. This was not the *Cain* of *Cain Mutiny* fame. It was an aircraft carrier in peacetime only a half hour's flight away from North Island. But Hoy had convinced himself and his followers that they could and would win. The ship was out of control, and they would save it.

Why play the game? To salvage his career by taking command of a carrier?

Hardly. His career was over, and he knew it.

To destroy Dave Cronin?

Not very likely, not at least as the main reason for his activities.

Why then?

Because, as the man said of Mount Everest, it was there. Because "Digby" Hoy was driven by his own inner demons to do it. Because it was possible to do it.

NIS had dryly observed that the events of March 5 to 8 might not have happened if the captain had relieved the XO immediately. But that was hindsight. Who knows what would have happened if he had replaced Hoy with Commander Dempsey. There might have been active mutiny with the marine guards arresting Hoy and his supporters.

That's what happened in the diocese. The chancellor moved into the bishop's office and the staff barred the door to the bishop. The priests of the diocese, as priests do, equivocated. But the police removed the chancellor and his gang and restored the bishop to his office in the now-empty chancery. The malcontents sent a petition to Rome. Baffled, the congregation of the clergy said to Sean Cronin, whom they routinely contact only when there's a major mess, to in effect find out what the hell is going on out there.

So he issued his usual "See to it, Blackwood" command.

Under my direction, the bishop finally suspended the chancellor, fired the rest of the chancery office, and appointed new people. Rome rejected their petition. The civil courts threw out their suit. The chancellor now has a parish way up in the mountains in a distant diocese. The lay staff have scattered to the winds.

I forbade the poor bishop ever to hire any of them again.

That's what might have happened if Captain Cronin had fired his XO.

Instead, murder happened.

On the afternoon of March 5, Hoy reported to the security officer that there were threats against his life, verbal threats whispered behind his back. The security officer, Lieutenant John Larkin, in turn reported these alleged threats to the captain; he told the captain that he thought Hoy had turned paranoid. Nonetheless, he urged the captain to provide Hoy with an escort of marines and to post a guard at the door to his cabin that evening. Hoy came to supper in the wardroom with Lieutenant Ericsson. He was pale and edgy, twitching, one of the marines later reported. Ericsson tried to reassure him, but to no avail. Hoy was convinced that the captain had put out a contract on him and that the marine guards were in fact the assassins assigned to kill him.

There had been a scene in the wardroom when the captain entered as the XO was leaving. Hoy had accused the captain of plotting his murder. Still trying to be reasonable, the captain tried to explain that he had no such intentions, and that the marines would protect him. Hoy replied that the marines were killers. Captain Murray, the C.O. of the sea marine detachment, who was present, told Hoy that he was a fruitcake. The skipper had to separate them. Hoy screamed that he would bring charges the next day against Murray.

The rest of the wardroom watched and listened in horror. Commander Carlson, the engineering officer, urged the captain to lock Hoy up for the night and ship him out on the morning COD for psychiatric observation at North Island. Captain Cronin agreed that if there were no improvement in the morning, he would do just that.

The NIS report, enjoying the luxury of hindsight, criticized the captain for not following that advice. However, it did quote Carlson as saying that he understood the captain's decision to give Hoy "one more chance."

"Digby was clearly around the bend, but he didn't seem a threat to himself or to anyone else. I thought he should be locked up merely to preserve order on the ship."

The marine guard was changed during the night. The two men in each shift had excellent records. They had taken and passed lie detector tests in which they had reported that no one had entered the XO's cabin in the course of the night, except Lieutenant Commander Wade and Lieutenant Ericsson, both of whom had papers for Hoy to sign. Lieutenant Ericsson left first and then, perhaps a half hour later, Commander Wade.

At that time, the XO seemed more composed and confident. However, one of the marines noted that his eyes were still dancing nervously. No one else had entered or tried to enter his room.

Except the mailman, as in G. K. Chesterton's famous Father Brown story.

Had Wade and Hoy made love in that half hour? Apparently, the NIS had not thought the question worth asking. Perhaps that was understandable. I would not have thought of it if it had not been for the chancery office incident.

"He doesn't so much enjoy screwing women," my virtuous sibling had warned me, "as dominating them.

Tormenting them. Not quite S-M, but something that edges close to it. Clammy hands type."

Commander Hoy did not emerge from his cabin at six hundred as he usually did. His neighbor, Lieutenant Commander Shorter, the deputy supply officer, had emerged from his room shortly thereafter and had joked with the marines that the XO must be really nervous because he had locked the door to their joint bathroom, thus forcing Shorter to use a common lavatory down the passageway and around the corner.

At nine hundred, a distraught Commander Wade had arrived and pounded on the door to the cabin. There had been no answer from the inside. She accused the marines of harming Commander Hoy.

The lance corporal in charge of the two-man detachment summoned Captain Murray and Lieutenant Larkin, who were unable to arouse the XO. Murray, who had wisely come with two women marines, in his turn summoned the C.O., who finally ordered the lock opened. Lieutenant Larkin reported that the master key that would open the door had disappeared. The C.O. then ordered that the door be opened with an acetylene torch. The C.O. and the other officers had entered the room and found no one and nothing.

Commander Wade became hysterical, accused the captain of kidnapping the XO, and physically attacked the captain. Captain Murray ordered the women marines to remove her to sick bay where she was sedated.

The crew searched the ship for the next three days and found no trace of Commander Hoy. The search appeared, according to NIS, to be thorough and professional.

Commander Hoy's friends and colleagues made repeated accusations against the captain and other senior officers of the ship and against the admiral and his staff. No proof was offered to substantiate the allegations. Wade and Ericsson formally accused the captain of murder. They alleged that the XO had proof of the captain's dereliction of duty, but the nature of the dereliction and the proof were insubstantial. NIS concluded that Hoy's friends were suffering from a mixture of paranoia and hysteria.

An understatement, it seemed to me.

The NIS conducted its own thorough search of the ship and found no trace of Captain Hoy. It concluded that either he had fallen or thrown himself overboard or had, by a ruse, escaped ashore on a COD before anyone was aware he was missing. The COD crews, however, reported that no one who might resemble the XO had been on the plane in the course of the day.

The report paid no attention to the locked-room mystery. It simply didn't exist.

And what was a "thorough" search of the ship? How could you search a fourteen-story, three-football-field-long ship with so many spaces that no one knew the exact number? Patently, repeated searches had not found either Wade or Ericsson. Might "Digby" Hoy still be on the ship? Dead or alive?

A city of six thousand people would provide many hiding places for someone who had allies who wished to hide him.

Someone knocked at my door.

"Yes?" I said suspiciously.

Another knock.

I put aside my notes, sighed loudly as is my wont, and walked to the door.

"Yes?" I repeated.

The knocker was a petty officer in a navy blue uniform, jacket and tie included.

"The Naval Investigative Service requests your presence in the lounge of the captain's wardroom immediately, sir."

"Do they, now? Well, tell them that I will join them shortly, as soon as I finish the work in which I am presently engaged."

"I have been instructed to accompany you, sir."

"Well, then, sailor, you can wait outside till I am ready to be accompanied."

The young man shifted nervously.

"I have been ordered to accompany you immediately, sir."

"Young man," I said politely but firmly, "Please inform your superiors that they try to intimidate me only at considerable risk to themselves."

I closed the door and locked it.

Normally, I get along fine with cops, so long as they are not bent cops. On the basis of their record, I must presume that the NIS is bent, that its masters have perverted it so that it's main goals are to cover up navy mistakes such as the perennial scandals at the Academy or, even worse, to fabricate explanations, as in the case of the turret explosion on the *Iowa*.

One look at me, and they would assume that I was ineffectual and incompetent. Maybe they would be in for a surprise. With an even louder sigh, I went back to my work.

On the morning of March 8, Wade and Ericsson did not report for work in the morning. Commander Dempsey, who had been appointed temporary XO, reported their absence to the captain. He, in turn, ordered Lieutenant Larkin, the security officer, to investigate and informed the NIS agents who were still on board.

Their cabin mates reported that neither had slept in their beds that night. Once more, the crew searched the ship as did NIS.

"As thorough a search as humanly possible," the NIS report informed its reader.

They had excellent reasons for resenting the nosy little bishop who had discovered not one but two bodies.

Two bodies . . .

I picked up my phone and dialed the captain.

"Skipper, Blackie."

"Yes, Bishop," he said with what I thought was understandable lack of enthusiasm. "Have you figured out where Digby Hoy is?"

"Hardly. However, I do want to confirm that Commander Wade was raped."

Dead silence.

"How did you figure that out?"

"It fits a pattern that is beginning to emerge."

"I suppose," he said wearily. "We can't keep it a secret much longer. If I had told Mary Anne, she would have said I should have informed the crew immediately before the rumors spread."

"That would be excellent advice."

"Roger. I'll do it."

"Ask her how to do it."

"I'm not that great a fool, Bishop, that I would not ask."

"And she was raped?"

"Her body was naked when they found it. She had been repeatedly raped and sodomized. By several men."

"God save us!"

I meant that. Evil was rampaging through the ship. The poor woman. Another victim in the long history of masculine brutality.

"Have there been many such attacks on the ship?"

"None in either our cruise to the Western Pacific nor on this cruise. A couple accusations of molestation and harassment in San Diego. We have dealt with them appropriately. This is a safe ship for women." He paused. "Well, it used to be a safe ship for women."

"It is dangerously unsafe now," I warned him.

"I know that, Bishop. We must find the bastards."

"Oh yes, Captain. And find them we shall."

"I'm going to put the ship on a full security alert. Obviously this will terrify the women."

"Not without reason."

I returned to the notes I was making from the NIS report.

Their conclusion was that the most probable explanation of the events on the *Langley* was a collective suicide of three officers who were plotting mutiny and whose plot had been discovered.

"Bullshit!" Someone had written across the offending paragraph. Night Plane Lane, to judge by subsequent comments he had initialed.

They concluded by suggesting that lax discipline on the ship had contributed to the deaths and that the "personal relationship" between the captain and Lieutenant Keane may also have played a part in "this bizarre case."

Admiral Crawford had written in neat script, "Discipline on the ship was never lax. Innuendo against captain unjustified."

Night Plane Lane's scrawl was more vivid.

"These final remarks are nothing more than NIS's attempt to cover its own ass for its abject failure to solve the crimes. *Langley* has an excellent reputation. Neither captain nor crew are responsible for behavior of a borderline personality who should never have been sent to sea at this time. There is no foundation for allegations about captain's personal life. What may have happened ashore is no one's business."

Precisely.

There were further handwritten notes from Admiral Lane.

"March 12, Captain Cronin has advanced the next officers in line to the positions vacated by the disappearances on his ship. Thus Commander Dempsey becomes acting XO and Lieutenant Keane becomes acting public affairs officer. He had no need to consult me on these appointments but thought it wise to do so under the circumstances. I had no problem with his decisions. All are excellent officers."

No note about Lieutenant Keane.

"March 15, I write this note with some hesitation. Captain Cronin reports paranormal manifestations on the ship. Apparently Digby won't stay dead, but haunts the ship, particularly women on the ship. I don't know what the United States Navy is supposed to do about that. It is disturbing. Something is terribly wrong out there."

"March 20, Captain Cronin asks permission to invite on board a distant cousin who is a Catholic bishop, a certain John B. Ryan. The bishop will come aboard under the guise of administering confirmation. However, he is also supposed to be an expert in the solution of locked-room mysteries. Fine with me. Though maybe we need an exorcist.

"I checked on him with a guy I know in the Pentagon who is, or at least is supposed to be, an expert on Catholic clergy. He tells me not to be fooled by this guy who looks utterly harmless and most of the time badly confused. He also says that he thinks he's the son of the late Admiral Ned Ryan, one of the great characters and the great heroes in the history of the United States Navy."

"Harmless and most of the time badly confused." Well, fair enough.

I wondered again what the old fella was thinking of this excursion of mine.

I pondered my notes. There were a number of pertinent questions:

1. What had happened to E. Rogers "Digby" Hoy? Who had reason to kill him?
2. Why the locked-room mumbo-jumbo?
3. Why the gruesome and apparently needless murders of Wade and Ericsson?

I had begun to see the vague outline of an explanation. I didn't like it. The smell of evil on *Langley* was turning truly ugly. It made little sense. That was the problem. Why such viciousness?

I consulted the card next to my phone and dialed the public affairs office.

"Keane," said the voice at the other end. No intervening secretary.

"Blackie."

"I've just talked to the skipper. I'm working on a statement. . . . Do you know what the fear of rape means to a woman?"

"Only as an outsider."

"We will have more than a thousand terrified women in a half hour. They are already frightened by Digby's wandering ghost. They'll see Wade's fate as a strong suggestion of what's going to happen to them. I know it's a risk we take when we go to sea on a warship . . ."

"Or when you walk down the street at night."

"That's right, Bishop. We have to find the men who did it."

"That we shall."

But having found them, how would we obtain evidence to convict them?

"Have you talked to the NIS people yet?"

"Oddly enough, I haven't quite found the time yet. I'll probably wander down there in a couple of minutes."

"They'll be furious."

"Doubtless. After that, it will presumably be time for lunch."

"I will meet you in the wardroom. See if I can find Father."

"He is elusive, is he not?"

"Strange man, but a good priest."

I let that go.

"I note from the noise outside that the planes are flying again."

"There's a front coming through, not a bad one, but

there'll be rain and maybe a little fog tonight. Relatively calm seas."

"The proper authorities will cancel flights?"

"Oh, no. It will be good flying weather. These young people have to learn to land at night in bad weather . . . which may be one reason why I decided I didn't want to be a pilot."

"Prudent decison."

"Just now, I'm not so sure."

Before facing the navy cops, I turned my attention to the question Josh Williamson had raised earlier in the morning: Did I want young women pilots, like Margaret Mary Monahan, killing people?

The answer to that was a flat-out no. But then I didn't want young men killing one another, either.

Still, there was a difference. For many millennia humankind and indeed prehumankind had worked out a division of labor in which men had done the fighting when fighting needed to be done and women had taken care of the children, often to be the prizes of war should their men lose. There were exceptions to this cultural custom, of course; humankind is a plastic and flexible species, capable of a wide variety of adaptations. Yet generally there seemed to be a cultural bias against those who bore life taking part in its destruction. For much of human history, there was no choice. Pregnant and nursing women could not fight.

Now, for a combination of reasons, this position seemed to be changing. Women were joining armed services around the world. In most countries, they were excluded from combat, even in Israel, as like Sparta as any modern country could be. But in the United States, women demanded combat roles on the grounds that they would never achieve equality in the services unless they did everything men could do.

They thus put themselves at great risk should they ever become prisoners of war, much greater than their male colleagues would face. They would be challenged by those men who would say that they would not have the steel nerves required of a killer in a situation when killing is required, if only as a means of self-defense. One knows, of course, that many men lack such steel nerves, too, and often do not kill in combat even though they have enemies in their rifle sights. Combat women would also be challenged by men and women who would argue that it was against everything a woman should be to kill in combat.

What they thought themselves, how they resolved these questions was not at all clear, in great part because they are so frequently on the defensive, especially from attacks by men who hated women, as does a substantial proportion of male humankind, and by women who hate other women, as does a substantial proportion of female humankind (though for different reasons).

Perhaps I would ask Megan. Or perhaps I would listen and she might eventually tell me. One thing I did know was that the solution to these delicate questions would have to come from them. No male had the right to venture an opinion, which of course would not stop them from venturing the opinion.

With these confused thoughts filed for further reference, I tore up my notes, which I had committed to memory, and sallied forth to do battle with the Naval Investigative Service.

CHAPTER 10

BEFORE I BEGAN my moment of truth with the NIS, I found my friend Martha, the mess steward from the previous night, and persuaded her to show me how to work the ice cream machine.

Chocolate. Naturally,

I entered the lounge they were using for their office, slobbering up ice cream.

"You gentlemen wanted to see me?" I said between scoops—the characteristically bumbling, ineffectual bishop who often had trouble finding his way back to the cathedral rectory (without even trying to get lost).

It will be said that I was baiting them and there would be a considerable amount of truth in such an assertion. However, it would be utterly erroneous to assert that I was gratuitously baiting them, though I am on occasion capable of such behavior. In point of fact, I wanted to determine a number of things about this crowd of navy gumshoes: in the room, a commander, a lieutenant, a lieutenant, a chief who took notes, and a seaman at the door with a side arm. All wore blue uniforms.

- I wanted to find out how dumb they really were.
- I was curious as to whether their mission was a cover-up of the sort that NIS is required to do every time there is a scandal at the Academy, which is usually almost every month.
- I wondered whether their betters had already

made a decision about the outcome of the investigation.

- Finally, I wanted to ascertain whether they knew anything I didn't know, a very unlikely possibility.

"This is a very serious matter, Mr. Ryan," the commander began.

"Dr. Ryan would be more appropriate if we are using secular titles."

"Several major crimes have been committed on this ship, and we are charged by the secretary of the navy to solve these crimes."

"Personally?"

"Personally, what?"

"Mr. Dalton call you into his office and tell you get out here and solve the rape and murders, just like you solved the disappearance of Commander E. Rogers Hoy?"

He turned an unbecoming color of purple.

"Such assignments need not come directly from the secretary. . . . The fact that you are a Roman Catholic bishop will have no influence in our search for truth in this matter."

"Catholic will do just fine. Some of us find the adjective *Roman* to be a prejudicial nativist stereotype. . . . And I take it that you mean that Mr. Dalton doesn't tell you to go over to Annapolis and cover up the latest dumb thing those idiots have done."

Everyone turned purple.

It will be said by those who criticize me that I was loving every second of this exchange.

Guilty!

"Sir, I would remind you that you are involved in a crime."

"I've been on this boat," I glanced at my watch, "less than twenty-four hours, and as far as I am aware, there have been no crimes, certainly none in which I was involved."

"You were involved in the discovery of the bodies of two naval officers, one of whom had been brutally raped."

"Where I come from, Commander, that's called solving a mystery and indeed solving a mystery that NIS was unable to solve."

"Isn't it true," the Jaygee, an obnoxious little punk who was probably a lawyer, demanded, "that you are a relative of Captain Cronin?"

"Only of Admiral Ned Ryan."

"Never heard of him."

"I would assume not."

"We find it odd that you would come on this ship for a religious function and within twenty-four hours, discover two bodies."

"And I find it odd that NIS would not have immediately searched inactive aircraft."

I searched for a place to put my empty ice cream dish. I ended up putting it on the floor.

"You are not here to engage in criticizing navy personnel."

"As a modest taxpayer, I propose to exercise my right to criticize manifest incompetence whenever I choose."

These guys were truly dumb cops. If they'd had any sense, like John Culhane back in Chicago, they'd ask directly or indirectly for my help. Instead, they figured on intimidating it out of me. They could have proved useful in digging out information. Now I just wanted them out of my way.

"We could hold you as an accessory after the fact to these crimes for refusing to cooperate with us."

First words out of the lieutenant commander. He obviously wasn't a lawyer.

Three bad cops, not a single good cop. These guys didn't know how to do it; but then, you didn't have to be very good to cover up scandals at the Academy.

"Not for any more than five minutes, and your young friend the lawyer here knows it, even if you don't."

I stood up.

"Stay out of our way," the commander barked.

"I'd tell you to stay out of my way," I said as I left the lounge, "but I don't think you're capable of getting in my way."

I found a quiet corner of the wardroom, removed my portable phone from my Bulls jacket, and punched in a number in the Beltway that I have had reason to call on occasion.

"Blackie," said the man on the other end of the line, "What the hell is going on out there?"

I told him.

"Why did those assholes send NIS out there?"

"They work for the government, not for me."

"How long will it take you to clear it up?"

I took a big chance.

"Two or three days at the most. Maybe less."

"OK, I'll keep those dolts out of your hair."

"Fine."

I hung up, as the protocol of such conversation requires.

I went back to the wardroom and obtained another dish of chocolate ice cream.

Then I waited for Lieutenant Mary Anne Keane to arrive for lunch, since I had no reason to expect that Father O'Malley, my other escort, would show up.

What was he all about? I couldn't imagine someone who read Angela of Foligno being involved in rape and murder. But even by clerical standards, he was a strange one.

"Chocolate ice cream as an appetizer?" Mary Anne asked, slumping into a chair next to me.

"It beats salad."

"How did your interview with the gestapo go?"

"As I might have expected."

"They're trying to blame David and me."

David now, was it?

"I think we can preclude the possibility of success in that strategy. As you of all people realize, the media will want a better explanation."

"I know that. But the publicity could destroy David's career, not that I think anyone should stay in the navy for their whole lifetime."

"We can avoid that outcome by the simple expedient of solving the mystery and seeing that he gets credit for it."

Unasked, Martha appeared and began to serve our lunch. She giggled as she removed my empty ice cream dish.

Mary Anne Keane considered me as though she had seen me for the first time. I was, she was deciding, clearly devious enough to be a bishop after all.

Half again and more, my dear, but that's not yet the point.

"You think you can swing that?"

"Arguably."

"You've got to solve the locked-room business, don't you?"

"That should prove no great problem. The question is why the killers bothered with it."

"Do you know who they are?"

"I have plausible explanations for that. I don't understand the motives, to say nothing of the motives for the other two crimes, and especially for their brutality. Herein lies incomprehensible evil."

She nodded as if she understood. Patently, she did not, because neither did I.

In retrospect, my error, one of the many, was to underestimate how great was the evil which already had spun out of control because of the concatenation of various energies, each of which might have been minor in itself.

Martha served us a salad. I declined on the grounds I was not a rabbit.

"This afternoon, Bishop, you are to interview Chief Larsen of my office, Lieutenant Chisolm of our television station, and Lieutenant Commander Shorter, the acting supply officer."

"Indeed."

"And you have a confirmation at 5:00."

"Which ceremony will include the ineffable and virtuous Megan in the role of a sponsor."

"Nothing really important can go down on this ship without her being involved. . . . Might I suggest someone else? Immediately after lunch?"

"Certainly."

"It's Lieutenant Johnny Larkin, our chief master at arms. He, too, worked for Commander Hoy."

"Yes, I believe I saw his name on the list of those cited for insubordination."

"And with more reason than your friend Megan. Johnny is, well, you'll have to meet him. He's the one person under the XO who was totally unaffected by the—well, whatever it was. Johnny is a very special kind of character."

"And what does the chief master at arms do?"

"Security. He has his own people and the sea marines work for him, too. They're all over the ship now in our security alert. Johnny, among other things, is very impressive at his job."

"Indeed . . . Perhaps I could interview the engineer, too."

"Commander Carlson . . . He was one of the most vigorous proponents of action against the XO. Too bad David didn't listen to him."

"Arguably. . . . Do I understand correctly that your, ah, relationship with the skipper did not antedate Christmas?"

She turned pink and indeed remained that color for the next several exchanges.

"It was . . . I mean, we made love only that week. I'm afraid I formed a crush on him the day he arrived on the ship. I assumed that he didn't notice me. He claimed he did, the night there was a party for him when he took command."

"Indeed."

"I still can't believe that he would notice me."

"Men don't notice you, Mary Anne?"

She squirmed uncomfortably. "They didn't use to. Apparently they do now. I don't quite understand it."

"Mmnn," I said.

"I was driving out of the parking lot at North Island on Christmas Eve. I saw him looking forlorn. Apparently, someone forgot to pick him up. I offered him a ride and then, recklessly, Christmas Eve dinner. He had no Christmas plans. I felt sorry for him."

"Ah."

"We made love before dinner. Almost as soon as we got to my apartment. I'm afraid I was the aggressor."

"Indeed."

"We did go to Mass. He said he thought it was all right to receive communion. So we did. . . . What do you think, Bishop?"

"I'm not going to question the decision you made in good conscience."

Not that in the circumstances either of them had much freedom to make any other choice than they did.

"It was wonderful. I did not know that love could be like that. . . . Then it was time to embark on the ship again, and we had to stop."

"Ah."

The flush faded from her face and her shoulders slumped again.

"Don't sound very penitent, do I, Bishop?"

I ignored that pietistic comment.

"You could, of course, bring about the, ah, validation of the relationship."

I finished the large and delicious hamburger Martha had provided me and decided in the interest of self-restraint not to ask for a second one. She did, however, bring me two glasses of iced tea.

"I can hardly do that now, especially with Hoy's charges and the murders and the NIS all over the place."

"Can you not?"

"You're saying I should?" She feigned shock, poor dear, lovely woman.

"Not at all. I'm merely questioning your claim that you cannot draw the relationship to an appropriate moment here on the ship."

She puzzled over that possibility. Fortunately for my determination to avoid the role of a guardian of morals, Commander Hilda King, the navigator and senior woman on the ship, joined us at the table.

"Hi, Bishop, hi, Mary Anne," the navigator greeted us with characteristic exuberance. "It's clouding up outside. Air officer will love it."

"Rain and fog tonight?" Mary Anne asked.

I perceived what should have been obvious as soon as I came on the *Langley*: not only was this a crowded and mysterious city, it was also, for many of its inhabitants, a sunless city. Rarely did many of the crew, Lieutenant Keane included, see daylight. Six months at sea without sunlight in dense and cramped quarters with very little privacy: no wonder the crews often went wild when they finally hit shore.

"Yep, air officer will love it even more. Give our kids some practice with bad weather and relatively calm seas. . . . Take their minds off what we found last night. . . . Johnny's got his usual crowd of good guys all over the ship. . . . Reassure everyone."

"Do you really think so, Hilda?"

"No, I don't really think so. I'm whistling in the dark.

All we need is one more incident, and the women on the ship will panic. They'll see themselves as trapped on a ship with rapists and killers on the loose. They'll call their families on shore with their cellular phones and the media and Congress will be all over us. We'll be in deep doo-doo for sure. And I don't think that for all his spit and polish and elegance and wit, Johnny Larkin can prevent another rape. If a couple of men want to rape a woman badly enough on a vessel like this and get away with it, they probably can do it. They could do that back in San Diego or New York, as far as that goes."

Suddenly, pieces began to fit together; not all the pieces, but enough to make me uneasy. The evil began to take shape and was more horrible than when it was still shapeless.

"Why?" I asked.

"Who knows?" Hilda shrugged grimly. "They could have thrown poor Wade overboard. They left her there the way she was to scare the women on board. Pretty sophisticated, if you ask me. They knew how tense the ship was after Hoy's fun and games. Now they've doubled the ante."

"Good God," Mary Anne exclaimed. "I've never thought about it that way. . . . Who?"

"If we knew that, we'd know it all, wouldn't we, Bishop?"

"Better if we knew why."

"Look, Mary Anne, I stopped by to say that I don't want anything to happen to you. The women on the ship admire the way you stood up to Hoy. . . ."

"I didn't really stand up to him."

"Yes, you did, dear. You're a heroine in their minds. They also think you'd be good for Speed, but that's mostly irrelevant. If I were a couple of madmen, or I suppose I should say mad people, I'd want to go after you. Don't take any chances. I've asked Johnny to put a guard on you. Don't get out of his sight, understand?"

"Yes, Hilda," Mary Anne agreed solemnly.

"Make her do what she's told, Bishop."

"I'm scared, Bishop," Mary Anne Keane turned to me, her eyes wide, when the navigator had left our table. "She's right, you know. If they want me or any other woman or group of women on the ship, they can rape us and kill us."

"Only if we let them," I said with more confidence than I felt. "The captain and his officers are not without resources. I'm sure Commander King has shared her fears with them. You will be well guarded. You must not, for any reason, slip away from your guards."

"No fear of that," she said fervently.

In the back of my mind, still unformed, was the beginnings of a suspicion that whoever or whatever was trying to terrorize the women on the *Langley* would try something different this time. In retrospect, it was incredibly stupid not to have figured out what they would try.

Whoever they were.

I finished my iced tea.

"Come on, Bishop." Lieutenant Keane stood up from the table. "I'll take you up to Johnny Larkin's office on oh-three level. That sailor at the door with the side arm is undoubtedly my guard."

I thanked Martha for her ministrations and followed the public affairs officer to the door of the wardroom.

"Hi, shipmate," she said to the armed guard. "Don't let me out of your sight. I'm going up to your boss's lair to introduce the bishop to him. Then I'm going back to my office on the gallery deck."

"Yes ma'am," the sailor grinned. "It's a pleasure to follow you around, ma'am, and not get in trouble for it."

She touched his arm. "I'm sure you'll follow me around respectfully, shipmate."

"No other way, ma'am."

As we picked our way through the passageways and

up the ladders to 03 level, I began to hate this weird, science fiction city with its bright, artificial light, obscure trails, mysterious humming sounds, endless if slight swaying motions, ominous if obscure threats, and grim and unrelenting beige walls. Despite the courtesy of the citizens of this improbable city, it was finally a depressingly inhuman place. Its six thousand inhabitants dwelled there to make it possible for some eighty aircraft, highly sophisticated technological masterpieces flown by no more than a hundred and twenty men and women, to rain destruction on enemies, should there be any such. It made improbable science fiction and even more chilling reality.

Yet the city was no more dangerous and inhuman, I supposed, than the London of Dickens, the Chicago of Mr. Dooley, or many Third World cities of the present. There was less disease, better sanitation, infinitely better health care, and women were safer here than they would be in some of the mean streets of America, streets on which some of them had grown up.

So there wasn't any sunlight. There were worse things in the world.

Still, I didn't like this science fiction metropolis. Not one bit. I would have to get out of it soon, before my admittedly aging gray matter stopped working completely.

CHAPTER 11

"GREETINGS, MOST HOLY One," Johnny Larkin bowed deeply, "and Most Wondrous Princess to the humble shop of the chief master at arms. What can I sell you? Pikes? Lances? Crossbows? Sabers? Scimtars? We have all these fabled weapons within the mysterious walls of my store. What's more, I can get them for you wholesale."

"Call me Blackie."

"Certainly, all reverend person. Not as in Boston Blackie, I assume?"

"Not with someone who is clearly Boston Irish despite his efforts, only partially successful, to sound like Alec Guinness in *Lawrence of Arabia*."

The office of the chief master of arms was on level 03, a small, beige cubbyhole with a tiny metal desk and the usual computer. Above the desk were a range of TV monitors on which various sections of the ship appeared in rapid order. During our talk, Johnny Larkin never took his eyes off the monitors. In an even smaller hole in the bulkhead, a woman yeoman was answering phone calls from various patrols of the master of arms. In fact, the only arm in the room was a small-caliber handgun strapped to his waist. The pikes and crossbows and scimitars, such as there might have been, were discreetly hidden away.

Three o'clock and all is well, modern form.

"Look, Bishop, get this straight," he now had become

155

Edward G. Robinson, who was long before his time:
"I'm the boss around here, see? What I says goes, see? I
don't want no backtalk from people like you, see? And
that goes for this gorgeous doll you brought along, see?"

I knew Johnny Larkin well. He was your Irish American barroom/wake stand-up comedian and seanachie. At
the most an inch taller than I and so slender as to appear
almost fragile, wavy black hair, dancing dark blue eyes,
pale skin, perfect teeth, a handsome, mobile face with the
palest of skin, he was, in fact, however temporarily, a
lieutenant in the United States Navy. But he might have
been a precinct captain or a litigating lawyer or a
bartender or a cop or a priest (of the sort who would drive
his superiors crazy). His comic act—involving shifts
from Bogart to Eastwood to Wayne to James T. Kirk and
sundry other male heroes—was not really an act so
much as the result of a comic view of life, a vision that
the Irish had in great measure before the advent of
Christianity. As my sister Eileen (the federal appellate
judge) remarked once of her husband, "There will never
be a wake at which he doesn't make people laugh and
that will include his own."

"I'll leave you two comedians to entertain one another," Mary Anne said. "Johnny, give me a ring when
the bishop is ready to go on to Commander Shorter."

"From the rising of sun to the going down thereof,"
Johnny was Alec Guinness again.

Then he added à la John Wayne, "You know, pardner,
"If the skipper ever is so dumb as to give up that there
woman, I'd sure be pleased to pursue her myself."

"Indeed."

"Yep. She and that red-haired marine brat do power-
fully affect my fantasy life, with all due respect, your
reverence."

"Then you have good, albeit, heavily Irish taste. . . .
Tell me about the so-called Digby Hoy."

"Varmint." Now he was Eastwood. "He tries his little

game on me, and I says to him, 'Varmint, I'm a J. D., that's doctor of laws. When I finish up with the Yewnited States Navy, I will specialize in admiralty law in my father's admiralty law firm. If you mess with me, I'll have your fat ass hung from the highest spar in our radar tower.' That did the trick."

"So he did not penetrate the security apparatus on the *Langley*?"

"Ah, no. But he was—how to say it—weird, and he had all the weird people in executive following after him. Did I not say to Skipper San that soon I personally would have to put down a mutiny?"

He was now either Peter Lorre playing Mr. Motto (though he was a little young to have seen those films even as reruns) or Albert Finney as Hercule Poirot. The characters blended seamlessly.

"And you think he was murdered by someone he had threatened dangerously?"

"Tell you the truth, preacher man, I figured he was holed up somewhere on the ship with them two sidekicks of his. Seemed like the rest of his uns could hide him for a few days. Reckoned that he'd reappear with more reasons for taking command."

"Yet you were not able to find either him or the bodies of Ericsson and Wade?"

"We're kind of shorthanded here at Fort Apache, white man. Got me a few sea marines that aren't much good at anything but looking like marines. Mah men in blue are just raw recruits. We keep up a pretty good show, but if the natives come riding over the hill, this here aint gonna be no Rork's Drift."

"The crowd out here in the passageways and on the ladders looks impressive."

The Boston Irishman, worried about the direction of the comedy, made a brief appearance.

"Sure, Bishop. I told them to look impressive. And they're more useful than the NIS stumblebums. My guys will reassure the women on this ship until the next shoe falls, which please God it does not."

The prayer would go unheard, mostly through my intolerable failure to use the intelligence that Herself gave me and thus require Her perhaps to intervene directly which, according to one theological reading at any rate, She is reluctant to do.

His phone rang.

"Spock here."

Someone at the other end spoke for a few moments.

"I agree, Captain, that it is most illogical. . . . The holy man? Yeah, he's right here."

He handed me the phone.

"Captain James T. Kirk wants to talk to you, O Most Holy One."

Now I knew what the *Langley* was. In its antiseptic and crowded gloom, it was the starship *Enterprise*.

In which I was, in fact, Spock.

"Blackie? Dave."

He now reminded me very much of his cousin the cardinal, except rarely if ever does Milord Cronin sink to the vulgarity of my real name.

"Yes, Captain."

"I hear from Admiral Lane that NIS has had its wings clipped slightly. They are to finish their forensic tests and remove the bodies on the late afternoon COD. They are to refrain from further interrogation of the crew for the next thirty-six hours. We have that much time to wrap this case up."

"Arguably, that will be adequate."

"Someone seems to have tilted the playing field back in our direction."

"Perhaps."

"Have supper later on? We'll secure air ops and begin again when it's dark."

"Grand." Before I hung up, I added, "Live long and prosper."

"I told them to search every plane on the ship," Johnny Larkin mused. "I guess they figured the old A-6 wasn't a plane."

"What kind of groups exist on the ship, Johnny Larkin? I mean informal groups."

"What you mean, son, is self-help groups. We have more of them than you could shake a Phoenix rocket at. Everything from bird watching to bible reading, including history study groups, navy pride groups, prayer groups, language groups, self-control groups, which is what we call your addiction and therapy groups. We could find one for you, son, just name your poison."

"I am thinking in particular of right-wing groups."

A flicker of interest crossed his face and he turned his eyes away from the rows of monitors to briefly, very briefly, examine my face.

"This is the Yewnited States Navy, pardner. We don't hold with none of your left-wing groups."

"I'm thinking of maybe a fundamentalist prayer group, Christian or Islamic, which has a high degree of interest in maintaining the good, old-fashioned navy pride, like it used to be."

Johnny nodded thoughtfully and became once again the Boston Mick, which accent some would think the most comic of all.

"Couple of those around, all right. High on the navy, but don't think much of the federal government of which the navy is part. They have no monopoly on that in this ship or in this navy. They're a little stronger than some of the others. Nothing like your militia types. Not yet."

"Not yet?"

"Well, amigo, you know how it ess. In ze navy, we do not spy on people, yes? But we keep ze eye on them, no? When they start to read ze really serious antigovernment stuff, perhaps we watch zem a leedle more closely, eh?"

"I understand."

"And, so most holy and learned and wise one, you want to know whether any of the crowd around Commander Hoy were of that persuasion. Ah, you have so many interesting ideas. But in this you may not see beyond the veils of illusion. These men are, how should I say it, mostly career noncoms. They have too much respect for authority to be involved in something that looks like a plot against a captain, any captain, even when the captain is James T. Kirk."

He opened a file cabinet in his desk, removed a folder, and glanced through its contents.

"Well," he said in Bostonian again, "I erred. Chief Larsen, Lewis, was indeed a bridge between the two groups. Twenty-eight-year man. Big farmer from somewhere in the plains. Heads the printing room in public affairs. Stolid, serious, not overwhelmingly bright, but not quite a character out of *Fargo*, either. Commanded one of them damn river gunboats in Nam. Never quite got over it, they say. Not really much good at line duty anymore. Skipper gave him the print job to see him through his last two years. Worships the skipper."

"Yet he was party to what you yourself have described as a scheme to remove the skipper from command."

"Yeah."

Still the proper Bostonian, Johnny Larkin drummed his fingers on the folder in front of him. "On the margins. Damn strange."

"Arguably."

"Nelly with the sweet blue eyes!"

"Sir!"

"Would you hunt down that no-count deputy of mine, Lieutenant Junior Grade Roosevelt Cartright, tell him to get his black rear end out of the saloon and over here to the sheriff's office. Pronto. And I mean *pronto*!"

"It will be done as you have commanded."

"It won't hurt, will it now, to keep an extra eye on some of those Clinton haters? You know, exalted one, there are not many Democrats on the ship besides present company, Nelly of the pretty blue eyes and the gorgeous young body included. Skipper, air officer, maybe the CAG, and the cheesehead from Green Bay who flies the F-16, the Empress Maria Anna . . ."

The aforementioned Nelly flushed but smiled content-edly.

Johnny Larkin in a wedding Irish tenor voice (the kind you hear after a good deal of the creature has been taken), sang a couple of verses of the Victor Herbert song which proclaimed his Nelly's blue eyes to be brighter than the stars in the sky.

"May have to marry the child," he whispered under his breath to me, "but that's another matter."

"Would you describe the presumably late Commander Hoy's physical appearance?"

He frowned, hunting for words.

"Truth is, pardner, he didn't look like much of any-thing at all. Five feet ten maybe, skinny, plain sort of face, big mustache of which he was enormously proud. Possibly a fake. Pale blue eyes. Kind of sickly looking. You'd hardly notice him, like a lot of varmints."

"Do you ever see on your monitors his troubled spirit, which allegedly roams the ship at night?"

"Roams the women's quarters especially, if the stories are to be believed . . . Our monitors are discreet, Holy One. They don't probe into the places the ghost likes to appear. Shower rooms for example."

"So the monitors never pick him up?"

"Sir, our monitors are not designed to record ecto-plasm, even if there be any of it out there. . . . But even when he was alive, Digby Hoy knew where all cameras were. That varmint was a sneak and a spy. Loved to appear in unexpected places and catch poor folks. Really wanted to find some lesbian activity, if you ask me."

"There is such?"

"Figures to be." He shrugged like John Wayne. "Figures to be."

"One more question, Johnny Larkin. Tell me about the parish priest of this starcraft."

"Father O'Malley? Odd one. Works hard. Women all swear by him, including my Nelly, who is from New York and hence talks almost as funny as you do. Prays a lot, with which there is nothing wrong. But kind of unpredictable, even haunted."

"He has study groups, too?"

"Nothing of that sort. Mostly prepares people for the sacraments: baptism, confirmation, marriage. Not much interested in politics, though strong on racial justice and harmony."

"Yet he himself told me that he was an admirer of Captain Hoy."

"Yeah, I know. Father's got this odd notion that there's a moral breakdown in America. He doesn't push it on you, but he's convinced of it. . . . What do you think, Bishop?"

"Relative to what golden age of virtue?"

"Yeah, that's what I think, too. . . . Hey Nelly, Nelly Bly," he sang the young woman's name as though it were a line in an Italian opera."

"Sir," the very attractive yeoman bounced into the cubbyhole. I noted that she was wearing a massive sidearm and a marksman's medal.

Or should one say marksperson?

Only after recording these data did I observe that she had curly black hair, a pretty elfin face, twinkling blue eyes, and an acceptably curvaceous figure.

"Would you conduct this wise and holy man to the office of our beloved colleague, Lieutenant Commander Glendenning Shorter, a.k.a. Tubby Shorter?"

"Yes, sir," she replied. Her lips were twitching with barely restrained laughter. She had seen Johnny Larkin's act, arguably ad nauseam, and could still laugh at it. Yes, he would be well advised to marry her.

"I'll see you down in the saloon, pardner," the chief master of arms said by way of farewell.

"My name really isn't Bly," the virtuous yeomen assured me as we walked down the corridor. "Watch it, Bishop, there's a knee knocker right around this corner."

"Neither was hers."

"Yes, but she was a seaman, just like I am."

Not a Brooklyn accent but Queens. Incurable.

"Elizabeth Cochran Seaman to be exact . . . You are going to college when you're finished with the navy, Yeoman . . ."

"Regan, sir. Yeoman First Class Julia 'Nelly' Regan. You bet I'm going to college. We have lots of kids at home. I figured I could pay for my education and see the world."

"Did you see the world, Nelly Regan?"

"Some of it. And a lot of that office. As Dr. Chisolm said, serving on a ship is like being in prison with the added danger of drowning."

How many yeopersons, first class, could quote Samuel Chisolm?

"And I've had a chance to watch Lieutenant Larkin's act. . . . He doesn't do it with everyone, sir. Just those with whom he thinks he can do it—or those who he knows will hate it."

"It hasn't bored you?"

"Not yet, sir. He's also very good at what he does on this ship, and he's a first-rate lawyer."

"Indeed."

"He's also a gentle man and a gentlemen."

"One might suspect that you have lost your heart, Yeoperson First Class Julia 'Nelly' Regan."

"Arguably."

Little witch was mocking a bishop! Shame on her.

"But the present crisis is a serious challenge to the order of the ship, is it not?"

"Scary, Bishop. Terribly scary. We pretend that we have it all under control, but we don't know who or what we're fighting. If there's any more trouble, the ship may have to return to port early."

"With humiliation for all concerned?"

"Especially Captain Kirk. Who deserves better."

"Indeed."

"I sleep with this weapon at my side every night. In lieu of any other company. Here's Commander Shorter's office."

An image flashed through my mind, one that tied everything together and threatened grave danger, danger that Johnny Larkin's flair and ingenuity could not avert.

I groped for the image. It eluded me. It slipped back into my preconscious to remain there as a torment and a threat.

"Are you all right, sir?" Nelly Regan asked me.

"Fine. I just lost an image. It will come back. Thank you, Yeoperson, for the escort."

"Yes, sir. . . . Sir, may I say something?"

"Certainly."

"Lieutenant Larkin did his top act for you. He only does that for kindred spirits." She was grinning proudly.

"I would assume so."

"Yes, sir."

Tubby Shorter, as I ought to have anticipated, was not Tubby at all. Rather, he was tall and lean and crew cut and erect and unbearably stiff—Robert Duval as a naval officer—and as much unlike the chief master at arms as a fellow human being could be.

"I'd be glad to answer your questions, sir," he greeted. "I'm not sure, however, what light I can shed on this ugly business."

"You shared the same suite as Commander Hoy. Do you have any idea what might have happened to him?"

"We shared the same bathroom, sir. But we were not close to one another. My department is not under the XO's command. Supplying a ship this size is a huge task, as you can well imagine. The supply officer necessarily reports directly to the captain. We are responsible for food, fuel, weapons, replacement parts, the desalinating system—everything that it takes to keep the ship running and the various other officers well supplied with what they need. As you can see from the computers in here and in my outer office, it's an enormous task. I don't have much time for socializing with anyone."

"I see."

He was reciting a part he had played before.

"I had nothing against Commander Hoy. I probably shared many of his feelings about the way the navy was going, though he never did describe them to me. If the rumors are true that he planned to assume command of the ship, then evidently he was a very sick man. I must say, however, that insofar as one can know someone with whom one shares the can and little else, he seemed ordinary enough. A little tense, perhaps."

"He did not seem to be afraid of the enemies he was making?"

"Not until the end, sir. When he demanded the guards. That's when I felt that the strain of his . . . his perspectives had become too much for him."

"You speak of the ideas about the navy?"

Glen Shorter stirred uneasily.

"I guessed that he was not happy with the way the navy is going. We are in deep trouble, sir. The constant politics in the Pentagon, the games the president plays with us, the insensitivity of Congress, the threat of rampant liberalism—all of these are tearing the navy apart."

"I see."

His smooth-shaven jaw became tense as he talked. "Fifteen years ago, we were promised a six-hundred-ship navy, the best in the world. Expectations were high. We thought that the federal government finally understood after all these years of neglect that the navy is and always was the first line of defense. Vast sums of money were appropriated. Then, sir, nothing happened. The money was eaten up in corruption and bureaucratic wrangling. The CNOs were weak, the secretaries of the navy incompetent, the media hounded us with alleged scandals. Changes were imposed on us that the navy did not want."

I wondered why he was telling me all this. Perhaps because his feelings were so deep on the subject he could not help but talk about them. Presumably many others felt the same way.

"For example?"

"Gays and women, sir. They are both utterly demoralizing on a ship. I suppose they are all right ashore, but women are not meant to fight wars. This is a warship, sir. I'm not sure how many of our women personnel understand this. My judgment would be that most of them do not. They view the United States Ship *Langley* as something like a college dorm or sorority house."

"I see."

"Mind you, I believe in civilian control. If the government wants to permit women on a warship and sodomy between shipmates, I will not refuse to obey the orders that make such things possible. However, the government ought to realize that there is an upper limit to how much we who are career officers can take. The government should not forget that we can always leave the navy."

"I have heard this dissatisfaction from a number of officers," I said cautiously.

"Consider this statistic, Reverend. Last year, fifty-three percent of the postcommand commanders in naval aviation left the navy rather than continue their career. These are the men who have proved themselves for twenty years. Every one of them was a possible future admiral. They are the elite of our officer corps. They left, Reverend. They left because they couldn't take it anymore."

"That certainly sounds like bad morale."

"I was an aviator, Reverend. Until my eyes gave out. I still wear these wings proudly. My twenty years are up in eighteen months. I was too young to fly in Nam. I flew in the Gulf War. My shipmates in those days were some of the finest men I've ever known. Most of them are gone. Fed up. How can you take naval aviation seriously when the government and the media let the Tailhook scandal get out of control? It was worth a few days' publicity. Only a few guys were involved. So now we're all disgraced. Is it any wonder that guys take a walk?"

Beads of sweat had appeared on his high forehead as he talked.

"You're going to leave next year?"

"I don't know, Padre," he sighed. "I'm confused. This mess just makes it worse. It could never have happened in the old navy. The government should decide which is worse, Tailhook or the present condition of this ship."

"You blame the captain for this?"

"Speed? Hell no, Reverend. Excuse my language. He is doing the best he can under the circumstances. I wouldn't be surprised if he wants out when his twenty years are up. He's trying to preside over a zoo that Washington has created out here. He can't afford to offend anyone. That's not fair to a bright young officer like Speed."

"Everyone seems to like him, though the late Commander Hoy didn't."

"It wasn't Speed. It would have been any C.O. . . . I suppose you heard that I took myself out of the running to be acting XO? I knew it was either me or Dempsey. But as I told Speed, I thought I had better not give up supply until I had a trained replacement here. Dempsey's competent enough, even though he wouldn't have made it as far as he has if he were white."

"Can you remember the events the day the XO disappeared?"

"I've described them so many times I don't think I'll ever forget them. A marine lieutenant knocked on my door as I was getting up. Had I seen or heard the XO? He had not shown up in his office. The door to his quarters was locked, and he did not answer knocking. I'm a heavy sleeper, so I hadn't heard a thing. I tried the bathroom door. It was locked from the other side. The marine knocked on it. No answer. I got into my uniform and went out into the passageway. The captain had just arrived. He ordered the machinist mate who was standing by to cut out the lock. They opened the door. There was such a crowd that I didn't bother to try to look inside. The XO wasn't there. The bathroom door was locked on his side, too. The marine guards swore that he had not left his quarters during the night. I understand that they later took lie detector tests."

"How do you explain this phenomenon?"

He rubbed his forehead with a tissue from a box on his desk.

"Damned if I know. Excuse my language, Padre. It's impossible, but it happened."

"You didn't actually look in the room?"

"No, but I believe the skipper and the master at arms."

He rubbed his hands over his face.

"I don't know what happened to Hoy. I don't know who killed the other two. I don't understand any of it. I only know that in the old navy, these kinds of things simply didn't happen."

"So I understand."

"You wouldn't believe the change would come so quickly. During the Gulf War, there was a spirit among the air crews that was just unbelievable. Our aircraft weren't what we needed. Our ordnance was inferior.

Still, we did a good job. We all thought that we were finally breaking out of the hangover from Nam. Now it's all fallen apart."

"Most unfortunate."

"I'm not the only one who feels that way. The CAG, the air officer, Josh Williamson, they all agree with me. We're not getting good young pilots and the older guys that are any good are all leaving. You don't know when it will stop."

"You're not impressed by the younger pilots?"

"What man worth his salt as a pilot would want to fly in an outfit where that crazy redhead cavorts around in an F-18?"

"Ah. You mean Lieutenant Monahan."

"She symbolizes what's wrong with the navy today. She doesn't belong in a Hornet, she doesn't belong on this ship."

"I have been led to believe that she is a competent pilot."

"That's not the point, Padre." He sighed. "That's not the point."

I did not ask what the point was, because I think I knew it.

"I have heard that there have been certain, ah, psychic manifestations on the ship since the XO's disappearance. I wonder if you have, ah, observed any such phenomena."

"No way," he said firmly. "The only difference is that now I have the whole can to myself. No one wants to sleep in his bunk. Other men tell me strange tales. I don't believe any of them. The dead don't walk."

"If they're dead."

"Digby Hoy is dead, Padre. We're kidding ourselves if we think any different."

"Arguably."

We both stood up.

"I feel sorry for Speed. Some woman is going to make

a complaint against him. With a thousand of them on the ship, there's no way he can avoid it. Then he's finished. One of the finest men in the navy was forced into retirement because one senator wanted to ask a question about why one woman helicopter pilot was washed out. Another man was taken off the admiral's list—and his career ended—because of one anonymous phone call alleging he told dirty stories about women. Why bother trying when they can do that to you?"

"Deplorable."

The first incident he mentioned was indeed deplorable. However, the decision was made by a new CNO who apparently had a score to settle. No point in my arguing.

"Or take the Naval Academy so-called scandals. It's not the navy's fault that young people are selfish, dishonest, and hedonistic today. They do the best with what they get. A few midshipmen act up, and the whole institution is blamed. Our weak leadership won't step up and defend them. The Academy is still one of the finest educational institutions in the country, but no one is willing to say that anymore. It's all those liberals in the media."

"Lamentable."

In a sense, the poor man was right. Like other government agencies in the age of constant media attention, the navy alternated between stonewalling and collapse. Moreover, the behavior of some men and women did not discredit either the whole Academy or the whole navy. Finally, Washington journalists were not so much liberals as carrion.

"Well, good luck, Padre." He sighed sadly. "I hope you can straighten this mess out."

"Oh, I think things will clear themselves up."

Mary Anne was waiting for me in the passageway beyond the outer office, in which six young men were poring over computer screens. Her armed shadow lingered behind her, a big grin on his face. You don't get to follow a beautiful woman around all that often as an action in the line of duty.

"Did Glen smile once?" she asked me.

"I thought he was going to weep."

"We Academy people take the navy very seriously," Mary Anne observed. "Too seriously probably, but it's our life. Or maybe our mother who we know is going to betray us eventually but whom we'll always love anyway. What for most of us is a mild obsession, for Glen is a fixation. He can think of nothing else but all the things that are going wrong. I suspect that people like me are part of what he sees as wrong."

"Especially if you fly aircraft."

"The skipper is right: Every generation has its own complaints about the collapse of values. As he says, the lyrics change a little, but the music is the same."

"Wise skipper."

"He didn't go to the Academy, so it's different for him. I almost added, thank God."

"Is it true that our peerless skipper chose Commander Dempsey over Commander Shorter to be acting XO?"

"He's not peerless. Well, not quite. . . . Did Glen tell you that?"

"More or less."

"David doesn't discuss such matters with me. Obviously. But there wasn't a moment's doubt that Dick was the man for the job. Don't let the charm fool you. He may just have the highest IQ on the ship."

"Besides the skipper."

She flushed attractively.

"Well, naturally . . . Glen is only kidding himself if he thinks he would ever rise any higher than his present responsibilities. He's a good supply officer because he's compulsive, but he's too compulsive to do anything with broader responsibility."

"Indeed."

"These are my offices. The photo lab is over there. I

had to restrain the kids with the cameras. They're all over every guest who comes aboard. I hope you don't mind if some of them work the confirmation?"

"They should take many pictures so I can convince my siblings, children, and grandchildren that I actually was on the ship. One at least on the skipper's chair on the bridge."

Somehow she thought that was funny.

"Go easy on Chief Larsen. He's not too swift anymore, poor man. But he runs a good print shop and is quite harmless."

"Yet he fell under Commander Hoy's spell."

She thought about that. "So maybe not completely harmless."

"This is the captain," a voice boomed on the public address system. "The chief master at arms tells me that the ship is secure. We will maintain that security. I ask that from eighteen hundred to oh-six hundred no one on the ship be alone, either in their quarters or in the passageways, or in any space on this ship. This a precaution. I think we will all rest easier because of this precaution. I am grateful for your cooperation."

Stars shone in Lieutenant Keane's eyes as she smiled approval at the skipper's wisdom.

CHAPTER 12

IN HIS OWN slow, heavy style, Chief Petty Officer Lewis Larsen took great pride in his section of the public affairs office. A massive man, at least six feet four and well over two hundred and fifty pounds, with huge hands, little hair, and the solemn face of a bishop about to fall asleep during a long liturgy, he seemed to assume personal responsibility for the sophisticated printing system and the marvelous photographic equipment (which, strictly speaking, was not his domain), as though he himself had designed it all. He brushed dust, frequently invisible to the naked eye, off each piece of machinery and then polished it with the sleeve of his khaki shirt.

"We didn't have anything like this equipment in Nam, sir," he said. "Not that we'd want to take pictures of what happened on the Mekong River. The navy is much better than it used to be."

The young photo crew and the other ratings in the office treated him with enormous respect but deftly skirted around him to get their work done. There was a conspiracy to pretend that he was in charge so that he could serve out the final months till his thirty-year retirement in dignity.

"Patently," I said soothingly.

"You want to ask me some questions about Commander Rogers Hoy?" he said, his shoulders slumping and his hands coming together as if in prayer, a gesture that would prove to be frequent.

"If you don't mind."

"Not at all, sir. I'd be happy to be whatever help I can be."

He didn't sound happy, but I suspected he never did. His words were the automatic response of a seasoned petty officer.

He led me to a desk in the corner of his print shop and indicated a chair next to the desk for me.

"I'm sorry, sir, that I don't have one more comfortable."

"This is fine. . . . What happened to Commander Hoy?"

He shook his head sadly. "Overboard, sir. That happens more than they let on. The strain becomes too much, even for a dedicated man like the commander. A lot of men do it. I had a C.O. on the Mekong, only a jaygee he was, who went over the side of our boat with a weapon tied to his body so he wouldn't come up. Too many casualties, too much blood. Not like the pilots who didn't have anyone die in their arms."

"You believe he suffered from stress because of the responsibilities of his position?"

The chief frowned thoughtfully, as if chewing over that thought. "I don't think he could take it anymore."

"What couldn't he take?"

"All the conflict . . . In Nam, life and death were all that mattered. Now," he gestured helplessly with one of his massive paws, "there's so much politics. He was trying to straighten out the ship. Most of us thought he was right, and that the higher-ups were unfair to him. Too much politics."

"You think that if he had lived he would have attempted to relieve the captain?"

"No, sir. That would have been mutiny. Some people thought he should. But that was just more politics."

"And the deaths of Lieutenants Ericsson and Wade?"

"They knew too much." He lifted his paw again in a gesture of powerlessness. "The higher-ups had to get rid of them."

"Which higher-ups?"

"You can never be sure."

"The captain?"

"No, sir. The captain is a good man, even if he isn't a Christian. So is Lieutenant Keane a good woman; I think she'll become a Christian before it's too late. I wouldn't believe anything bad about either of them. I hope both will be saved."

No one would say anything bad about the skipper.

"They say Lieutenant Ward was raped."

He shook his head sadly. "You have women on the ship and that kind of thing will happen. It's too bad."

"Indeed."

"Commander Hoy was a fine officer. He ran a tight ship. The way a real officer should. The navy needs tighter ships. We all loved him. Any one of us would have died for him."

Tears formed in pale—and faintly aimless—blue eyes. He clasped his hands together.

"If we'd known he was that troubled, we would have stopped him. But he didn't seem like he was the kind who'd go overboard."

"Do you think the higher-ups might have killed him?"

"Maybe . . . It's all politics."

"Some say that the commander still walks the ship at night. Have you ever seen him?"

The chief's brow furrowed in a deep frown, as if he was trying to sort out a complex puzzle.

"Not exactly. But when I'm praying hard, real hard, I kind of feel that he is still with us, watching over the ship. Know what I mean? Do you Catholics pray, sir?"

"Yes, we do. A lot."

"I know you don't read the Bible. . . . Do you

believe that God hears your prayers even though you're not saved?"

"We believe that God loves all of us humans like a parent loves a child, like a spouse loves the other spouse."

His eyes opened wide in surprise. "I don't think Christians believe that."

"They do if they read the Bible. . . . Do you pray a lot, Chief?"

"Yes, sir. I want to be ready when the Rapture comes. We pray every day in our prayer group to be ready. It could happen any day now."

His thoughts were those of a fervent fundamentalist, but his tone did not change. He was still the petty officer with too many memories.

"I see. . . . Was Commander Hoy a God-fearing man?"

"Yes, sir. He certainly was. He saw the sinfulness of this ship. He knew it was a modern Sodom and Gomorra. Like Lot, he finally fled it. Those of us who remain must not forget the fate of Lot's wife."

I would learn very little more from Chief Larsen. Mary Anne, however, had made her point: For the weak and the troubled in his domain, E. Rogers Hoy was a messiah figure.

I found her in her cubbyhole, reading an A.P. dispatch about O. J. Simpson.

"Your friend the skipper must know that he has to clean out the Hoy crowd as soon as he can. They're an undigested and indigestible lump in the crew."

"I don't know," she said, putting the story aside, "what he intends to do. Commander Dempsey knows it, however. I'm sure David will follow his suggestion."

"What will happen to Chief Larsen when he retires?"

"His sister is married to a farmer in Nebraska. He'll retire to the farm and tell stories to anyone who will listen. Help out on the work. Pray a lot. Sit on the porch and wait for the Rapture. He won't be any trouble to anyone."

"Do you happen to know why there were riverboat squadrons in the Mekong?"

"Some admiral's bright idea to make a name for himself . . . It was a catastrophe. That's what happens in war."

"If there were another war, what would you do?"

"Like Nam? I'd resign."

I thought it better not to pursue the subject.

"The chief thinks you have a chance to be saved."

She smiled. "If I become a Christian and confess the Lord Jesus before the Rapture. He doesn't think Catholics are Christians or can be saved."

"Is he dangerous?"

"Chief Larsen? Heavens, no, Bishop. He's just a worn out man, old long before his time. He'll never get over Nam. He wouldn't hurt a fly."

I wasn't so sure of that. "He seems harmless enough, all right. Still, there seemed to be a touch of the fanatic in what he said."

"You don't know many Christians, do you Bishop? They all sound that way. But they're no more fanatics than we are. Just a different set of symbols."

Hey, young woman, I'm the one with the degree in philosophy. "I take your point. Still, I'm wondering whether he might be the kind who could rise up and smite the Amalecs or the Philistines or some such tribe if the occasion were right."

She pondered for a moment. "I don't think he would take that kind of passage literally."

"Did he kill people in Nam?"

"Probably. That's what they did on the riverboats. . . . Surely you don't suspect the chief of being involved in the murders. He's not bright enough to concoct the locked room, is he?"

"Arguably not. Maybe you're right. We don't have too

many of those kind in my parish. They scare me, just the same. Perhaps they remind me too much of our own right wing."

"Don't worry about the chief. Now I'll introduce you to our TV man. He's really quite gifted, though he doesn't belong in the navy. But then, who does?"

"And what navy."

Her eyes flickered for a moment. "You're beginning to catch on, Bishop Blackie. There's four or five navies on the ship."

Lieutenant (J. G.) Carl Chisolm was the first officer I had encountered on the ship who did not wear khakis. Instead, he was dressed in fatigues, light blue work shirt and jeanslike trousers, a gold bar the only sign that he was not a rating. He was a thin young man with watery eyes and sparse brown hair, puny looking despite his brave handlebar mustache. He spoke with the cynicism of the college sophomore, which he must have been only a couple of years ago. Clearly, he didn't like the navy or his job.

"The equipment here isn't bad, Father," he said going listlessly through the motions of showing me around his shop. "We have a small TV studio in which we can make tapes for various purposes. We maintain the TV operation throughout the ship. Pick up a lot of stuff from the satellites to entertain the crew. Off the coast here, we can provide them with twelve channels of American programming. And, of course, we monitor what happens up on the flight deck. I always have two or three camerapeople up on the flag bridge and a director who shifts from one camera to another, like in NFL games. Technically, we're pretty good. Nothing artistic, but what the hell, this is the navy."

That was the end of his tour. He sank back into his chair in front of the control panel like a man who had been awakened from a nap.

"Surely you are getting experience that will be an asset when you return to civilian life."

"Only if I want to be a station manager in the Oklahoma panhandle for the rest of my life . . . Well, they paid for my education, so I can't complain."

"Roger ball," said the monitor.

"I'll hear those words in a nightmare for the rest of my life."

"I'm sure the work can be monotonous."

"That monitor is about as close as I ever get to daylight. I suppose it's exciting to watch the traps. Believe me, after a week of it, it's a bore. Even the night traps become dull. Some days, I work eighteen hours. It wouldn't be so bad if it were hard physical work. I could take that. But this stuff is like watching paint dry."

"I'm asking some questions about the disappearance of Commander Hoy."

"Yeah, so I heard. . . . I suppose that wasn't so dull, was it? Might make a good mystery. Officer disappears from a locked room. Too bad Bogart is not alive. He'd fit the role. Get it?"

"You did not like the commander?"

He yawned. "Digby fascinated me. He was the kind of guy who could use the navy style to subvert the whole substance of their shit. Stirred things up on the ship. It was fun for awhile. Then it became a drag."

"What do you think happened to him?"

He shrugged indifferently. "Don't know. He got in the way of all the affirmative action around here. You saw who replaced him, didn't you?"

"Commander Dempsey?"

"You noticed his color?"

"African American?"

"Yeah," he sneered. "I don't mind them so long as they don't get any special favors. My folks had to work for everything they got. I do, too. They get an education for nothing and jobs that they can't do. I would be a better XO than Dempsey."

"And women, too?"

"Well, I don't mind Mary Anne. She's sexy and kind of interesting to talk to. Wasted in the navy. Not giddy like the rest of them. It's like living in a mixed dorm at school. Women dominate it. Never seen it to fail. A guy can't really relax and be himself, get it?"

"Arguably. . . . I assume you have no contact with the commander's spirit?"

"See, that's what I mean about women on a ship. They get off on fantasizing about Hoy's ghost and the rest of us are supposed to take it seriously. What shit!"

"If you were writing a script for the locked-room mystery on this ship, who would you make the killer?"

"That's an interesting way to put it. Never thought of actually doing that. Might be fun. My script would never make the air, though." He grinned cynically. "Not politically correct, get it?"

"Ah?"

"I'd say some of the Black Power people did him in. Threw him overboard. He was hunting down their little coke rings, get it? Anyone tell you that the people he busted were all blacks?"

"No."

"I didn't think so. Everyone pretends that it's only a coincidence, get it? And some of them say it was a frame-up, just like O. J. . . . They always want discounts."

Mary Anne was waiting for me in her office.

"You like our Generation X populist?" she asked me.

"Not especially," I said. "Yet he is the first one to tell me that those whom Commander Hoy apprehended were all African Americans."

"No one mentions it, but everyone on the ship knows it. We walk on eggshells."

"Unable even to think that race might be part of the problem?"

"Certainly we think about it. We just don't talk about it. A fifth of the crew are African American," she insisted. "Race relations on board are better than they are in the rest of the country, but you can't take racial harmony for granted. If there were evidence that race was a factor in the murders, we'd pursue the evidence. As it is, it is on everyone's mind, but almost no one mentions it."

"Are there black militant groups on the ship?"

"Sure there are. Not very militant, however. Black Muslims. Their men are the most disciplined people on the ship. They weren't involved in the drug bust, you can bet on that."

"Yet many whites on the ship are convinced that the murders are racial and many of the blacks know that and resent it?"

"Yes."

"And they also think that Hoy may have set up those who were arrested for drugs?"

"Yes."

"And the African American women think that whites feel there are black rapists on board, which of course they do?"

"Yes."

"And the African American women fear reprisals?"

"Naturally. One of my roommates is a black woman who works in ordnance. She is petrified. And won't talk to the rest of us."

As we talked, she glanced repeatedly at the inevitable TV monitor above her desk.

"The redhead," she said, as a plane—no, when in Rome—an aircraft split the ball and landed neatly on the deck. "Perfect, of course. I wish I could fly like that."

"You were a pilot?"

"I learned when I was in high school. My father and

grandfather were pilots, you remember. So I had to be a flyer. I have a civilian license."

"But you didn't go to navy flight school?"

"No way . . . Here comes Janie. Not fair that she should have a trap after the red witch. . . . Ugh! Another wave-off. She's lucky, I suppose. Won't have to be a combat pilot. . . . Lot of mist out there already. Waves are picking up. Night traps will be rough. "

She turned back to me. "We were talking about the African Americans. . . ."

"Commander Dempsey's appointment as acting XO does not reassure them?"

"Some say he's an Oreo. They would say that, I suppose, of anyone who gets as high as XO."

"No reason that gender and race should stop being America's defining problems when the ship sails out of North Island."

"It still works, Bishop," she pleaded. "The ship still runs. There is no overt conflict. If we can get beyond this crisis . . ." Her voice trailed off.

This public affairs officer was the mother of the ship. Even if she weren't in love with the captain, she would still be mother of the ship. One advantage of women being on the ship, I reflected, is that there is some mother love aboard—though whether that is functional on a warship might be open to question.

"Actually," Mary Anne continued, "Lieutenant Chisolm is a nice enough young man. Just doesn't belong on this ship. Or any ship. He's no more racist than anyone else. Just more honest about it."

Motherlike, she saw good in everyone. In turn, every-one, or almost everyone, loved her.

"How does Father O'Malley get along with the Chris-tians?"

"They bother him a lot. Poor Father is a man who is torn by doubts. I think he likes to be torn by doubts. It's part of his psyche. They have no doubts at all, at least not on the surface. They beg him to confess the Lord Jesus and be saved. He's not sure some of the time that there is salvation. One of the Protestant chaplains deals with the Christians, though some of them are not even sure that he's confessed the Lord Jesus yet."

"So we have gender and racial and religious conflict of a sort on a ship where there has been one disappearance and two murders."

"It's America, Bishop."

"Arguably."

"Did you encounter Commander Hoy last night?" she asked with a shudder.

"Not as such," I said. "You?"

"He was all over the women's quarters. My shipmates swear that he's real." She glanced at her watch. "It's sixteen-thirty. The confirmation is set for seventeen hundred."

"Ah. I must go back to my quarters to prepare."

"Your escort is waiting. . . . You heard what the skipper said. No one walks alone on the *Langley*."

"You will have an escort to the confirmation?"

She did not remark on my assumption that she would be there. Naturally not. Mothers go to confirmations.

"It's just down the ladder, but yes, I will," she said with a complacent smile. "The captain called me. He will escort me. So there, too!"

"Remarkable."

"Marvelous!"

As I was leaving, she called after me. "Bishop Blackie! Don't leave just yet. Sit down, please. I want to tell you some more secrets."

"So?"

"Not about me and the skipper." She blushed. "If there ever are any, I'll tell you."

"I will await them."

"Some of the Black Power people have been making themselves weapons. Knives carved out of files, like they do in prison. In case there is ever a race riot. Over rape. Of course the rednecks in the crew know that."

"The chief master of arms knows that?"

"Certainly. At some point, he'll have to confiscate them, but he won't let the confiscation turn into a pretense for a riot. Digby knew it, too. Was planning to go after them. There's only a handful, but if the other African Americans think we're picking on them . . ."

"Indeed."

"But that's not what I really wanted to tell you about."

"I didn't think so."

"There's a group of lesbians on the ship, too. Digby was planning to catch them in the act. That's when the threats on his life began."

"He managed to spy on everyone, didn't he?"

"If there can be gay lovers on shipboard, why can't there be lesbian lovers?"

"You tell me."

"Because they scare men."

"Arguably."

"You will never guess who the leader is."

"The navigator, patently."

Mary Anne Keane was taken aback. "Do other men know?"

"Not so consciously, I believe, that they are aware that they know."

"It would destroy Hilda's career. No one talks about it."

"Naturally, she made a pitch to you."

The young woman frowned. "You know too damn much!"

"Arguably."

"It was very subtle, very indirect, very . . ."

"Unsettling?"

"Very . . . I go through my life firmly convinced that I am not sexually attractive, then men and women suddenly seem to think I am. I turned her down, of course. Gently."

"Naturally."

"It was mostly disagreeable, but I wondered what it might be like."

"Naturally."

"Can you imagine what conservative congressmen would do if it should become public that there was a 'ring' of lesbians on the ship?"

"Was the late Lieutenant Wade part of the group?"

"Yes. I don't think Digby knew that, however. He asked me the morning of the day he disappeared if I knew anything about the 'nest,' as he called it, of lesbians on the ship. He kind of hinted that I was one of them."

"And you said?"

"I told him that I thought I had already established my heterosexuality with the captain and that I wasn't one of his spies. He sneered and gave up."

"You told no one of this exchange?"

"No. Not even David. I'm only telling you because it might be part of the solution to the mystery. I hope to God it isn't."

I rose to leave. "People might have been waiting in line to silence Commander Hoy."

"And there were surely others about whom we don't know," She rose to lead me back to the passageway.

"Lieutenant Mary Anne Keane, the *Langley* is a microcosm, a cosmos in miniature. There is no reason to assume that any segment of the human condition is absent from it."

"I know that. . . . Who am I on this mythological ship?"

"Patently, the goddess of spring. And don't you forget it."

My escort was a young, very young, African American marine who would not see his twentieth birthday for a long time.

"A happy ship, Corporal?" I asked him.

"Yes, *sir*. Despite all the troubles."

"Some tensions among the brothers and sisters?"

"No, *sir*. Oh, there's a few who are never happy. Always complaining. Most of us know that the navy has been good to us. And the marines, especially. For me, it was either a gang or the marines. They made a man out of me. My mom and dad are so proud of me. I don't have much time for this race talk."

"You think most of the men and women feel the same way?"

"Yes, *sir*. Some brothers do a lot of talking and maybe they make a little sense, sometimes. Usually, they're the kind who like to hear the sound of their own voices. But most of us just listen and go about our work. We have jobs and food and clean and warm quarters and good prospects when we get out. What's there to complain about?"

"Indeed."

"I sure do wish this Commander Hoy business would be cleaned up. It's hard on everyone, isn't it, *sir*?"

"Yes, it is."

"He was a strange man, sir. He didn't like the brothers and sisters much at all."

"I gather he didn't like lots of people."

"Yes, *sir*."

My corporal had, in fact, confirmed Lieutenant Keane's version of the racial situation on the ship but from a different perspective: *Langley* was sitting on a ticking bomb.

As I strove, with much effort but little visible effect, to gather together the vestments and paraphernalia required to administer the sacrament of confirmation, I pondered the impossibility of my task. I had interviewed so far only a fraction of the officers and a handful of enlisted personnel.

Commander E. Rogers "Digby" Hoy was a borderline

personality who, like some other such, had a magical influence on a group of people whose needs meshed with his own. He had disappeared. Then two of his closest allies had vanished. Later, the bodies of the latter two had been found on the ship. There was widespread gender and racial tension on the ship, for some of the officers reinforced by dissatisfaction with what had happened in the navy during the last fifteen years. Many of the officers I had interviewed would not have been too upset by Hoy's disappearance, but there was no reason to think they would have the motives for murder.

I knew, of course, how the locked-room trick had been accomplished. But so far, I had discovered no reason for it.

I was completely at sea.

At the most, I had thirty-six more hours to resolve the problem. Meanwhile, the rain and mists swirling around the ship heightened the tension. Something more was about to happen.

We were all waiting for the other shoe to drop.

CHAPTER 13

"IT IS NOW time," I told the confirmands, "for the bishop to ask questions so that he might determine whether you are prepared to receive this sacrament of the Holy Spirit. I warn you, I am a stern test giver."

Giggles from the group, which knew that the opposite was patently the case.

"Who is the Holy Spirit?"

Megan Monahan's hand shot up immediately. Brightest girl in the class. Sodality prefect, if they still had them. She had arrayed herself for the occasion in marine dress blues, dark blue jacket with red and gold tabs and trim, brightly polished wings, and a white woman marine's cap with her blazing hair discreetly tucked under it. Some traces of makeup were visible on her face and her scent was high school prom style, which filled the room. Her protégée, Tina by name (whose confirmation name would of course be Margaret), was in navy dress whites. Everyone else—with deplorable lack of elegance—was wearing the standard khaki.

"Margaret Mary Monahan," I reproved her, "sponsors can't answer."

"Ohh," she protested and spun around one complete turn in frustration.

"Tina, suppose you tell us."

"The Holy Spirit," the young Mexican American assured me, "is the third person of the Blessed Trinity. She is God's Love. She comes to us today in a special way so that we may show God's love to everyone we meet."

"Very good, Tina. Father O'Malley has done a fine job preparing you."

"Yes, Father . . . I mean Bishop."

The chaplain's anguished lips parted in a faint smile. As I was vesting, he was his usual self, alternately friendly and helpful and distant and resentful. There were five young people to be confirmed, a Filipino, Tina and a Mexican American man, an African American woman, and an extremely young white man with a long Polish name.

Oh beautiful for spacious skies and amber waves of grain.

The tiny daily chapel was crowded. The skipper and his lady were in attendance as promised, standing together at one side of the altar, enveloped in an invisible sheath of love, the kind of couple one encounters on occasion who radiate a passionate involvement with one another, that you know will never wane. It is in couples such as these that image of God's love as disclosed in human love is most evident. In his radiance Lieutenant Keane seemed peaceful and happy, truly the spring goddess of the *Langley*.

The usual suspects were also present and some other guests.

I asked my standard questions about why God wanted to be called love (because She created us out of passion), how God's love was different from human love (implacable), and why we needed a special sacrament for God's Holy Spirit (to remind us of the Spirit's presence among us).

Megan Monahan practically exploded every time someone gave an only partially correct answer and I refused to recognize her hand.

"Lieutenant Monahan," I said at the end of the

questioning, "did you want to answer a question I haven't asked?"

"You didn't ask why there are *sponsors!*"

"All right, Lieutenant, why are there *sponsors?*"

The answer was creative but hardly orthodox.

"So there'll be more people at the *party!*"

There may have been an orthodox insight in it, so I used it as a starting point for my own instruction that the Holy Spirit was also God's spirit of variety, a kind of divine Tinkerbell flitting through space with a magic wand and calling forth the superabundance of diversity which was creation: galaxies, stars, planets, moons, millions of species of animals and plants, and a wide variety of humankind, men and women, people of every hue and size, speech and hair color, even a few odd people with red hair (loud harumph for Tina's sponsor). God is exuberant. She loves diversity. She must especially enjoy the *Langley* with all its diversity. We pray that the rest of us enjoy the diversity, too. Because that's why God created it for us.

Thereupon, I signed them with the sign of the cross and confirmed them with the chrism of salvation in the name of the Father and the Son and the Holy Spirit Herself. There was no mighty wind, no tongues of fire, no speaking in foreign languages. Yet for a moment, I felt that the Spirit was present among us in a fashion different from Her ordinary mode and well aware that, like me, She had Her work cut out for Her.

The night would demonstrate that She knew this.

At the exchange of peace, the virtuous Megan kissed as many people as she could, including the blushing skipper, much to the amusement of the skipper's lady.

After Mass, there was a small reception in and around the chaplain's office: cookies (excellent), small petit fours (equally excellent), apple juice, tea, and coffee. I found myself talking with Captain Joe Holloway, the air officer who, I learned, was responsible for all air operations and who commanded the deck crews and everyone who services the aircraft. Built like a linebacker with a broad and perhaps honest face, a widow's peak, and penetrating brown eyes, he looked like an admiral should look. He had recently been promoted to captain and assigned to the office of the chief of Naval operations in Washington and would report in May. (Just in time, as it would turn out, for the suicide of the CNO who had been caught by *Newseek* wearing a trivial medal to which he was not entitled.)

"I suspect Speed will be at the Pentagon in a couple of months, too, and with his star. He has been a highly successful captain."

"Despite a few unsolved mysteries."

"You know what, Padre? That would finish a lot of four-stripers. But Speed is too good in the new navy for anything to stop him. They need him more than he needs them."

That was an interesting perspective. I often thought that was the only reason that Rome tolerated his cousin, Milord Cronin.

"You approve of the new navy?"

"Hell, yes. You gotta change to remain the same. Right? I read that in some Italian novel."

"*The Leopard* by Giuseppi Di Lampedusa. Turned into a film with Claudia Cardinale."

"Incomparable," he said with a sigh.

I could not but agree but felt it was unnecessary to do so.

"Great sermon today, by the way. Perfect description of the *Langley*. That's why Speed is indispensable. He can handle all the diversity without holding his nose or patronizing anyone. I'm not sure your Holy Spirit is orthodox, but I like Him."

"Her."

"I'm here because that young hellion insisted I come. I might have lost my job if I wasn't here. Most of the people you confirmed she roped in, not just that weapons handler. You guys should sign her up if she leaves the navy. She might be pope someday. And can she fly an airplane! Best pilot I have ever seen, bar none. More green stars on her chart than the rest of them put together. A real knockout, too, especially when she dresses up like she has for this event."

Diana and Venus were shipmates, it would seem. Or to do the proper mythology, Brigit and Sionna.

"Arguably. . . . Tina handles weapons?"

"Yep, she loads rockets. Wears the dark red shirt. I'd trust her to do it right more than any man."

"And what do you make of the disappearance of Commander Hoy?"

He stared at me thoughtfully. "I'm not sure he's gone, Padre. I don't mean any ghost, either. I think he's aboard ship somewhere, still stirring up trouble. He was most of the way over the edge when he embarked on this ship. I figure that when Speed finds him, it all stops."

"Where is he hiding?"

"There's a lot of spaces on this ship where a madman might hide, especially if he had some help. He'll turn up just as those bodies turned up. If you ask me, he's responsible for their deaths, too."

It was a new take on the mystery and one not entirely incompatible with one of my own models. I even had my suspicions where he might be found.

"I'll see you at supper, Bishop?" the skipper asked me. "In your quarters?"

"Actually your quarters."

"Only in port. You don't mind if I bring Steve Turner along, my duty officer of the day?"

"By no means."

"Now," he said with a grin, "if you don't mind, I think I might just engage in some low-key sexual harassment, not the sort of thing I would need absolution for."

"That might be a very good work."

He laughed and left me to collect the spring goddess of the *Langley*, who, womanlike, knew what was coming and was glowing with joy.

As a spring goddess should.

CHAPTER 14

"MORE CRAZINESS, BLACKIE," Captain Speed said when he strode into the captain's in-port cabin. "Would you believe necrophilia?"

"Lieutenant Wade was raped after she was killed?"

"Precisely! How did you know that?"

"I didn't. But I'm prepared now to believe anything."

Before he had arrived, I had restored my purple robes to their appropriate cases with serious intent not to wrinkle them and full knowledge that this good intention is of the sort with which the streets of hell are paved.

After that, I had removed the five iron from Captain Speed's golf bag where, in an unexpected gesture of neatness, I had replaced it that morning. I had placed it at the door to the cabin, firmly resolved that I would not leave to wander about the ship without it firmly in hand, armed escort or not.

Then I had engaged in conversation with the virtuous Martha and a white male mess steward on the subject of what the ship was saying about the disappearance of Commander Hoy.

"Everyone hated him," Martha had said, "but not bad enough to kill him."

"Not too many tears being shed," John, her colleague, surely not above fourteen, had agreed. "We worry about the skipper getting the blame."

"That's what Washington does," Martha had observed.

"They blame the good men. It's not an easy job to keep ships like this running smoothly. Skipper's great."

"And the racial situation?"

"Only a few people pay any attention to it," John had replied. "Only a few crazies on both sides. This is a happy ship."

"Absolutely," Martha had said with a vigorous nod of her pretty head.

"And your friends don't mind women on board?"

"Hey," John had grinned, "it's a much nicer ship because we have smiles like Martha's on board. Only the idiots who hate women complain."

"Thank you, John. My husband says the same thing."

A somewhat different perspective from the very young. And the very innocent. They probably spoke for the majority, but a silent majority. An angry minority of whatever race or gender or religion or sexual preference could make a lot of noise and cause a lot of trouble.

"I hear rumors about rape," I had said.

"That's why the skipper told us always to be with someone else," Martha had said piously. "Nothing terrible will happen tonight."

As it turned out, she was wrong. Something terrible did happen, but it wasn't rape.

Then the skipper had charged in, drew me over to a corner, and told me about the necrophilia.

"What does it mean, Blackie?"

"It means that for all the intelligence and ability on this ship, we are caught in a web of darkness of which we must dispose one way or another in the next twenty-four hours."

If only I could figure out how. In time. Before even worse evil occurred. In fact, we had less than twenty-four hours.

"As I threatened," he led me to the table that Martha and John had set for dinner, "I violated navy rules against minor sexual harassment."

"Harassment only if it is unwanted."

"True. I could claim active cooperation instead of resistance. More cooperation than I had expected . . . Anyway, I told the woman I intended to marry her."

"In so many words?"

"Course not," he smiled complacently. "I'm not that much of a fool. I told her that I wanted to spend the rest of my life with her."

"And she did not reject the suggestion out of hand?"

"Nope. Not at all."

"But you did not offer the ring which is taken to seal such intentions?"

"Not yet. I brought one on board with me when I embarked in December. I thought I'd give it to her maybe the week before we sailed back to North Island. It would be out of place to give it to her now with all that's happening on the ship."

"Tasteless."

"Yep. But I don't want to lose her."

"In my limited observations, that is unlikely."

He chuckled joyously. "I can't believe my good fortune."

Perhaps he had thought the same thing when he had been a student at Notre Dame. This time, however, his instincts were correct. The *Langley*'s spring goddess would always bring life to him.

"Commander Turner is here, Captain," Martha announced.

"Come in, Steve," the Captain said exuberantly. "This is Bishop Ryan."

He had better contain his exuberance or his immediate colleagues would think that his renewed suit of the fair public affairs officer had progressed farther than it had.

The duty officer of the day was a slim man in his middle thirties with wavy black hair, sallow skin, fine teeth, and a quick, intelligent smile. Presumably, he was one of the bright young men on the ship. He watched the skipper and listened to him with the alert attention that I suppose marked the loyal aide. He quickly noted Dave Cronin's upbeat mood and lifted a thick, dark eyebrow in approval.

So Zeus had kissed and caressed Venus and everyone would be happier because of that fact. Or in my metaphor Luhg had frolicked with Brige.

"Gentlemen," I said as we began our dinner, "I wish to propound a question. Do you think women pilots would actually kill people in combat? And if you do, do you believe that would be desirable?"

"Megan, for example?" Commander Turner responded.

"For example."

The captain frowned, his joy over what he took to be his (limited) sexual conquest spoiled by the question.

"I don't think we know the answer to that, Bishop Blackie. It's all new. Right now, women want full combat status. Whether they will continue to want it and how many will is anyone's guess. We'll just have to be very sensitive."

"If the ship were under attack," Turner added, "I don't think there's any doubt that a woman would shoot at the attackers. We're her family. Women would be, on the average, more fierce in defending the family than men."

The skipper nodded his agreement. "Right now, it's all a game. Our qualifying pilots are all kids. They know that combat is a remote possibility, but as they look around at possible adversaries, it doesn't seem likely that they'll ever have to shoot at anyone. So they don't worry about it."

"If there was another war like Nam," Commander Turner added, "I bet Megan would hand in her wings, like a lot of others of both genders. Too much killing."

"The secret story of Nam is how many men turned out to be poor combat flyers, some of the best and hottest pilots, at that."

"Ah."

"Do you mind a little navy history, Bishop?" the Skipper asked.

"Not at all."

"There have been four generations of navy pilots; the kids, the professionals, the killers, and now the professionals again. We lost most of our air crews in the early days of World War II. We had eighteen- and nineteen-year-old pilots at the end of the war and squadron leaders that were barely able to vote. They knew they would be in combat the day they signed up. They took it for granted. They were young enough to think they were invulnerable. Most of them actually survived because casualties were light at the end of the war—though a lot were killed in accidents. They were always kind of crazy. Fearless or forced to act like they were fearless. Korea and Nam didn't bother them in the least: being a naval aviator meant killing people or being killed."

"Not as crazy as the sub people from that era."

"No one was as crazy as them. . . . The men that fought and died during Nam were the professionals. I mean, they felt that flying an A-6 or a Corsair was a profession, just like being an accountant or a lawyer or a . . ."

"Commodity broker," I finished for him.

"Right. Then they found themselves off the coast of Nam thirty years ago. They had to fight a dirty kind of air war for which they had not trained with equipment that was not appropriate. They were in constant danger of death, POW camps, crash landings, running out of fuel, mechanical breakdowns. Moreover, the people back home turned against the war, including, in some cases, their own children."

"Neither of us were there," Steve Turner chimed in, "but we flew early in our careers with some of the men who were. The survivors."

"My point," the skipper continued, "is that a lot of

professionals bugged out. They didn't fly to their targets, they dumped their ordnance in the South China Sea or on rice paddies. Whole flights bugged out early in the war. Later, individuals somehow managed to get separated from their wing men time after time. People turned in their wings in substantial numbers and were given the silent treatment till they were able to disembark. None of this ever got into the media or even into official reports. The navy pretended that it wasn't happening. So, by definition, it didn't happen. Enough men hung in there to fight the war and that was sufficient. They were the killers, though not the carefree teenage killers of 1944. A lot of them got killed or went to the Hanoi Hilton, older men especially, since they were the ones who thought they were supposed to be good examples."

"It's one thing to be a professional navy aviator," the commander added, "and it turns out quite another to be a professional killer, especially when you're not a teenager. The skipper and I often wonder what we would have done."

"It seems you need one kind of man to fly carrier traps during peacetime and another kind to do the same thing during a war, especially a war like Nam. The pilots who deter war are often, not always mind you, but often not the kind who will fight it. Some of the best of our pilots bugged out."

"Why, Skipper?" I asked.

"Why did they bug out? Fear; some of them didn't want to die. Too much imagination; they weren't crazy teenagers. Revulsion at killing. There was a lot of that. I guess that's another secret about war. People deliberately avoid killing other people. Even during the Gulf War, a fair amount of ordnance ended up in the Gulf or the empty desert."

While we were having this revealing conversation, Martha and John served our dinner, Caesar salad, lamb chops, and rice, as I remember. We dutifully suspended our exchanges when they were close to the table.

"Officially," Steve Turner said, "we disapprove of such behavior as dereliction of duty. But we've come to understand that such things happen. We never force anyone to fly who turns in his wings. Let the one who does not have a coward lurking in his own heart throw the first stone."

"So, if women want to turn in their wings at the prospect of killing other people, I say they won't be the first ones to do so," the skipper waved his fork at me, much as Sean Cronin would have. "And if they dump their ordnance in some convenient place, they won't be the first ones to do that, either. My guess is that they would be less afraid of death than men, but more likely to rebel at killing. I could be wrong. I hope we will never have to find out."

"Right now," Commander Turner sipped his iced tea from a goblet which anywhere else in the world would have contained red wine, "the kids flying traps will be deterrence pilots who can't really imagine what combat would be like and really don't want to."

"So as to our Juno, my guess is that she would die for the ship, but would turn in her wings if we asked her to kill people that were not an immediate threat to us. Nor would I criticize her or anyone else whose conscience got in the way."

"Diana," I corrected him.

"Huh?"

"She's the Diana of the ship, not Juno. The public affairs officer is patently the spring goddess, Venus to the Romans and more properly Breig or Bride to the Celts. Or even arguably Oestern to the Anglo-Saxons, whence our name for Easter for the Christian Passover."

They both broke up laughing at that correction.

"You tell her that? Venus, I mean?"

"Patently. Though I prefer Breig, personally. After all, she did become a Christian saint."

He blushed happily and, as the Irish would say, half-changed the subject.

"Did she tell you that she has a pilot's license?"

"She did."

"She can fly a private jet if she wants to?"

"I believe that detail was omitted."

"She tell you why she's not a naval aviator?"

"She did not have to."

"And the reason?"

The skipper's gallowglass eyes, much like those of his eminent cousin, glittered with amusement and affection, as they did whenever we mentioned the public affairs officer.

"Too much imagination and too many memories of stories about her parent and grandparent."

"You do know practically everything, don't you? Just like the cardinal said?"

"Arguably."

The conversation had helped me to understand a little better what the navy and the *Langley* were all about. Useful background, perhaps, for the obligatory puzzle solving of the next twenty-four hours. It was now time, over dessert, when we Irish always do our serious business, to turn to my real interest.

"I wonder if you two gentlemen would mind giving me brief opinions about some of your officers."

"Off the record?" the skipper asked.

"Patently."

"Sure."

"The admiral?"

"Crawford was lucky to get his second star. He's out after this cruise. I wouldn't want to have to sail under him again."

"Too fussy and cautious," Turner added. "Good heart,

though. Occasionally decisive. Usually has to ask the skipper what to do next."

"Indeed. . . . The acting XO?"

"Dick Dempsey will be the first African American CNO. First-rate man. He'll be a captain soon."

"Skipper did not promote him to acting XO because he was African American. But he wasn't unaware, either, that it would calm some nerves after Hoy arrested those African Americans on drug charges."

"What did Commander Hoy look like, by the way?"

They looked at one another.

"Medium height," the captain said.

"A little less maybe."

"Big mustache of which he was very proud."

"Thick hair, which some people thought was a toupee."

"Brooding brown eyes, scary."

"More black eyes than anything else."

"Kind of hard to describe him. A nondescript kind of person. Larkin should have a photo of him somewhere."

"I see. . . . The navigator."

Again their eyes consulted each other.

"Hilda?" the skipper said, cautiously choosing his words. "She's first-rate at what she does. . . . Will get her eagle and nothing more, even though she's a woman. Probably could command some small depot or office ashore."

I chose not to push the sexual orientation matter.

"Air officer?"

"Bright, ambitious, charming. Not all that deep, but a good guy."

"He's off to the Pentagon when we put ashore," the chief of staff added. "Good at what he does, that's for sure."

"Engineer."

"A good engineer. One of the best. Nothing more than that. A pain in the butt, normally."

"Political reactionary, sounds like he's getting ready to mutiny. Which he isn't. At least I don't think he is."

"Acting public affairs officer?"

"I'll pass on her," the captain laughed. "Conflict of interest. Steve?"

"Who doesn't have a conflict of interest on her? Not a person on the ship who would not be proud to serve under her, spring goddess or not. . . . Sorry, I didn't mean a pun, Skipper."

"Forget it!"

"Chief master at arms?"

They both grinned.

"We'll lose him, of course," Dave Cronin replied, "to that law firm. Wish we could keep him. And that cute yeoman of his who probably knows more about the ship than anyone else."

"He's crazy like a fox, that's why he found that yeoman who was going crazy in supply because she wasn't supposed to think for herself. But I'm sure you have figured Johnny out, Bishop."

"Arguably. . . . The aforementioned supply officer."

"Glen Shorter is another pain in the butt," Turner said with a grimace. "Monumental. Obsessive."

"He could handle any supply operation in the navy, no matter how big. You'd just have to put up with his complaints about what's wrong with the navy and his pessimism."

"Complaints shared by others?"

"Sure, but not as obsessively as he harps on them."

"CAG, as I believe the wing commander is called."

"Frank Gill is a CAG with a heart. Hard to do, but he carries it off. He'll have a ship of his own soon, though maybe not a carrier."

"Lieutenant Colonel Williamson?"

The skipper frowned. "I don't know him all that well. Kind of hard to figure. A little slippery, too, if you ask me. At first, didn't like your friend Diana . . ."

"Erihu," I corrected him again. "Whence Erin or Ireland or later Kathleen Ni Houlihan."

"Arguably," the skipper replied, intolerably stealing my line. "But he changed his tune when he saw which way the wind was blowing."

"And which way was it blowing?"

"He discovered that she was the best pilot on the ship and immensely popular. Clever enough to want to bask in her glory. Can't beat 'em, join 'em."

"Indeed."

"Captain Murray of the marines."

"The sea Marines are the pick of the corps. And their officers are the best in the corps. Sound and sensible most of the time, till someone tries to criticize his platoon. Then he's a tiger. Would have torn Hoy limb from limb in the wardroom if Steve hadn't held him back."

"One tough, strong guy, Bishop," Steve Turner added. "I'd want his back against mine in a barroom fight. . . . Not that I've ever been in a barroom fight."

"If you will," I asked, finishing my iced tea and signaling the exemplary Martha for another dish of chocolate chip ice cream.

"And the senior chaplain?"

"Jay O'Malley?" The skipper seemed surprised. "He's a little strange, Bishop. Not as gregarious as a lot of chaplains. Kind of agonized. But he's a good chaplain. The crew like him. They have no trouble making allowances for his moods, if you can call them that. Some of them say he's saintly, not the usual judgment about chaplains. I'm sure he'll make captain the next time around."

"I'm sorry, Bishop," Martha said apologetically. "We don't have any more chocolate chip. All we have is rum raisin."

"On an allegedly dry ship of the United States Navy?

I am shocked. Nonetheless, I will have two scoops, if you don't mind."

"You don't seem to have much trouble with the calories, Bishop," Commander Turner commented.

"On the contrary, I have enormous trouble. During Lent, except when I'm traveling as I am now, I fast and lose no weight at all. On the other hand, when I eat as I have out of respect to the excellent food on this ship, I put on no weight."

"You're lucky."

"Arguably. . . ."

Martha served the ice cream with her usual smile of benediction. When she withdrew, I continued my questions.

"Would you go over that list in your mind and see if, in your judgment, any of them had sufficient motive to do away with Commander Hoy."

They paused, considered, and then glanced at one another.

"Most of them didn't like him," the skipper began.

"And not without reason."

"But as far as I know, their reasons for disliking him were not enough to lead them to kill him."

"But, Bishop," Commander Turner cautioned me, "Digby had made a lot of enemies. We've gone over these names before and added a few more. We end up by saying that there could be other people on the ship about whom we know nothing who might have had excellent reason for wanting to push him over the side."

I sighed. I had arrived at conclusions about the officers we had discussed that were, in some part, not different from their descriptions. Most of them might have disposed of Commander Hoy, but if they did so, it would have to be for motives that were unknown to us. Moreover, while I knew how the locked-room caper had been carried out, that did not furnish me with any explanations of why it had been carried out.

Martha and John removed the remnants of dinner and demurely departed.

"I should get up to the bridge," the captain said. "It's going to be a rotten night, but they need the experience. It'll be a lot worse out in the Indian Ocean during the monsoon. At least tonight the waves will only be a few feet high."

"We worry about losing people in night traps," his aide added. "But so far our safety record has been perfect. Almost miraculous."

"Hard work more than miracle," the captain observed. "Sometimes safety is a bore. Usually. All the more reason to be disciplined in our insistence on it. No choice."

"Patently."

At the door, Commander Turner went into the passageway. David Cronin lingered, as if for a moment's extra conversation.

"Personal matter, Bishop?"

"Certainly."

"Mary Anne, as you probably guessed . . . Is it possible for two people to pass in the night, touch one another lightly, almost casually, and then be bound together for the rest of their lives, bound with chains of steel, almost without realizing what has happened, without wanting it to happen, and indeed being terrified by what has happened?"

"Oh, yes." I said simply.

"The very first time we were together, almost accidentally, we both knew that there was no escape. When we embarked on this cruise, I told myself it was merely a passing incident. But I knew better."

"Hence you brought the ring when you embarked."

"A visible sign. But even if I hadn't, I would have been—what should I call the feeling—captured, besotted, trapped, swamped. Delightfully so, but irrevocably, even if neither of us ever said a word about that."

He frowned, searching for words to describe his emotions.

"She overwhelms me. Complex, intricate, demanding, vulnerable, fascinating. I'll never escape, not that I want to."

Emotions that are commonplace yet unique to every person who feels them.

"I'm almost afraid of my power to affect her. I can make her smile, laugh, cry with a single word. I touch her and it is as though my finger is a torch and she catches fire. The flames envelop me and I become like a firestorm. . . . Nothing like it has ever happened to me before. Will it always be like that?"

"Oh, yes, so it is when God touches the barren tree with the heat of summer and calls forth its luxuriance. He has surrounded us with members of the opposite gender so that there is a possibility that one of them might touch us the same way."

He nodded thoughtfully, realizing perhaps the inadequacy of words to describe his turbulent emotions.

"I sometimes think," he hesitated, again groping for words, "that I have changed her. Not that I wanted to or tried to. It just happened. When I first saw her, she seemed like a kind of plain Jane, wanly pretty, perhaps, but not all that exciting. Now she seems to radiate sexual energy. Irresistible. Can a man do that to a woman without even realizing it?"

"It seems to be built into the plan."

"Clever planner."

"Oh, yes."

"I don't want to lose her. Nothing the navy has to offer is as important. Is this what love is like, Bishop?"

"It is not an antiseptic emotion."

"You know . . ." He opened the door. "She even looks like Venus."

Patently, he meant with her clothes off, but was too much the officer and gentlemen to say so.

"I yield to your superior experience in the matter."
He laughed. "I have no intention of losing her."

If only, I reflected to myself, *we could get through this awful night.*

CHAPTER 15

MY FIRST STOP as I began my rounds that night, with my marine guard always in tow, was the office of the chief master of arms. Yeoperson Nelly Regan was in charge.

"The boss not here?" I said, with the characteristic Irish nod of the head toward the place where the boss should have been.

"Wandering about our guard stations like he was a monsignor walking the parish at night . . . Can you imagine, Bishop, he wanted to go out by himself. I totally wouldn't let him go until he found himself a marine to go with him."

She frowned angrily at the memory of her boss's impudence.

"And how did you prevent this imprudent departure?"

"I stood in the doorway and refused to move. He wouldn't dare push me, so what can I tell you?"

"I daresay he was flattered by your concern."

She blushed. "I suppose so, but still he has to keep his own rules, doesn't he?"

"Oh, yes. . . . There is one detail of the disappearance of Commander Hoy that puzzles me. As I understand it, the skipper was called to the door of the commander's cabin. He arrived with the illustrious and admirable chief master of arms. They were unable to gain entrance. So a machinist mate was summoned to cut a hole in the door. Is this correct?"

"I guess so. I wasn't there."

"There was no extra key?"

"We're pretty strong on privacy here, even if you have to share a cabin with eleven shipmates like I do. So we don't pass out a lot of keys. The ship is maybe too open as it is. There are master keys, of course. . . . Let me show you."

She opened a closet and then opened an inner door with a key of her own.

"Only Jumping Johnny and I have keys to get in this closet. Not even the skipper has one."

She opened a ceiling-to-floor panel. On a neatly organized metal wall scores, probably hundreds of keys, each hanging from a tagged label, stared ominously at us.

"These are the master keys. In case of an emergency, Jiving John or someone who has clout with him can get into a cabin, like if they locked themselves out. This is the one for that wing of officers' quarters."

"Then why wasn't it used the day of Commander Hoy's disappearance?"

"The key disappeared, too. Jazzman John couldn't find it. Mostly because it wasn't there."

"That happens often?"

"Nope," she closed the panel and locked it. "First time since I've been aboard."

"The NIS investigators asked about it."

"No way. Naturally, we didn't tell them."

She locked the closet and led me back to her cubbyhole.

"What do you think happened to it?"

"Someone took it and it wasn't the boss or me. And do we think it significant? Sure we do, but we don't know of what."

"Fascinating."

"Fer sure. There's a locksmith next door who has the codes for the keys. He made us the new master key that I just showed you. Just in case it disappears again," she opened a drawer in her desk, removed a box of tissue, opened the bottom, and produced another key, "we have a backup. Clever man, the Jolly Johnny, huh?"

"You suspect Commander Hoy had access to your key box?"

"You bet!" she nodded vigorously. "Moreover, as a clever gumshoe like you has already figured out, Bishop Blackie, the missing master key for that section of officers' quarters is still missing. Someone on the ship has it."

"Fascinating . . . Surely you had the keys to that closet changed?"

"Certainly, but if someone got into them once, it could happen again."

"Your locksmith a trusted man?"

"He used to be. Now we're not sure."

"I see."

"Toward the end, Hoy was telling people, especially the gullible types who were under his spell, that he was on a special assignment from a supersecret government agency that was monitoring abuses in other government agencies. I think he even had some kind of printed document to prove it."

"The skipper knew about this?"

"Only at the very end when he made up his mind to remove him."

"And the locksmith is in one of those 'patriot' groups?"

She nodded solemnly, her blue eyes wide. "Didn't used to be but is now. Don't worry, Bishop, we're keeping an eye on them."

Certain pieces were beginning to fit together, but the pattern was far from complete.

"Do you think you have on file a picture of the late Commander Rogers Hoy?"

"Sure, we've been giving out copies like he was a celebrity or something."

She opened up a file cabinet next to her desk and extracted a photograph.

"Doesn't look much like him," she said. "Doesn't show him as a sawed-off little creep with a potbelly."

In the picture Hoy wore no mustache and his hairline was receding. His facial features were unremarkable. I gave the picture back to her.

"You didn't like him?"

"Totally yucky! Sneered at me. I don't know what those other women saw in him. Crept around the ship like a mole."

"Other women?"

"You know, his fan club."

"Ah . . . There is no fan club, I presume, for the stalwart chief master at arms?"

"Yes, there is," she responded defiantly. "And only one member is permitted."

"He is aware of this exclusive club?"

"What can I tell you? If he is, he keeps it to himself. . . . He did kiss me when I blocked the door on him."

"Instead of pushing you aside, he kissed you."

"First time," she said with satisfaction.

"Not the last, I presume."

"I sure hope not."

The chief master at arms was a dead duck.

The name of the chief engineer, Commander Olaf Carlson, suggested a blond Viking, arguably with a battle-ax. But, the next man on my list of interviewees was, in fact, a thin man with rimless glasses and the demeanor of someone with a Ph.D in engineering, which, in fact, the chief possessed.

"Fascinating place, isn't?" he said to me as he swiveled around in his easy chair above a large room with a vast display of monitors and control panels. "We're responsible down here not only for the nuclear reactor but for all the energy on the ship. If the power goes off in one of the galleys, for example, it's our fault, and we have to restore it immediately if not sooner."

"The nuclear reactor provides no problems."

"Not yet, and indeed not on any of the Nimitz class carriers. They're far more reliable than the furnaces on other ships. They're cheaper, cleaner, safer, last longer, enable us to stay at sea indefinitely if we want to, and give us more room for aviation fuel. So we can't berth in Australia or New Zealand, which is their misfortune for listening to liberal ideology."

"Ah."

"There's no way that one of these can go Chernobyl, but you'll never persuade your nutty environmentalists of that fact. So we do what we can."

"Indeed."

"I didn't like Hoy. He had no authority over us down here. Yet he'd call a couple of days every week and demand to know the status of the reactor. You see that Negro kid over there, the one in front of that big panel?"

"Yes."

"Well, he and the guy next to him monitor the reaction eight hours a day, dullest job in the world, but they and their crew are probably the most cautious and careful men on the ship besides me. They don't need an asshole with three stripes harassing them.

"Hoy would never come down here. Afraid of the radiation. He'd avoid me in the wardroom because he thought I carried the radiation with me. A real nut case. Should have been sent ashore after the first week."

"So."

"You ask me, the problem with this ship is that the captain is too liberal. You hear nothing but good about him topside, right?"

"Pretty much."

"Yeah . . . well, down here, we think he's a hand-wringing coward. In my navy, the C.O. gives orders and is obeyed. All this business about balancing the women and the gays and the lesbians and the Negroes and the Hispanics and religious nuts is bullshit. If they want to be on this ship, they should do what they're told, and that's that."

"I see."

"Personally, I don't mind the Negroes if they do their job, and if they don't, they don't last down here, let me tell you. The gays and the women, you can have them. They don't belong on a warship. The sooner the navy finds that out, the better off we'll all be. If we keep having trouble like we do here, the navy's going to have to draw the line."

"You think it will?"

"If it doesn't, if it keeps sending out captains like our liberal friend up on the bridge," he nodded in the general direction of 05 level, "the navy is finished."

"Who might have killed Commander Hoy and his associates?"

"No one down here gave a damn about him. Topside? I'd start with the gays and the lesbos, to begin with. Then maybe some of the Black Power guys. They're furious at Hoy for breaking up their drug scam. Some radical women who were afraid he'd rape them . . . Hell, I don't know!"

"Did you agree with Commander Hoy's efforts to tighten up the ship?"

"Look, Padre, most of us on this ship who have been around twenty years figured that the ship needed to be a lot tighter than it is. We wouldn't mind seeing Cronin's career go down the tube. But Hoy was a nut case, a freak, a fool. There are a lot easier ways of getting rid of a weak captain than that. All he did was make it tougher to get rid of him, see my point?"

I did, indeed. I wondered what those other ways were, but I decided it was not wise to ask.

I chatted with him for a few more minutes about the

wonders of the engineering marvels on the *Langley* and then slipped quietly away.

A clever reactionary and a possible conniver. But perhaps not the kind who would dispose of Digby Hoy, whom he would figure was a fly not worth swatting.

My next stop was at the medical office where a young woman with blond hair, glasses, a ponytail, a voluptuous body shielded by a white medical coat and a name plate that said Sander replaced the motion sickness patch behind my ear. I assumed that she was a nurse but, on second thought, called her Dr. Sander.

"Well, at least you didn't think I was a nurse, Bishop. Most people do. They don't realize that with a thousand women embarked on this ship, we have to have a woman doctor."

"Patently," I said, complacent with my prudence. Fortunately, she didn't ask how I knew.

"How do your women patients stand up to the rigors of shipboard life?"

"I have men patients, too. I take care of the skipper when his knee acts up. Basketball accident. I'm sure Mary Anne insists he see the woman doctor."

"Indeed!"

"They are certainly going to be married. It will be good for both of them. It is probably even good that they practice restraint for awhile like they are now. Not for too long."

"You favor restraint?"

"You folks have no monopoly on it," she said, jamming her hands into the pockets of her white medical jacket. "Civilization depends on restraint. On the whole, the presence of two genders on a crowded ship like this is a good idea. Rubs rough edges off both genders. But it works only if a substantial number of men and women are willing to practice restraint."

A very intelligent and thoughtful young woman. More than just an M.D.

"How would you say that functions?"

"Well, if you're working with someone who is about your age and who is smart and very attractive and very nice, you'd have to be devoid of hormones to not feel a tug toward union. Do you Catholics admit that?"

"We call it a sacrament. Tells us about our appeal for God and God's appeal for us."

"So that appeal humanizes you, and if you have any sensitivity, you learn to admire that person as a person and not as a couple of sex organs. That experience enhances life, makes it more fascinating, more poignant, more dangerous, and more rewarding. And you learn something about persons of the other gender. Maybe there's a possibility of something more. Usually there isn't. So you both practice restraint, which only humans can do."

"And to be human one must do."

"Precisely," she clapped her hands. "You know how things are. It isn't easy. Harder for men. Maybe. Somehow, I have become kind of an unofficial chaplain. For women, of course, but for men, too. They come to me for advice, sexual advice. I provide them with the most elementary information about the sexual physiology and psychology of women. They're completely astonished."

"And delighted?"

"It would seem so. They keep coming. I don't know why they would ask me, except that I'm a doctor and hence maybe a little neutral."

"A woman doctor."

"That seems to be part of it." She shook her head, puzzled. "It's an erotically interesting role."

"Doubtless."

"Anyway, on a crowded little semiprison for men and women, you learn restraint and respect, or the whole idea doesn't work."

"You think it is working?"

She shrugged. "As well as anything in the human

condition . . . To answer your question about ship-board life, tonight every woman is scared. But generally, they do about as well as the men. They work hard, complain, enjoy their friendships, and keep their eyes open for a man who might make a good husband. Which is what most women do on shore. Men too, I suppose."

"And a good husband is?"

She paused and looked thoughtful, her eyes closed for a moment. She took off her glasses and put them in the breast pocket of her medical coat.

"Would intelligence and passionate gentleness do?"

"I should think so. Men would perhaps use a similar definition if backed into a corner, Dr. Sander."

"And mean something different but not altogether different. Therein is the agony and the ecstasy of the human condition, I suppose. And my name is Ellen."

"Mine is Blackie. And should you find such a good man on this ship, what would happen to your counsel of restraint?"

"If I was certain that this was the man, I'd go after him. Fuck restraint. . . . Does that shock you, Bishop, ah, Blackie?"

"Hardly."

She smiled. "Are you a philosopher?"

"If I remember correctly, I may have a degree in that subject."

"Suppose I find a guy that I'm willing to be unre-strained with, and suppose that he is a Catholic."

"All right."

"And suppose I asked you whether there would be room for someone who doesn't believe all that much in your church, would there be room for me?"

"Why should you be different from the rest of us? We Catholics really don't believe in all that much. What we do believe in, however, we believe in very strongly. Be sure you receive the collection envelopes and the holy water, however; those are the only things we give away free."

"Suppose that all this should happen, and it's a lot of suppose because the man in question doesn't have the most remote idea that I'm interested in him. And I'm not sure that I am. But suppose it does, would you do the wedding?"

"Seven nineteen North Wabash Avenue, Chicago 60611, Superior 7-9343."

Astonishingly, she grabbed a piece of paper from her desk and wrote it down.

"End of that part of our conversation," she said.

I returned to the subject at hand. "Did the late Commander Hoy attempt to hassle this department?"

"Sure," she shrugged her shoulders. "He tried to hassle everyone. Borderline personality fer sure."

"Ah."

"Chameleon. Charm the birds out of the trees one minute and rage at you the next. Classic. Those kind always find people they can suck into their vortex. Skipper should have put him in the brig the first day."

"You were afraid of him?"

She hesitated. "Any woman in her right mind would have been afraid of him. He'd rape you with his eyes." She shivered, as though a gust of cold wind had slipped down to 03 level.

"Fortunately, then, he is no longer on board."

"I don't believe in ghosts. I don't believe in much of anything, Bishop, but I know I don't believe in ghosts. Or demons. Or possession. Yet, even before what they discovered last night, I felt that his malevolence is stalking this ship."

"Malevolence?"

"Sometimes borderline personalities deteriorate rapidly. Something turns them on or turns them off and they become profoundly evil. I had a case like that once. Absolute madman. All the protective coloring gone, but more clever than ever. I know Hoy is dead, but what he did to this ship is still on board, lurking in every dark corner."

"Hmm."

"These patches give you pleasant dreams, Blackie?"

"Nightmares."

"Which my remarks won't help."

"They won't make them worse, either."

"May I ask why you are carrying that golf club?"

"Five iron, Ellen."

"Yes."

"I use it to exorcise demons. Thank you for the patch."

"And thank you for the philosophy. I'll see you around. Maybe around," she put her glasses back on and glanced at the note she had put on her desk, "Seven nineteen North Wabash."

"Area code 312, Su 7-9343 . . . I'll be waiting for the call."

"Can you find the way to hangar deck from here, Corporal?" I asked my marine protector, who was waiting for me in the passageway outside the medical area.

"Certainly, sir."

In the vast, brooding silence of the hangar, there were no hints, no warnings, no clues. *A space like this,* I told myself, *is too impersonal, too mechanistic to be subject to human emotions, particularly sick emotions. Hangar decks are simply not haunted. No way.*

Are they?

Above us, the aircraft thudded violently into the flight deck as the night traps continued. A nearby TV monitor repeated the now monotonous incantation, "Roger ball."

"Now, Corporal, the Catholic chaplain's office."

Jay O'Malley was hunched over his desk, reading St. John of the Cross.

"Very good confirmation class, Jay," I began.

"Thank you, sir," he said formally. "I try to work hard

on preparation for the sacraments. It's mostly a waste of time, but you never know when you're going to have an effect on someone."

"Indeed . . . It's not a particularly happy ship these days, is it?"

He closed the book on his finger, a hint that he would rather struggle through the dark night of the soul than speak to an itinerant bishop.

"No, sir. Ships like this are never happy. There's too many people, too much strain, too much lust. The only difference these days is that it is all out in the open. Even in the chapel."

I waited for further denunciations, but none were forthcoming.

"Have you solved the mystery of the XO's death?" he asked me politely.

"There are certain pieces of the puzzle that are beginning to fit together."

"I don't think he had anything to do with those murders," he said. "He was basically a good man, like I told you yesterday. At least not a hypocrite. Toward the end, it was all too much for him, I'm afraid."

"Indeed."

"Do you know this fellow, Bishop?" Finger still marking his place, he lifted the book off his desk.

"I've read him."

"Powerful stuff."

"Shocking erotic imagery."

He considered that. "Yeah, I guess so. I never noticed it though."

"Ah . . . There are those who say that Commander Hoy's spirit walks the ship at night."

"Maybe he does, Bishop. Maybe he does. I wouldn't be surprised. Hauntings occur in places that are permeated by evil. The *Langley* sure fits the bill."

"I would have said permeated by humanity."

"What's the difference?"

On that happily Augustinian, not to say Manichean, note I left Chaplain O'Malley to pursue San Juan de la Cruz, now convinced that he didn't understand the saint at all.

My next stop was the captain's bridge, crowded and dark for the night landings in the rain and the mists. The navigator and the officer of the deck were gathered around the young woman at the helm. Their faces illumined in the lights of the various instruments seemed spooky, like aliens on the starship *Enterprise* (or the *Voyager,* if one wishes). In the background, shadows in the dark, lurked the talkers, enlisted personnel who reported to the captain on the communication traffic on the ship and between the ship and the air.

The skipper himself was perched on his comfortable high chair overlooking the flight deck. He watched intently as each aircraft emerged from the dark over the fantail and almost instantly careened into the deck. Then his head would turn and he would glance forward as in a roar of engines and an explosive hiss of steam the catapults would hurl an aircraft off into the murky darkness that surrounded the ship.

"Bishop's on the bridge!" one of the talkers announced.

"No demonstrations, please," I said, amid much laughter.

"Sorry it's so dark up here, Bishop," the captain said. "We don't want any extra lights confusing the kids, and its easier for me to watch the operations down on the deck. . . . We're doing pretty well tonight. For aviators who are scared stiff, they're doing a good job, aren't they, Hilda?"

"Sure are, sir. Weather says that it will get worse after midnight."

"We'll secure air ops by then. . . . Bishop, there's your friend Megan in that Hornet that is taxiing on to the cat. She's had a couple of fine traps. Crazy woman loves night flying."

"Red witch," I murmured.

"You've been talking to someone I know."

A big screen rose as if by magic from the deck to shield the blast of the Hornet's twin jets. Everyone seemed to hold their breath as steam oozed out of the slot on the deck beneath which the cat prepared to do its work. A deck hand slipped out from underneath the aircraft, having completed the final touches of uniting place to cat.

Then Megan's Hornet dribbled forward as if a giant hand was holding it back.

"Bad cat! Bad cat!" the captain screamed.

For a moment, the F-18 lifted unsteadily off the deck, then suddenly, as if giving up a bootless effort, it nosed down plunged out of sight into the darkness of the night and the Pacific Ocean below.

CHAPTER 16

"RIGHT RUDDER, SLOW speed!" Dave Cronin bellowed. "Air Boss, secure air ops!"

"Aye, aye, sir," a couple of people said.

"Did anyone see an ejection?"

"Second angel airborne," a talker said calmly.

An SH-60 (or Skyhawk as I later learned) emerged out of the thickening mists and thundered over the island. One of the two was always airborne during operations.

The massive window wipers swished back and forth with implacable indifference.

"No ejection, sir," Hilda murmured.

"Too much mist and rain to tell, sir," Steve Turner replied.

"I thought I saw something, Captain," the helms person said.

"Admiral asks if you want to detach the *Spruance* and the *Fletcher* to search.

"Certainly!"

He turned to me. "Why did the idiot have to ask? Did he think the frigates should just sail ahead?"

"Air officer," he shouted into his hand-held mike, "Secure all cats till further notice. I want a complete investigation of that launch. . . . Yes, I know the holdback bar broke. . . . They don't break on this ship, understand?"

"Air Boss! Report on flights! . . . Three low on

225

fuel . . . how many pounds? . . . Five more in the air? . . . Give us a few minutes. . . ."

"Cat captain one reports no ejection observed. Cat two thinks there might have been an ejection. Too much rain."

"She had maybe a tenth of a second, maybe less to pull the handle," he said to me. "If she didn't, the ship crushed the plane and her and sent them both to the bottom of the sea. If she did, she might have broken her back. Or landed ahead of the ship and been chopped up by its screws. Or drowned in its wake."

"The ejection seat," Commander Turner said grimly, "Is a NACES—Navy Aircrew Common Ejection Seat—a Martin-Davis Mk Fourteen. Within one second of the pull on the release handle, an explosion blows off the canopy, straps automatically restrain the pilot's arms and legs, a barostatic device measures the altitude and speed of the plane, and the rockets eject the pilot. At one point five seconds, the drogue parachute has already been released. At two seconds, the seat is detached from the pilot, and at two point five seconds, the pilot is floating back toward earth. Sometimes in ejections during traps or cats, the pilot can guide himself back to the deck of the carrier, though usually only in good weather and in daylight. There are some three hundred ejections a year, and the survival rate is ninety-four percent."

"There are no data," the captain said, "about night ejections in bad weather. My guess is that much of that other six percent occur in weather like tonight."

Dante would have cherished the scene. Rain, darkness, floodlights, an aircraft sliding off the front edge of the flight deck, people talking strange languages.

Dave Cronin did not lose his cool, though his face was twisted in anguish. The radiant young woman who had only a few hours before celebrated the coming of the Holy Spirit was dead, crushed or broken or drowned or maybe all three.

"The ejection device, if she pulls it and if it works," he explained to me, "blows the cockpit out of the plane and sends her tumbling into the air, maybe even fifteen hundred feet. It even automatically opens her chute. She takes a tremendous pounding in the process."

As I fingered the rosary in my jacket pocket, I warned the Holy Spirit that this was not an acceptable outcome. We needed this young woman; all of us did. We must not let the enemy take her away from us. Admittedly, I had bungled badly in not realizing that they would sabotage her plane. But I had embarked on this ship only a little more than a day ago. It was not my fault that I didn't see all the possibilities. The Spirit was demanding from me what was beyond all reason. Therefore it was Her responsibility to make up for my frailties.

Right?

Talk to God that way?

One must talk that way to lovers who are demanding too much—even if it does one more good than it has effect on the unpredictable lover.

The bridge was silent, the only sound now the swishing of the mammoth wipers that swept away the raindrops and permitted us brief views of the flight deck and the planes parked on the front of the ship.

Finally, one of the talkers, a woman's voice, said, "Angels report no contact."

"Very good. Resume previous course. Air Officer, resume ops. Air Boss, bring them in. Officer of the Deck, can you see the angels or the frigates with your glass?"

"No, sir, just an occasional flicker of light in the distance."

"Very good. Let's get the others on board."

A few minutes later, a dim outline of a Tomcat appeared on the TV monitor. "Roger ball," announced Paddles, as the landing officer was called in memory of the time when his predecessors used real paddles to guide a plane in.

"CAG's plane," the chief of staff said.

The skipper nodded grimly.

"No prize, but he's in," he said as Frank Gill's aircraft thudded hard against the deck, skidded, and then crashed down.

"A bit high," said the officer of the deck.

"More than a bit."

Two more aircraft quickly followed.

"Nothing from the angels?"

"No, sir," said the talker.

I wondered whether I should say the prayers for the dying, murmur a distant absolution for the red witch.

No, we would not give her up that quickly.

"I can imagine what the media and Congress will do with this," Hilda observed.

"Excuse my language, Hilda, but fuck the media and Congress."

Nervous laughter rocked the bridge. Apparently, the captain rarely used such language.

"Yes, *sir*." Said a number of people on the bridge.

"Still nothing from the angels?"

"No, sir," the talker sounded like she was choking back tears.

"Air Boss, we had better bring all the others in before the weather gets worse."

"It's not supposed to get worse than this, sir," the navigator observed.

"Get them in anyway. No point in taking any more chances tonight."

"Sir," said the talker, her voice choking.

"Yes?" said the skipper mildly.

"Angel Two reports," she struggled and then controlled her voice, "contact with life jacket radio beam."

"Patch them in. I want to hear this."

To me he said, "Keep praying, Blackie. We're not out of the woods yet. The jacket might just be floating around in the wreckage with nothing in it or maybe only a lifeless body."

"The water is cold?" I asked.

"No, not really. We're off Baja California, and it's March. Not a whirlpool, but it won't kill you."

"Repeat, Angel Two, this is Big L, please repeat."

We were now listening to the conversation between the air boss and the two copters.

"Angel Two to Big L." Static and noise made sound seem distant and weak. "We have a strong signal. Repeat, we have a strong signal. Request help from Angel One."

"Don't you two bump into one another out there!" yelled the air boss. "Maintain prudent distance. And stay routine altitude above the waves, unless you find pilot. Understand?"

The only response was two bursts of static. And then a faint, "Roger that."

"They are not going to obey that. They're practically surfing out there."

"Air boss asks whether he should secure from landings?"

"No, continue the traps until we know more."

We waited for the length of several eternities and back. The only sounds on the bridge were the static of the helicopters' communications, the thud of the landing Hornets and Tomcats, and the monotonous chant, "Roger ball."

Then there was a loud burst of static and the voice of the angel pilot as clear as though he were on the bridge with us.

"We have a flare! We definitely have a flare! The pilot must have seen or heard us! Repeat, we have a flare!"

"That means she's alive!" Steve Turner exulted.

The younger talker person was audibly crying.

"Sorry, sir," she murmued.

"No problem, Alice. That's the way we all feel."

"Roger, Angel Two. You have a flare. Do you see the shroud? Repeat, do you see a shroud?"

A negative burst of static.

"Say again?"

"No shroud yet."

"She carries a knife to cut herself out of the shroud. She can do that if she is not too badly injured, if she remembers the knife, and if she doesn't lose the knife in the water."

An excited burst of static.

"Say again Angel One!"

More static

"Say again!"

"We have the shroud. We definitely have the shroud. No sign of personnel."

"Just one. It was a Hornet."

"Roger that."

"You have no pilot, Angel one?"

"No pilot yet."

"Roger."

More static, sometimes loud, sometimes soft and distant.

"Say again, please, Angel One!"

Yet another roar of static.

Then very faintly, "We have a pilot, Big L! We have a pilot! He's waving at us, shouting, by the looks of it. . . . Sorry, Big L, *she's* waving at us!"

There were cheers on the bridge and echoes elsewhere on the island.

"This is the captain," Cronin's voice boomed on the public address system. "The angels report that they have found the lady leatherneck and that she is waving and shouting at them. Those of you who have been praying, it looks like your prayers may have been heard. Now we must get her on board the copter and bring her in. Safely."

Cheers rose up from every corner of the ship.

I continued to pray, this time the Glorious Mysteries of the Rosary.

"Prepare to rescue her," the air boss ordered. "She's probably unable to climb your ladder by herself."

Thick static in response.

"A ladder flapping in the wind and the engines of the aircraft," the skipper told me. "They'll probably have to send one of their men into the water and secure a breeches buoy on her."

"Not a chance," I said.

"Air officer orders you to go into the water to pick her up. She can't climb the ladder."

More static.

Then the clear voice filled the bridge again.

"Pilot's climbing up the ladder. We're taking her on board. She's still shouting."

"Secure from further air ops until we bring the angels back."

"Estimate survivor's condition," the air boss demanded.

"Vigorous! She's shouting two messages for the captain."

Dave Cronin was grinning now.

"This is the captain," he said. "What are survivor's messages?"

"Sir, she says that the hold-back bar broke and that she wants her scarf."

"Tell her that we know it was the hold-back bar and that she will get her scarf. I don't happen to have a supply on board."

"She's very insistent about the scarf, sir."

"I can imagine. . . ." Then his voice boomed on the public address system. "This is the captain. Lieutenant Monahan has apparently embarked on the angel under her own power. I think the ship can relax. For those of you who were praying, it seems definite that our prayers were heard."

Cheers once again rose from the bowels of the ship.

"Secure the patch, Alice. Megan gets away with what she gets away with because she is everyone's favorite teenage hoyden daughter."

"Scarf?"

"The company that makes those ejection seats, Martin-Davis, English firm, awards a very expensive tie to everyone who survives an ejection. Recently, they decided that they would give women survivors a scarf and an expensive jeweled pin. . . . Air Boss, secure further landings so they can bring her in."

It could only have been a few minutes, but it seemed like half of the eternity we had already endured till the Sikorsky appeared out of the dark just above the island and gently settled to the flight deck below us. I pressed my nose against the window of the bridge and watched the scene immediately below us as the big wipers swept away the rain, only to have to repeat their battle a few seconds later.

Dr. Sander, rain slicker over her medical coat, was standing next to a gurney, ready to take the survivor to sick bay as soon as the crew of the angel handed her out. That, however, was not the scenario that the survivor had worked out.

Megan, bedraggled and waterlogged, was the first one off the copter; indeed, she jumped off it. She hugged Dr. Sander, flicked a salute at the bridge, and then led the way, very much under her own power, into the island amid the loudest cheer of the night.

Next to me, Dave Cronin saluted in return and sighed. "Naturally, that's the way she'd do it."

"How else?"

The Spirit had done her work well. Now she was showing off, just as Megan was.

"Tell the air boss to resume ops. Get everyone down." His voice now was weary. "It's been too long a night."

"And we have to find out what went wrong down there," Steve Turner said.

"Tell the air officer I want him to take personal charge of the investigation, and I want it to start now."

"Aye, aye, sir."

"Then, Steve, maybe you'd better go down to sick bay and reassure her that the scarf is on the way. I suspect it's a little noisy down there just now. . . . Blackie, you want to go along with him?"

"Oh, yes."

"Tell her we'll have a scarf within a week."

"Won't do. Not with that one."

"How soon then?"

"Tomorrow."

"How do you propose to do that?"

"With the help of the exemplary public affairs officer."

Now all we had to do was to get through the rest of the night. We—well, mostly God—had stymied the other side. The media would have played it as the death of another woman pilot; that would have raised new questions about women in carrier aviation; it would certainly have destroyed Dave Cronin's career. Clever trick, extremely clever. It had not worked.

If they had any sense, they'd back off and rethink their strategy.

But they didn't have any sense or they wouldn't be involved in such a mad enterprise.

CHAPTER 17

A GAGGLE OF women marines stood at the door to the medical offices, heavily armed and somber women marines.

"CAG is inside, sir," one of them said to Steve Turner. "Captain Murray, too."

"Good," he replied.

"Why are you carrying the golf club, Bishop?" Another asked me.

"Five iron."

"Why are you carrying the five iron?"

"They're standard equipment for fighting off and in urgent cases exorcising demons, ghosts, haunts, spooks, and creatures that go bump in the night."

They giggled uncertainly.

"Especially," I added, "when the five iron is in the possession of the little man who wasn't there."

"You're here, all right, Bishop," Commander Turner assured me.

"Arguably."

The CAG was waiting for us, his square and honest face relaxed in a contented smile.

"Ellen Sander is in there checking her out. Mary Anne is with her. Naturally. It looks pretty good. She's talking a blue streak."

"Naturally," I said.

"Indestructible young woman," Captain Murray, the Marine C.O., said. "Thank God."

"Oh yes. . . . I trust that band of armed and dangerous young women out there are to remain here through the night?"

"You bet. . . . Do you think it was attempted murder, Bishop?"

"Doubtless."

Dr. Sander emerged from her inner sanctum.

"She's all right, gentlemen. A few bad bruises, but nothing broken and no internal injuries. We'll do some more X rays to be sure. Fortunately, she is young and strong and in excellent physical condition."

"Thank God," the Marine C.O. said again.

Dr. Sander shrugged, not sure about God's role in the matter.

"She's sky high now, enormous adrenaline flow. Babbling. In an hour or so, she'll collapse and sleep for ten hours. I could sedate her now, but it's better to let the process follow its own course. She'll wake up with a hundred aches and pains. . . . It might be worth my life to say so, CAG, but no traps for her. Indefinitely. Not till the aches and pains are gone."

"Absolutely," Frank Gill agreed.

"You can go in and see her for a few minutes, if you wish. Not too long. I want her to begin to calm down."

The four of us filed into the tiny "hospital" room, almost filling it. Megan, in hospital gown and robe, was sitting up in bed, her hair wild, her emerald eyes glowing ferociously—the red witch just home from battle. Behind her, Mary Anne watched protectively.

That's what women do: they bond against the rest of us.

Megan opened her mouth to pour out her story. Then she stopped and pointed her finger at me.

"Bishop Blackie, what are you doing with that golf club?"

"Five iron."

"All right, what are you doing with that five iron?"

"From the skipper's golf bag."

"All right, what are you doing with the skipper's five iron?"

"For fighting demons."

"Like the men who tried to kill me?"

"Indeed."

"Why did they try to kill me?"

"Because they are evil."

She nodded, as though she understood.

"Hit them hard."

"Hard enough."

"Good . . . Well," she began to babble, "I knew as soon as I felt the aircraft move that the hold-back bolt had broken, so I thought of getting my scarf and pulled the ejection handle and the next thing I knew I was floating down toward the ocean and the skipper must have turned the ship away or it would have run over me and I remember my knife and when I hit the water—and it was warm—honest—I inflated my life jacket and got dunked by the ship's wake and hacked away at the shroud and the ropes with my knife. I finally cut myself loose and floated around waiting for you people to come and get me. Then I remembered to activate my radio signal and I just waited because I knew you'd come and then I heard the two angels and so I fired off my flare and they came and got me and I climbed up the ladder and they were real nice and I want my scarf."

"And diamond clasp," I added.

"Absolutely. And diamond clasp."

"We will have it for you within twenty-four hours," I promised.

Mary Anne frowned, thinking I was promising too much. Which I never do. Except when it is necessary. But this time it wasn't.

"And, CAG, I want to fly traps tomorrow. I'm fine. I can't let myself get rusty or lose my nerve."

"Margaret Mary Monahan!" I shouted.

"Yes, Bishop," she said respectfully.

"Cool it!"

"Yes, Bishop."

"Captain Gill will put you back in the air only when the inestimable Dr. Sander says it's all right. Understand?"

Her shoulders slumped. "Yes, Bishop. You're meaner even than the skipper . . . oops, sorry, Mary Anne."

"And you will not hassle Dr. Sander. Or the Skipper. Or Lieutenant Keane. Or me."

"Yes, Bishop."

"That's better."

"Yes, Bishop . . . I gotta act like a grownup, huh?"

"The Holy Spirit worked overtime tonight, and we're not going to put Her ingenuity to the test again. Understand?"

"Yes, Bishop . . . I prayed a lot out there. When I wasn't thinking about my scarf. I felt very close to God in the dark and the rain and waves. And I'll never get the salt out of my hair. Never."

"And did God reply?"

"Oh, sure, He usually does. You know what He said?"

"What did he say?"

She perked up.

"He said, Margaret Mary Monahan, cool it. They'll come and get you. And I knew they would, but some of the time I was scared and I told Him I was scared and He said he understood and it was all right and that He loved me and so did some of the people on the ship and I said not the ones who broke the hold-back bar and He said they weren't typical and I shouldn't be afraid of the waves and the dark, because everything would be all right. Then it became very peaceful and I was filled with light and joy and hope. I even laughed. I knew everything would be all right."

A mystical experience floating around in the dark off

the coast of Baja California! No accounting for God's ways. Dr. Sander listened with wide eyes.

"A religious experience, Meg?" She asked.

"Oh, I have them all the time. I wouldn't exactly call them religious, would you, Bishop?"

"Whatever one calls them, they're neat."

She nodded vigorously and lay back in the bed. "They sure are. Will you give me a blessing, Bishop?"

"Megan Monahan, may Brigid and Patrick and Columcille and all the holy saints of Ireland watch over you and protect you, may God continue to be pleased with you and Mother Mary continue to delight in you, and may they all grant you good health, long life, and much happiness. Father, Son, and Holy Spirit."

"Amen," she replied fervently. "Thank you, Bishop."

Dr. Sander nodded us toward the door.

"Lieutenant Keane," I said, "could I have a few words with you?"

"Certainly, Bishop."

As he was leaving, Steve Turner said, "Skipper asked me to tell you he'd be down later to see you, Megan."

"He has to get all the traps down before he can leave the bridge," Megan agreed.

In Dr. Sander's office, I said, "Ellen, Mary Anne and I must do a little spin doctoring. Do you think you could give that group of heavily armed marine women a quick look at Megan, just to reassure them?"

"Certainly, Blackie. I'll stay with her, Mary Anne, while you're doctoring the spin."

"Excellent," I said slipping into a relatively comfortable chair and feeling very tired. "We must put the proper spin on this event to make it seem that it was a highly successful navy operation, the rescue of a crack woman pilot at night in the rain. We must give the skipper full credit for it. We must, above all, make it clear that the crash was not the fault of the pilot who behaved brilliantly under pressure. Moreover, you must find the

phone number of the Martin-Davis Company which
makes those ejection seats and suggest to them that they
should fly a representative over on the Concord and out
here on the afternoon COD to make the presentation of
the scarf. Finally, you must communicate to the relevant
media that Lieutenant Monahan will be available for
television interviews from San Diego, day after tomorrow."

I glanced at my watch.

"Well, I mean tomorrow. Since it is already morning."

Mary Anne's lovely mouth hung open.

"Why should they do that?"

"The Brits?"

"Yes."

"Because our lead will be based on Megan's line that
she felt the hold-back bar go, thought of the scarf, and
pulled the release lever—all in a tenth of a second."

"You think if there wasn't the promise of a scarf she
would not have ejected?"

"Certainly she would have ejected. But, in fact, the
symbol of the scarf is there, and that gives the story
powerful interest. Makes it a much better story. Unless
Martin-Davis are devoid of public relations sense—and
the fact of the ties and the scarves suggest that it is not
the case—they'll love it."

"Right." She turned on Ellen's computer and set to
work.

"Early on, you must quote the captain as saying that
she had less than a tenth of a second to eject but that he
is not surprised that she was able to do it because it is
typical of her superb skills as a pilot. Then we will have
quotes along this line from the CAG and the air officer.
The former will say that she has more green stars on her
board than any other pilot, and the air officer will say
she's the best pilot he has ever known. Both have said
those things in my presence, but you should confirm
them. Then the skipper can say modestly that the year

and a half record of the *Langley* not losing a single member of its air crews continues to stand. . . . That is true, isn't it?"

She nodded. "What about the hold-back bolt?"

"Single sentence near the end saying that the investigation of the malfunctioning of the catapult is continuing."

"Got it!"

She began to type.

"One must note that we are not changing the truth at all, merely shaping its presentation. We thus defend the skipper, defend women pilots, defend the navy, and defend the ship in part against future bad publicity."

She stopped typing and looked up at me. "You really think it was attempted murder?"

"Doubtless. If I had not been drugged with this motion sickness medicine, I would have anticipated something like this."

"Do you think they'll stop? To kind of regroup? Whoever they are?"

"Arguably."

I was, to put it mildly, not functioning with a full deck of cards. By now, the reader has doubtless solved the whole mystery. Even then, the solution was floating around somewhere in the back of my drug-addled brain. But I somehow could not hold it long enough to let it take form. As to Mary Anne's question, I assumed that they would hesitate before striking again. That would have been a rational strategy. We were not, however, dealing with rational people. It should have been obvious to me even then that their madness was tumbling out of control, as surely as Megan's Hornet had when it plunged into the Pacific.

"OK. Here it is," Mary Anne announced, pushing a key and thus initiating the printing. Now what do we do with it?"

"We wait for the skipper to come down, we show it to

him, we prevail upon him to awaken Admiral Night Plane Lane, who will in his turn awaken his public affairs officer and, perhaps over his objection, order him to release this story immediately."

"What do you think?"

She handed me the printout.

"Admirable. . . . How much trouble will the skipper give us?"

"He'll know that it has to be done this way."

"Excellent. Now, the Martin-Davis Company. We can add their response to the release if they can deal with it quickly enough. Being Brits, they probably cannot."

In this judgment I was flat wrong. It took the valiant Mary Anne only a half hour to get through to the managing director of the company. She turned on her not inconsiderable sexual charm and sold him the idea. He would fly out himself and see us later in the day. He looked forward to meeting her. Yes, of course he would bring choices of jeweled clasps. There were no choices in the scarves, however. Did the young woman really come out of the water demanding her scarf? She must be remarkable.

Naturally.

"Well done," I said.

"I can't believe I turned on the sexy voice the way I did. I never did that before. What's happened to me?"

"I hardly think I need to answer that question."

She turned crimson.

"I suppose not. . . . I can't understand, Bishop," she said hesitantly, "I just can't understand how a woman could walk out on a man who is such a skilled and sensitive lover."

"That must not have been high on her list of priorities."

"How could it not be?"

"People are different."

She shook her head. "I guess they are."

"What kind of conspiracy are you two up to?" The aforementioned skilled and sensitive lover entered Dr. Sander's office.

"Spin doctoring," I replied.

"The bishop has corrupted me."

"She is easily corruptible."

"I know," Dave Cronin said with a broad smile. "Let's see what you've done."

Lieutenant Keane's crimson hue returned. She did not, however, seem displeased with the skipper's judgment.

"It might be more appropriate after you've seen our resilient lady leatherneck," I said.

"OK."

"Can the skipper say hello to her?" Mary Anne stuck her head into the bedroom.

"Sure," Ellen came to the door. "Good evening, sir. Come in."

"Good evening, Ellen. How's our patient?"

"Mostly out of it."

"Medication?"

"No, natural weariness. It's all caught up with her. Come in."

Naturally, the public affairs officer went in with the captain. So, for that matter, did the inoffensive and hardly noticeable little bishop.

Megan was sleeping the sleep of the just one, looking like she was perhaps fifteen.

"Meg." Ellen Sander touched her shoulder lightly. "Skipper's here."

"Hi, shipmate."

Megan opened one eye.

"Oh, hi, Skipper. Thanks for fishing me out of the water. I knew you would. . . . I'll be a good patient because Bishop Ryan says I have to act like a grownup. Hi, Mary Anne."

"We'll have your scarf by tomorrow afternoon," the public affairs officer said.

"Cool."

She closed her eyes and went back to sleep.

"She'll be up and around tomorrow, Skipper," the doctor said, "but she'll ache a lot for a week or so. I'd just as soon keep her here most of the time. By the day after, she should be on her own. No flying till I say so."

"How long?"

"Two weeks. Maybe."

"Fair enough . . . Now, let's see what you conspirators are up to."

"'Nother blessing," Megan demanded, her eyes still closed.

"Megan, may God hold you in the palm of his hand and may you be in heaven a half hour before the devil knows you're dead."

"Amen," everyone responded, including this time our infidel Dr. Sander.

"Let's see that press release," the skipper insisted when the three of us were back in Dr. Sander's office.

"You're the public affairs officer, Lieutenant," I passed the buck.

She handed it to him without comment. He read it, frowned deeply, glanced at both of us, read it again, smiled ruefully, and gave it back to his lady.

"You two are diabolical."

"I had thought we were on the other side."

"I see what you're up to. It's very clever. I don't like the way you make me sound like a hero."

"Have to," I said. "Got to. Must. No choice."

"Yeah. I guess. What are you going to do with it?"

"It's what you're going to do, Skipper," Mary Anne insisted.

"Me?"

"You," I said complacently.

"You are going to call Admiral Lane on my mobile phone." She handed it to him. "Wake him up, read him this, and tell him that it's essential that it go out now."

"So we get in the morning news broadcasts," I continued. "The lead on CNN will be that a quick-thinking woman marine pilot saved her life and the safety record of her ship when a launching system failed."

"Wake up the admiral?"

"Oh, yes," Mary Anne said, "don't forget to tell him that he should get color pictures of Megan on the lines. The media will love that, even if it's only the evening news."

"We thus inoculate the ship," I concluded, "against possible bad news in the next day or two."

He nodded. "I'm not so dumb that I don't see that. OK. Here goes."

He dialed the admiral's home number from memory, rolled his eyes, and waited.

"Hi, Admiral," he spoke very rapidly, "Dave Cronin here. Sir, we lost Megan overboard tonight on a bad cat in the rain. Hold-back bar. Picked her up fifteen minutes later. She climbed the ladder herself. Wants the scarf immediately. My PAO and your friend the bishop have cooked up a press release, sir. They want it to go out right away. With a color picture of her. . . . She's resting peacefully now. Bumps and bruises and scratches . . . Yeah, thank God, indeed. You want to hear it?"

The admiral must have said yes because the Skipper picked up the draft.

"I should say, sir, that this embarrasses me. Makes me kind of a hero. . . . Yes, sir; they do mention the Skyhawk crews."

He read our draft in a firm, neutral voice.

"Yes, sir," he said after the admiral had reacted, "I think it's damn clever, too. I'm not sure which of the two of them is the more clever, though I do have some prejudices in the matter."

Mary Anne turned purple.

"No, sir. I don't think we want to clear it with the Pentagon. . . . Fax it to your office? And you'll be there to see that it goes out? Very good, sir. . . . Yes, sir. I'll say hello to Mary Anne for you . . . and Megan, of course . . . I agree, sir, no reform can be all bad when it puts personnel like them on a ship."

"I'll take it down to my office and fax it ashore," Mary Anne, said rising from her chair.

"I'll accompany you."

"That won't be necessary Captain," she said firmly.

"You have an escort?"

"No, Sir." She looked away from him.

"Isn't there an order that no one should be out of quarters by themselves tonight?"

"Yes, sir. There is."

"Well?"

"I see the force of your argument, sir." A very slight smile played at her lips.

"Thank you very much, Bishop," Dave Cronin turned to me. You've been an enormous help."

"Now all I have to do is solve the Commander Hoy puzzle."

"I'm sure you'll do that tomorrow."

"Doubtless."

"Let's look in on Megan," Lieutenant Keane suggested.

"Sleeping like a child." Dr. Sander looked up as we entered. "Which is what she is."

"We'll leave our detachment of marines outside," the skipper said.

"Yes, sir . . . You're doing all those exercises that I prescribed?"

"Certainly, Doctor," the captain grinned. "Almost every day."

"Every day, shipmate," Ellen Sander ordered him. "You hear me? Every day!"

Her eyes flickered at Mary Anne, telling her that she

should insist. Women bonding once more. Against the rest of us.

"Yes ma'am. . . . Lieutenant? Shall we send this fax off to Admiral Lane?"

"Yes, sir."

The skipper bowed her out of the door, gender taking precedence over rank. Sexual electricity crackled as they left. God bless them both.

I found my marine guard and withdrew to my own quarters. Only when I had sipped my small ration of grog, prepared for bed, and offered my prayers of gratitude that we had not lost Megan, did I realize that I no longer had my five iron. Left it in sick bay.

So I went again to the skipper's golf bag and pondered my choice between a six iron and a four iron. The latter was certainly too heavy, so I chose the former and placed it reverently on the bed next to me. I suspected little trouble tonight, but one could never be sure.

I had made up my mind that I would reflect on the mystery I was supposed to solve before I slept. I would have to clean it up tomorrow. But the motion sickness medication was too much for me. Nothing would happen tonight. I would need a clear head for the morning.

The presence slipped into the cabin. I told it that I had no time for frauds, and it departed without protest, but lingered on the fringes of the cabin and the ship.

"Tomorrow you will be finished," I told it.

I imagined that it laughed at me.

CHAPTER 18

SOMEONE WAS STALKING me as I walked from my quarters along the passageway and down the ladder to the wardroom. I heard his footsteps behind me, a monotonous click-clack on the metal deck. When I slowed down, his click-clacks lessened. When I walked faster, the click-clacks came faster. Firmly gripping my trusty six iron, I turned around to face him. Maybe eight yards behind—where the Bears usually are on second down—was a marine with sergeant's stripes. He looked like a professional noncom, older than most of the marines, with pale empty eyes, a hard stare, and bright red hair—though not as bright as Megan's.

He stared at me. I stared back at him. He blinked first. Then he turned and walked away.

As the grammar school kids say, you always blink when Father Blackie stares at you. Otherwise you'll burst out laughing. This marine didn't look like he was about to laugh.

I had awakened with the sensation that during the night all the pieces had come together in a picture that would solve the puzzle. But awake, the picture faded. The pieces were all there, but the fit had eluded me.

It would come back. Eventually, they always did. I felt there was no rush this time because after the attempt to kill Megan, the other side would pause to regroup.

The wardroom was tense and quiet. Men and women were eating their bacon and eggs and pancakes and drinking their coffee with the solemnity of a congregation in church waiting for the funeral liturgy to begin. Martha appeared next to my table.

"What would you like for breakfast, Bishop?"

How could anyone smile that happily at that hour in the morning?

"Many thanks, Martha, but I have yet to reach that age of infirmity at which I cannot get my own breakfast."

"Lieutenant Keane said I should. She'll be right in. She wants an English muffin and a cup of coffee."

"Far be it from me to argue with Lieutenant Keane."

I ordered a modest repast of two rashers of bacon, two heaps of pancakes, a large glass of grapefruit juice, and a pot of tea. Not what I'd usually eat at the cathedral, but I didn't want to create scandal and explain my odd metabolism again.

Mary Anne joined me, looking tired but very happy.

"She's still asleep. Ellen has her on Tylenol for her aches and pains. There's a new threesome of marine guards in sick bay. The X rays were all negative as Ellen thought they would be. She will be up and around in a day or two."

"Excellent," I said, finishing the grapefruit juice.

"The three networks want her on TV tomorrow from San Diego. Morning programs. That means we have to get her in by oh-five hundred. Very early COD flight. Ellen is not enthused and insists on coming along."

"You will go too?"

"Of course. I'm the public affairs officer. This is the best story I'll ever have."

"Has the skipper made any progress in determining what happened last night?"

"The air officer's people found the remains of the hold-back bar up on the flight deck. It had been filed down so that it would break under pressure. They're questioning everyone in secret, but there are all kinds of rumors. Some people say that other pilots in the squadron did it as a practical joke."

"I think we can dismiss that explanation as highly improbable.

"The word is all around the ship that it was an attempt at murder. That's why everyone looks so glum."

"Not without reason."

"Digby was everywhere last night."

"Ah?"

"All over the women's quarters, prancing and leering and laughing."

"Indeed. You saw him?"

"No. I tried to keep track of some of the reports. He was at the opposite end of our section of the deck at the same time, as though he could be in two places at once. Is that possible, Bishop?"

"Granted that it is possible that the dead walk, anything else might be possible. But I doubt it."

"You think we're experiencing hysterical delusions?"

"Perhaps. In part."

"The sun is out and it's a lovely day," she said in an abrupt change of subject.

"You have been topside?"

"No, but that's what the air crew people are saying."

"It is then the report of good weather that has created your happy smile."

"No," she turned deep red. "I suppose it's the fact that I was kissed good night last night."

"Doubtless a brief and light kiss."

"Neither!" she flared.

Then, realizing that I was joking, she settled down. "I think I have him, Bishop Blackie. I don't think he'll ever get away from me now."

"I'd be willing to wager he would say the same thing."

"Probably," she said with a satisfied smile. "We're going to be married as soon as this cruise is over."

"He has agreed to this?"

"No, but he will. . . . Do I sound irrationally confident?"

"Confident? Yes. Irrationally confident? No."

"So despite all the hellish nonsense on this ship, I still feel unbearably happy. . . . Can you imagine anyone being so crazy as to want to kill Meg?"

"As we agreed last night, if a person were willing to do anything to challenge the navy's determination to accept women as combat pilots, that would be a brilliant strategy."

"We've got to stop them."

"We will," I said with a good deal more confidence than the present situation justified.

On the way back to my cabin, I stopped in the gallery deck at the office of the chief master of arms. Nelly Grey, as she was being called that morning, was in John Larkin's office. They were both puzzling over a list. One might have thought for a moment that she was the commanding officer.

Both of them were wearing side arms.

"Ah, Most Holy One," Johnny bowed deeply. "I hail your superior wisdom in all things. You have taught us knowledge, truth, and wisdom, you have revealed to us secrets hidden from the ages; well, at least hidden for all these weeks."

"Indeed?"

"He means that the kid who slides under the plane at the last minute to secure it to the launch mechanism is a member of the patriot discussion group. So, too, is our beloved locksmith and Chief Larsen of Public Affairs."

"The yeoman san speaks truth, O Holy One, however inelegantly. Moreover, we informed the skipper and the air officer of these facts. They are questioning that unfortunate young man right now. He stubbornly refuses to talk. He believes that he is doing all things under secret orders and has sworn the most solemn oath never to reveal a word of them."

"Secret orders?"

"Yes, sir," the good Nelly said. "If he has to die for obedience to those orders, he will. Don't tell anyone that. We don't want the rest of the patriots to know what's happening."

"I assume that your master key is missing again," I said, a light beginning to explode in my head.

"Master key?" Johnny said, startled by the question into talking straight English, as best as a Bostonian could. "But it was there yesterday, wasn't it, Nelly Grey, when you showed it to the bishop?"

"Yes," she said. "Wasn't it, Bishop?"

"Indeed. But I put it to you that it is not there now."

Anxiously, she opened the door to the key locker and then the locker itself. Sure enough, one of the key hooks stood out like a skin eruption on a perfect face—empty.

"Wow!" Johnny breathed softly. "We'll have to act on this at once."

"Patience," I said. "There are one or two other details I must think through."

"You've solved the mystery, Bishop?" Nelly demanded.

"I must think about it for perhaps another half hour. You two stay here and watch those monitors."

"Has our secret master key disappeared, too, Bishop?" Nelly asked.

"I think not. Look for it."

She opened the drawer, looked under a stack of papers, withdrew the key, and held it up.

"Nope, still here."

"Only the woman and I know about it," Johnny assured me.

"Tell no one else.

I walked down the corridor toward the ladder up to my cabin. The stalker was behind me again. I felt a warning on the back of my neck. We went through the same routine of click-clacks. He was right behind me. The warning grew louder. I turned again to face him, six iron firmly in both my hands.

"Something I can do for you, Sergeant?" I asked.

He hesitated, stared at me, sadly, I thought, shook his head in the negative, and murmured, "No, sir." Then he turned and walked slowly away, his click-clacks fading away as he turned a corner and disappeared down a cross passageway.

I climbed up the ladder, walked past the admiral's mess, entered my cabin, and paused to reflect on what I had learned.

The phone rang. My portable phone. I scrambled into the bedroom of the suite and grabbed it.

"Father Ryan."

"Took you long enough to answer it, Blackwood."

"Indeed!"

"What the hell is going on out there!"

"You mean the curious matter of the lady leatherneck?"

"Yeah. If I ever saw a story that had your spin all over it, this is the one."

"It is all true."

"Doubtless, as you would say. It's not the whole truth, however."

"Oh, no."

"Is she really that great a pilot?"

"The only sign of an absence of virtue in the young woman is that she is a Green Bay Packer fan. Lamentably."

"That story about the scarf is true?"

"Absolutely."

"I know some women like that."

"Don't we all."

"When are you coming home?"

"With God's grace, on the red-eye tomorrow night."

"With mystery solved?"

"Arguably."

"David will be all right?"

"Unquestionably. You can count on that. One way or another."

"What does that mean?"

"I'll explain to you day after tomorrow."

"Wind it up. See to it Blackwood!"

He favored me with his manic chuckle and hung up.

I walked back into the parlor of the suite, poured myself a cup of tea from the pot some thoughtful mess orderly had brought me (doubtless the exemplary Martha), and once more tried to analyze the converging pieces to make sure I had every detail right.

Another ring of the phone.

"Father Ryan."

"Blackie, what the hell is going on out there?"

"That is an issue that seems to concern any number of people."

"Is that kid for real?"

"Oh, yes."

"You getting her on TV tomorrow morning like I hear you are?"

"You betcha."

"She as good a pilot as they say?"

"I have had the privilege of watching some of her traps. She's flawless. Nary a bolter."

He paused, surprised, doubtless, that I knew what a trap was, to say nothing of a bolter.

"Someone try to kill her?"

"Indeed."

"They know who?"

"It would appear so."

"Are we going to get a lot of bad media out of this?"

"Arguably not. I believe that the good Megan will, ah, tilt the playing field in our direction."

"I sure hope so. . . . If Cronin can sew this up, he's a cinch to make the admiral's list. We need him."

"That I do not doubt for a minute. He's a remarkable man."

"Yeah . . . He going to marry this woman?"

"Does the sun rise in the morning?"

"He didn't show much sense the first time around."

"He does this time."

"Yeah? Did she write the ingenious press release or you?"

"Every word was hers."

"With some help from you?"

"Arguably."

"Can you clear it all up out there today?"

"With good fortune, by noon, Pacific Standard Time."

"Yeah? Well, don't let me take up too much of your time."

Once more I tried to check out the pieces of the picture.

The keys were certainly the key.

Then I saw it all.

The cause was now urgent.

My phone rang.

"Johnny here, Bishop. Lieutenant Keane has disappeared. A rating saw a gunnery sergeant muscling her down a passageway. We don't know where he took her."

"I do. Johnny, summon the skipper. I will meet you and him in officer's country on level oh-three. I urge you to come swiftly. Mary Anne is in grave danger. But come stealthily, lest we aggravate the danger."

I hung up the phone, grabbed my six iron, and raced out the door.

Then I raced back in, looked up Johnny's number, dialed furiously, got the engine room, hung up, and dialed again.

While the phone was ringing, I jotted down on the back of an old Bears ticket that happened to be in my pocket another number.

"Chief master of arms, Yeoman Regan."

"Johnny has left?"

"Yes, sir."

"Get that master key and go after him."

"*Yes*, sir. He told me I couldn't come."

"Get that key to him."

"Yes, *sir*."

Again I went out the door, hoping that I hadn't forgotten anything else.

CHAPTER 19

I ARRIVED AT the passageway where most of the commanders lived before my allies had arrived. I pondered for a minute the use of such a small force. *Surprise would be what counted, not size,* I said, trying to reassure myself.

I flexed my six iron and hoped I would find the courage and the quickness to use it if necessary.

The skipper and the chief master of arms, Yeoperson Regan in tow, appeared at the same time. The latter two wore side arms. I noted Nelly's marksman's medal with some feeling of gratitude.

"What's happened to her, Blackie? Is she still alive?"

The captain's face was ashen as well it might be.

"I believe she is, but we must move quickly. There is every reason to think that she is in Commander Hoy's room, bound and gagged doubtless, but being preserved alive for later amusements. We must enter that room and free her quickly. There may be a guard in the room with her and he may well be armed. We must disarm that guard instantly. Moreover, we must open the door to that room and burst in so as to take the guard, should there be one, by surprise. Finally, we must approach the door with utmost stealth so that he will not hear us. The chief master will turn the master key quickly and silently and we will thereupon charge in."

Was there any other alternative strategy? I thought not then, and I still don't think so. Might I have been wrong about where they would imprison Mary Anne? Most likely not. *Please, God, don't let me be wrong.*

Quietly, we approached the door, the skipper in the lead, Johnny right behind him, then the ecclesiastic with a golf club for a crosier, and finally a grim-looking Nelly Regan.

"My responsibility, sir," Johnny edged the skipper out of the way.

After that, everything wound down into slow motion, a deadly drama in three acts, which spilled across the screen of my consciousness in the fashion of a leisurely ballet.

Johnny inserted the key gently, turned it cautiously, eased the door partially open, and then charged in, the skipper right behind him, and the Skipper's golf club in third place.

Inside, we saw a scene of terror. Mary Anne was strapped to a bunk, a rag shoved in her mouth. Her shirt had been torn away and her bra pushed aside. The marine sergeant had jammed a thirty-eight-caliber cruelly against one of her breasts. His face hung over hers, only a few inches away.

On the night stand next to the bunk, a razor lay open.

Surprised and startled, the sergeant spun around to face us, his head still only an inch from Mary Anne's, slowly raised the gun, took careful aim, and pulled the trigger.

Just as his finger tightened on the trigger, Mary Anne butted her head, the only free part of her body, against his. He jumped with surprise and jerked the gun slightly as he fired. In front of me, Johnny Larkin spun around and fell back out of the door of the cabin, a blossom of blood on his left shoulder.

The skipper would be next unless someone hit the marine with a six iron. So, with unnatural agility, I shoved the skipper aside, raised the club in the air with all the force I could command—actually not very much—and brought it down on the gunman's wrist.

A resounding crack indicated that I had broken his wrist, which was my intention. He screamed in terrible pain. The gun leaped out of his hand, spun to the floor, and discharged another bullet, which ricocheted around the room and then smashed into the television set above the desk.

"He only winged me, kid," I heard John Wayne say behind me. Glancing out of the corner of my eye, I saw Nelly Regan tenderly holding her wounded C.O. in her arms.

In the crowed room, now thick with smoke and the acrid smell of guns, the skipper scrambled for the gun. The marine grabbed the razor and moved it quickly in a slashing motion toward Mary Anne's breasts.

It was therefore necessary for me to break his other wrist. He dropped the razor, which fell harmlessly on to her stomach.

He screamed again, and again, and again: the terrible wail of the damned, and collapsed against the door to the bathroom into something like a fetal position.

"Commander E. Rogers Hoy," said the skipper, as with one hand he pointed the gun and the other pulled the gag out of Mary Anne's mouth, "I arrest you for mutiny, sexual molestation, rape, attempted murder, and murder."

Hoy, his wig askew, wailed even more loudly.

"I'm all right, Dave," Mary Anne gasped. "I'm all right."

"No, you're not, my darling," he replied as he gently cut the ropes that bound her and moved the remnants of her clothes back into place. "But you will be all right."

End of Act One.

The second act was already under way. The door of the cabin next to Hoy's slammed open. In a moment, against the frame of the door to Hoy's cabin, Glendenning Shorter appeared, massive, rigid, and taut with rage. He pulled a twenty-five-caliber pistol from his belt and swung it toward the prone Johnny Larkin. His usually impassive face broadened in a contented smile, hinting at sexual pleasure.

Then, in frame-by-frame action, I watched Nelly Regan tenderly lay her boss's head on the deck, unholster her massive forty-five, raise it in both hands, take quick aim, and blow off the top half of Shorter's head. He collapsed like a broken puppet to the floor. Blood and brains spewed all around, and dense smoke and the smell of death swirled around us. As he fell, Nelly, taking no chance with her beloved C.O.'s life, fired twice more. The bullets, at such close range, tore great, gaping holes in his body. His blood soaked the corridor and all of us in it, as he fell over Johnny's legs.

Another Irish goddess, Morrigan, the queen of battles— who was at the moment vomiting her breakfast.

I emerged into the corridor, weapon in hand, in case I was needed on that flank of battle.

All of this violence and gore happened almost instantaneously, in only a few seconds, and far less time than it takes me to recount it.

"Johnny, don't die on me!" Nelly Regan begged, the smoking forty-five still in her hand.

"Well, OK, ma'am." Still John Wayne. "But you'll have to take care of me for the rest of my life."

"Silly! I was going to do that anyway!"

In the cabin, the skipper and his public affairs officer were clinging to one another. Love amid the gore, life reasserting itself in the face of death.

End of Act Two.

"Look!" Nelly Regan screamed, signaling the beginning of the third act.

Chief Larsen had appeared at the other end of the passageway, an automatic weapon carefully cradled in his arms like it was a newborn child. He walked toward us with slow, dumb determination. In his cabin, Digby Hoy was still sobbing.

"Stop!" Nelly ordered.

He turned the gun toward us and lifted it to fire.

Nelly fired first.

Her gun jammed.

Chief Larsen moved the gun in an arc which would sweep us away in a tide of bullets.

I couldn't move, paralyzed in the face of certain death.

"Stay inside," I shouted at the captain.

No bullets.

Larsen was fiddling with the weapon, perhaps releasing the safety.

It occurred to me that I should charge him.

That proved unnecessary.

Just as he turned the weapon back in our direction, a wild cry of rage shook the passage way and a terrible apparition appeared behind him—a berserker with red hair, dressed in a hospital gown, waving a five iron like it was a Viking pike. Erihu to the rescue.

She hit Larsen in the face with her battle-ax. He dropped the weapon and clutched his face. Blood streamed between his fingers. His screams were an antiphonal chorus with the cries of Rogers Hoy.

To make sure of her victory, the red witch hit Larsen on the head with the five iron. He fell to his knees and, still clutching his face, tumbled over on the floor on top of the body of Glen Shorter.

Blood, smoke, stench, screams—someone should restore a semblance of order. Moreover, there might also be more armed allies of Rogers Hoy swarming around us. I removed the bit of paper on which I had scribbled a number, peered at it through my thick lenses, picked up a phone on the wall, and made my announcement.

"This is not a drill. I repeat, this is not a drill. Mutiny under way. Sea marines, security, medical personnel to officers' quarters on oh-three level. This is not a drill. I repeat, this is not a drill."

"Quick thinking, Blackie," the skipper said as he helped his chief master at arms to his feet. "We could use a little help around here."

"It's only a scratch, boss," John Wayne protested. "I'm fine."

"That's what they all say."

As our reinforcements swarmed in all around us, the three goddesses, Brigid, Erin, and Morrigan, hugged one another and wept together.

If it had not been for them, the skipper, Johnny, and, arguably, a harmless auxiliary bishop, might be dead. Oh, yes, there was room for them in the United States Navy.

There had better be.

Heaven help anyone, I told myself, *who dares to threaten those women. Or those whom they love.*

CHAPTER 20

SOME CONSIDERABLE SPIN doctoring was required to account to the public for what had happened on the good ship *Langley*. Needless to say, we told the truth, though not the whole truth.

There was no mention of the presence of an inoffensive little bishop, armed with his six iron. Nor did we mention the three Irish goddesses, in battle arrayed, since, even without the mythological allusion, their behavior would have seemed to the media world improbable.

We presented the skipper as the hero who had arrested the leader of the mutiny in his hideout. We hailed the courage of the wounded chief master at arms. We depicted Commander Hoy as a man driven to madness by the stresses of his work. We suggested that he had duped the three people who had died—Commander Shorter, Lieutenant Commander Wade, and Lieutenant Ericsson—by his forged orders from a nonexistent government agency. He had also duped some of the members of the patriot study group on the ship who were under investigation, especially for the sabotage of First Lieutenant Margaret M. Monahan's plane. The Pentagon and the NIS were only too happy to sign off on these explanations. The media had a second great story on the *Langley*, which was connected to their first story, and they had no interest in questioning the details we provided.

The aforementioned Lieutenant Monahan (soon to receive her second silver bar and become Captain Monahan) was the key to our successful spinning. Early the next morning while it was still dark, a COD had landed on the ship and had taxied to the island. The three women who were going ashore, Megan in marine blue and Mary Anne and Ellen in navy white, had shaken hands with the skipper and asked for my blessing as they boarded the plane.

"Are you sure the cats are working again, Skipper?" Megan had asked as she boarded the plane. She had not waited for an answer.

"It is altogether a good thing to have people like those three on a ship," he had said to me.

"Oh, yes. They complicate life, but they make it more interesting."

Megan captivated the nation by her TV interviews the morning after the final shoot-out at the OK Corral. She was a considerably restrained Megan, a smooth blend of a crack lady leatherneck pilot and a novice in a religious order, dressed in her Marine blues (skirt and woman's cap) and sporting just the right amount of makeup.

I imagined the prom-night scent.

She praised the skipper and the Skyhawk crews for fishing her out of the water, the air officer and the chief master at arms for solving within twelve hours the mystery of the hold-back bar, and the whole crew of her "wonderful shipmates" on the *Langley*. She had encountered no more sexual harassment in the navy than in civilian life, less in fact. Certainly she intended to continue to fly. Could hardly wait to get back in a new Hornet. She did not know whether she would remain in the service for the rest of her life. She might become a nun for a few years. After that, she might marry, if the right man came along.

Who might the right man be?

Well, she didn't think her standards were too high. He

had to be sweet and intelligent and rich and Irish and Catholic and a Green Bay Packer fan. Yes, she supposed the last requirement might be negotiable; and she really didn't care whether he was rich or not, it was just fun to say that.

That answer was delivered with a perfectly straight face and a leprechaun twinkle in her green eyes that won the hearts of the nation.

Could she believe that men would so resent a woman marine aviator that they would try to kill her?

It wasn't just herself, she replied. They wanted the navy to rethink the issue of whether women could and should fly planes like the F-18. Moreover, it was only a few poor sick men. She didn't blame all the men in the navy for what a handful had done.

"Their plot wouldn't have worked, anyway," she added. "The navy won't and can't change its mind. The Marine Corps never changes its mind. Or never admits it has. Women are here to stay. The marines always knew that. Besides, even if God and Captain Cronin and the Skyhawk crew had not fished me out of the water, the men who tried to kill me would not have gotten away with it. The air officer found the broken hold-back bar that very night; it was a clear case of deliberate sabotage."

Did she think Captain Cronin would be made an admiral?

"That's not for me to say," she replied crisply. "I'm sure all his shipmates hope he will. He's a superb officer and wonderful human being."

We no longer needed to worry about tilting the playing field any further.

"She sure gets us off the hook," Johnny Larkin, his arm in a sling, said to me as we watched Megan's performance.

"Absolutely."

That afternoon, I returned to the March snowstorms of Chicago.

Prizes were awarded. Dave Cronin was selected for the admiral's list. Johnny Larkin and Mary Anne traded in their silver bars for gold oak leaves. Yeoperson Nelly Regan became chief yeoperson. Well-informed sources reported that she was sporting a massive diamond ring, big enough to sink the *Langley*.

Commander Hoy and Chief Larsen were incarcerated in the psychiatric wing of the North Island Naval Hospital. Both spent most of the time weeping, the chief silent tears, the commander loud sobs. It was thought that neither of them would stand trial and would instead spend the rest of their lives in the hospital. The three enlisted men from the patriot group were awaiting trial. They had readily admitted their offenses but justified them on the grounds that they were working for a secret government agency that had sent Commander Hoy to the ship to restore traditional navy values. There were whispers about a plea bargain that would protect the navy from its own mistake of sending a man who was clearly deranged as XO on a ship at sea.

So all things had arranged themselves, as the French would have said.

I had been intolerably slow in my analysis. But one grows older and the gray cells do not function quite as well when they are desensitized by scopolamine.

I did not feel any responsibility for the death of Commander Shorter. He would have gone on shooting in any event. I should not have let Johnny Larkin rush into the cabin. But, as he said, he had only been winged.

I still have nightmares about the gunfight at the OK Corral and senseless dangers to innocent lives. On the other hand, if Erin and Morigan had not insisted on charging into the fray, there might have been more deaths.

I consoled myself with the thought that the Spirit had

taken over the *Langley* during the confirmation ceremony and was determined that, despite my follies, She would get it right.

The much-heralded catapult launch was an anticlimax. The COD huffed and puffed till it got up to full speed. Then we were hurled into space, tossed toward any Goliath that might be lurking in the sky. Facing backward, I was slammed somewhat unceremoniously against my seat harness as the pilot pointed the nose of our Greyhound toward the firmament. That was that. No big deal. Blackie Ryan, experienced naval person. Many stories with which to regale the grandnieces and the grandnephews.

As for the United States Ship *Langley*, CVN 90, which, if I could have seen it, was rapidly growing smaller behind us, I found that I was experiencing a certain sadness at leaving it. A floating semiprison perhaps, but my shipmates were wonderful people.

CHAPTER 21

CARDINAL SEAN CRONIN likes to entertain. But in limited numbers, so that he can preside at the head of the table. Preside, not dominate. He especially likes to do so when some of the guests are attractive women, which is more than I can say for some of his colleagues in the hierarchy. He presides over his small dinners usually on his own turf and not on mine, as he puts it: at the Cardinal's House on North State Parkway, next to Lincoln Park.

So the night before the marriage of Admiral David Cronin and Lieutenant Commander Mary Anne Keane, there was one such dinner. It had been arranged that the cardinal would officiate at the marriage and preside from the throne while his auxiliary bishop and cathedral pastor would lead the Eucharist and preach.

"Tell them your strawberry story, Blackwood. They'll love it."

In addition to the happy couple, the two principal witnesses for the marriage, Commander Richard Dempsey and, it goes without saying, Captain Margaret Mary Monahan, USMC., were present.

(The wedding party for this "official" marriage was the same as that hastily assembled in the in-port cabin on the *Langley* before I was hurled from the catapult. I suggested to the two of them that perhaps this might not be a bad idea. They agreed enthusiastically. Only the four members of the party and I realized that the ceremony in the Cathedral the next day was merely a legal and ecclesiastical validation of a union that already existed in God's complacent eyes. A glance at the radiant Mary Anne, however, revealed her joy. She was patently one of those fortunate women who are transformed by being the subject of passionate sexual worship.)

The naval foursome wore civilian clothes, the young women smart suits in spring pink and gray. Captain Monahan also wore her paisley scarf with its jeweled clasp, which I was told she wore on every possible occasion. She was the awed and respectful novice sitting at the left hand of the cardinal prince of the Roman church. Her dangerous green eyes glinted only when she scored a demure point against that worthy lord spiritual, especially when he perceived only dimly that he had been hit with a verbal lance.

Milord Cronin had dressed for the occasion in crimson zuchetto and cummerbund, and black cassock with crimson buttons and a short cape lined in crimson.

Also lurking on the fringe of things was an unobtrusive, virtually invisible little auxilary bishop, a sweeper, as I have said, in the sense of Harvey Keitel's role in *Pulp Fiction*.

I hardly need add that the china, the crystal, the silver, to say nothing of the wine and the food, were appropriate for a prince of the church, that is, one with good taste (which most of his princely colleagues lack).

Over the dessert (*tiramisù* as the current fashion demands), he turned to me.

"Well, Blackwood, we all know that you're dying to explain how you solved the mystery of the locked room. Moreover, your kind of Irish never say anything important until dessert. Why don't you tell us about it?"

Needless to say, I had assumed that there would be such a challenge and had prepared myself for it.

"I can say in defense of my slow wits after I had embarked on the *Langley*," I began apologetically, "that the scopolamine put me in a kind of blissful trance in which it was hard to translate thought into action. . . ."

"Slow at swinging Skipper's five iron," Megan interrupted me.

"Six iron. You had the five iron. . . . In any event, it seemed evident to me from the very beginning that there was one very easy way to accomplish the locked-room bafflement. Commander Hoy merely withdrew from his own quarters, secured the bathroom doors, and went into Commander Shorter's cabin. He waited there in presumed tranquillity until he heard the noise of the machinist's mate cutting open the locked door. Then he climbed into the upper bunk of the cabin, closed it from the inside, and remained there until he was informed that it was no longer necessary to hide because the searchers had departed. Whenever either noise or Commander Shorter, who was his accomplice, warned him there was danger, he tumbled back into the bunk. An uncomfortable position but tolerable for brief periods of time."

"So Glen was in the plot from the beginning?" Dave Cronin asked grimly.

"Oh, yes, at least if this hypothesis is right. Since the courageous Nelly Regan dispatched him, we can only speculate about his motives. He certainly wanted to discredit the experiment of a thousand women on a carrier at sea. As far as I am aware, he had no malice against you, Skipper. It may be that there was a synergy between his obsessions and Commander Hoy's growing insanity. He may also have believed, as Hoy himself probably came to believe, that the Office of Special Services, whose existence Hoy had created and whose credentials and instructions he had forged, actually existed. Somewhere deep in the government there was an agency that stood for the American way, the navy way, the patriot way."

"Was Digby opposed to women on the ship?" Mary Anne asked.

"I doubt it. He was interested in power, a power that was far beyond his reach in the real world but within his grasp in his fantasy world. I suspect he persuaded Chief Larsen to create those persuasive credentials in the print shop and was so impressed by them that he came to believe they were real, probably by the time of his disappearance."

"So you had two crazies, driving each other further round the bend?" the cardinal observed. "You do manage to get yourself into the damnedest situations, Blackwood."

I resisted the temptation to comment on who assigned me to such situations.

"I assumed that at night, when it was reasonably safe to move around, he went to another hiding place. When the wondrous Nelly told me about the puzzle of the keys, I began to have a vague sense that something else was going on. Why take the master key out of its locker? Finally, I realized that there were two reasons for doing so. The first was that the noise of the cutting away of the lock would alert him to the presence of the captain and the chief master at Arms. The second was more important. Once a lock had been reinstalled in the door, he could enter his own quarters at leisure and thus hide in the one place where no one would search for him—the locked room from which he had disappeared."

"He was hiding in his own room all along, then?" Dick Dempsey exclaimed.

"Most of the time. He thought he had outsmarted everyone. Once the NIS investigators had left the ship and the new lock—with the same code as the old one—was installed, he assumed that he alone could gain entry to the cabin. When you and I entered it, Mary Anne, he was apparently out on one of his explorations of the ship. Perhaps Shorter told him about it. Or perhaps he had sensed your presence, from a trace of scent possibly. I speculate that he went into panic and then into total insanity, hence the attempt on your life, Megan, the next night."

"Poor man, he was really sick." She shook her head sadly.

"Oh, yes, he was all of that. And the genius of his sickness, if I may use that term, is that he is the kind of borderline personality who can link his sickness with that of other people and create collective sickness. . . . I should explain, incidentally, that unlike fictional detectives but like most people in the real world, I do not reason logically to the conclusions. Rather, the pieces flit around in my brain and then suddenly I see a picture. It fades and comes back and then it freezes in and I see it long enough to take it apart and see if it fits reality. . . ."

"It's all in his dissertation on William James," the cardinal observed genially.

"He was Irish, too," Megan informed us.

"Mother's name was Walsh, though as the saying goes, they kicked with their left foot. . . . In any case, the keys were the key, so to speak. The image began to form when the good Nelly Regan explained to me the odd matter of the keys. One disappeared with keys only if one intended to remain alive, on the ship, and use the keys for a hideout—though it took me too long to figure that out. Then I remembered the various descriptions of him I had heard from different people. They did not correlate. He was the protean man, shape shifter, a chameleon, as someone said."

"Not literally?" Dick Dempsey asked.

"Not like the fellow in *Deep Space 9*. Rather, his very blandness made it possible to take on many different psychological appearances, depending on the needs of the person he was dealing with. He manipulated and manipulated and manipulated, as borderline personalities must do to fight off the enemies in the totally hostile world in which they perceive themselves as living."

"They used to call them sociopaths," the Cardinal

observed as he poured dessert wine for the bride-to-be and her maid of honor, with more ceremony than I thought the occasion required. "One out of five of my brother bishops are at least somewhat in that category."

"A conservative estimate . . . I was struck by the difference in the descriptions and how the picture of him in the chief master at arms' office didn't fit any of the descriptions. Then I recalled several people saying that he crept around the ship spying on possible offenders. Perhaps he had learned how to maneuver in the three thousand plus spaces on the ship with skill and ease. Moreover, maybe he had learned how to disguise himself to facilitate his investigation of malefactors. . . . I'm sure that you did not see anyone like him skulking outside your apartment at Christmastime, Mary Anne, yet there is every reason to believe he was there even then in some sort of simple disguise."

"And so we found those disguises in his room?"

"Precisely. By the morning of the shoot-out, I had determined that the locksmith, the young man who worked on the hold-back bar, and Chief Larsen, the printer, were all members of the patriot study group. There were two possibilities. Either Commander Shorter was the leader of a mutinous group, or the late and lamented Commander E. Rogers Hoy was alive and well, neither late nor lamented, and pursuing his reign of terror by more direct methods. He was using his cabin, the last place in which anyone might have expected to find him, as a base and then roaming the ship, perhaps as he had already done, in various simple disguises."

"A seaman, first and a Marine gunnery sergeant," the skipper said. "Ingenious."

"Oh, yes, nothing if not ingenious. How many seamen first are on the ship? Scores at any rate. He could join the food line and fit right in, an older career rating, so bland and ordinary that people would hardly notice him, sit at the table and eavesdrop, and no one would recognize what he was doing. If they should ask where he worked, he would have been vague and then quietly drifted away. He could slip into almost any section of the ship unnoticed and slip out again. Presumably, the only difference in this behavior before and after his disappearance was that after, he was presumed dead and was actually hiding much of the time in his own cabin. A bland, innocuous, seemingly harmless little man that one would not normally notice any more than the postman in G. K. Chesterton's famous story."

"Seems to me," the cardinal interjected, "that is a pretty good description of the self-image of someone I know."

I ignored his thrust, though admittedly it was well taken.

"Still, it was damn risky. He could have been caught," Commander Dempsey pointed out. "Eventually, he would have been caught. The seaman's role he could have gotten away with a little longer, but the gunny disguise was reckless. There aren't that many gunnies on the ship, air crews from the VMFA and sea marines."

"He could pretend that he was with the other whenever he encountered marines. On the one occasion when he saw the two together, he simply would drift back into the environment like he had done so often before. I would not be surprised if somewhere on the ship there was also a set of women's clothes, so that he could at ease slip into the women's quarters, too. Hence the rumors of his frequent sightings."

Both the women gasped.

"Are you sure, Blackie?" the bride-to-be exclaimed.

"I think it probable, but I can't prove it. Perhaps one of the patriots destroyed the evidence before we apprehended them. Or a woman ally of whom we are unaware."

"XO is right," the admiral-to-be said firmly. "We would have caught him."

"Doubtless, but I put it to you that he may have wanted to be caught."

"Wanted to be caught!" Milord Cronin exploded.

"Just as your predecessor of notorious memory wanted to be caught. . . . We know nothing about the world of the borderline, or if you will, the sociopath. I suspect that it is much like Signor Alighieri's hell, isolated, cold, lonely, frozen in despair. The person trapped in this hell wants to get caught eventually. The demands of fighting off his enemies become too much. Better to finally let them destroy you. I note, milord, that your predecessor did just that."

"Yeah, but he was crazy!"

Somewhat hollow laughter from the dinner party.

The cardinal personally served coffee and tea to the company and then poured an expensive cognac into Waterford brandy snifters. He presented me with a snifter of Baileys Irish Cream, murmured something about "South Side Irish." Megan gazed lustfully at the Baileys. Maybe she lived on the South Side of Green Bay.

"You have any proof he wanted to be caught?" the cardinal renewed the conversation.

"Oh, yes. During the morning of the shoot-out, when the air officer was leaning on the kid who sabotaged Megan's hold-back bar . . ."

"And I admired his courage every day for crawling under the plane just before launch."

"Courage he had, Margaret Mary, but no common sense. He probably was sorry he had to kill you, but orders are orders, especially from the real patriotic group in government. . . . Anyway, Commander Hoy in his gunnery sergeant modality stalked me . . . indeed twice."

"What!" everyone said in some kind of unison.

"I was on my way to join Mary Anne in the wardroom. The picture was about to freeze in my head, I was on the edge of seeing it clearly, when I heard someone walking the gallery deck behind me. I stopped and the someone stopped. I felt a warning prickle in the back of my neck. I turned round and saw this somewhat superannuated marine with red hair behind me, maybe ten yards. I knew it was Hoy, alive or dead, and probably alive. I stared at him, fingered my six iron . . . well, the skipper's six iron . . . and he turned and walked away."

"And then you saw all the pieces come together. No wonder you were so excited at breakfast."

"I did not think, Mary Anne, that he would be so dumb as to stalk you, especially since he was waiting for me after breakfast and followed me back to my cabin. I turned to him again, brandished my weapon, and said something of the sort of 'Get the hell out of here!' He did."

"You knew it was Hoy?" Mary Anne, white-faced, clung to her husband's hand.

"As sure as I knew that I was John Blackwood Ryan. I also knew that his number was up, that we had him, and that we would put an end soon to his reign of terror. I did not realize, alas, that it would end so violently. Perhaps because I was still underestimating how deeply he had deteriorated."

"He wanted to destroy everyone, didn't he, Blackie?" she said.

"He wanted rather to eliminate his enemies one by one. Whenever he disposed of one enemy there was another that bounced up in front of him, like the dummies in commando courses. You bayonet one and another is upon you. He was driven to destroy the various people he dragged before captain's mast because they were a threat to his reign as the best XO in the navy and his evidence of Captain Cronin's incompetence. But we must not underestimate the depths of his fear. And also his need for enemies to sustain his fear, which was finally the only motive he knew."

"So even his allies finally became enemies?" Mary Anne said.

"Right. Such terrible threats that he had to order their executions. I suspect we would be able to find in his past history other such collective neuroses, though none so spectacular as this one, at the end of which he broke those who were his strongest supporters and got away with it by using others to do it."

"Like that poor kid who killed Wade and Ericsson," Mary Anne said with a shudder.

The cardinal refilled her cognac snifter.

"And the others who raped her after she was dead. On his orders. He subverted five of the fifteen men in the patriot group, poor Chief Larsen, the locksmith, and three innocent kids. Ugh!"

"That only emerged as a certainty after we found the forged documents in his room, his credentials from the OSS as he called his fantasized organization, using the same initials as the World War II predecessor of the CIA—including an order to execute them as traitors. The same credentials and orders that his accomplice showed the air officer when he was accused of sabotaging Megan's F-18."

"Poor, poor men." Megan sighed with a Mother Superior's piety. Sincere piety of course.

"How could they have believed that?" Commander Dempsey wondered.

"They wanted to believe that somewhere in the government there was an agency of "good guys" who were looking out for American ideals, the kind of secret and all powerful group so beloved by films and TV. Your mission, Mr. Phelps, should you choose to accept it . . . Moreover, we know how skillful he was at discerning and manipulating the weaknesses of his victims."

"One of my predecessors did that to the whole Archdiocese of Chicago," The cardinal remarked, "for seventeen years. To the end, to the absolute bitter end, he continued to manipulate people successfully."

"And," I added, "toward the end, he wanted to get caught and was caught."

"After that second encounter, I knew that I had seen Digby Hoy, that he was alive, and that he was behind much of the mischief on the ship. I went back to my quarters, clarified the picture in my head, and realized that just as he was disguising himself as someone who would never be noticed, he was hiding much of the time in the last place we would have looked, his own locked room from which he had disappeared. It was an ingenious scheme, madcap and destined to fail, as you say, Skipper, but dazzling in its elegance and simplicity. I mistakenly assumed that he was in retreat, though it wouldn't have made much difference in the outcome if I had realized how crazed he had become. Then Johnny Larkin told me about your being hustled down a corridor by a marine gunnery sergeant, Mary Anne, and I knew we had to take quick action."

"Which you surely did." She smiled in gratitude, which I certainly did not deserve.

"If I had known there was going to be a firefight, I might have told Johnny to bring his whole gang, but they might have got in the way in the corridor and we would have suffered worse casualties."

"Don't worry about Johnny," Megan admonished me. "He has a medal for bravery, a brand-new oak leaf, the woman he loves, and enough stories to tell the rest of his life."

"And the two crazy men will be locked up for the rest of their lives," the cardinal said, as if to reassure me.

"Will they?" I said skeptically. "I wonder. It may be that the will to manipulate has been extirpated from Rogers Hoy. Perhaps he will merely remain in the hospital wing of Portsmouth Naval Prison for the rest of his life, weeping every day, as surely Chief Larsen will.

But consider Hoy's success at spinning a dangerous collective neurosis on the *Langley*, a neurosis that was responsible for three deaths and for the destruction of the careers of several naive young men. If he decides to manipulate the navy and the law and psychiatrists, I wouldn't bet against him."

Mary Anne shivered. Milord Cronin offered her a refill on the cognac; she waved it off.

"Not as long as I'm an admiral in the United States Navy," Dave Cronin said vigorously. "No way."

Patently, he meant it.

"What will happen to the sailors who fell under his spell?" the cardinal wondered.

"The aviation machinist's mate who tried to kill our fair maid of honor will get some credit for spilling out all the truth when he learned that Hoy was a wounded and captured fraud. The men who executed Ericsson and Wade and raped her dead body will receive precious little leniency when they argue that they thought they were doing the work of a supersecret government agency. Long prison terms, at best."

"Very long," the new admiral agreed. "Perhaps some clemency later on."

"Digby really was prowling the women's quarters?" Mary Anne asked. "It wasn't just our imagination?"

I sighed. "Doubtless he was but there were too many apparitions, some of them, as you remarked that final morning, of his being seen at the same time in different places. I submit that there might have been two Rogers Hoys wandering the ship, two wraiths, one human and the other not."

"Two!" Milord Cronin protested, as he usually does when faced with evidence of the uncanny.

"Indeed. The first was the demented human who enjoyed tormenting and violating women. The second . . . Let's call it a psychic energy convened by the fear and the terror on the ship, the collective neuroses, the hatreds he had stirred up, and a psychically sensitive individual who, as it were, gathered together all these swirling emotional energies and projected them into an image of terror for those especially afraid of Commander Hoy."

"Like me," Mary Anne observed ruefully.

"With reason," her groom assured her.

"Someone did that deliberately!" Commander Dempsey exclaimed.

"Probably not. Such individuals are intense, easily confused, and generally unaware of the projections they are capable of creating. The cardinal and I have not been without past experiences of such phenomena."[1]

Mary Anne raised an eyebrow, ever so slightly. I nodded even more slightly. We agreed that the channel was Chaplain O'Malley.

"The spooky Commander Hoy won't still be on the ship when I go back?" Commander Dempsey wondered.

"Not as long as the real Commander Hoy is still alive."

"Let me summarize . . ." Dave Cronin began.

"My husband," Mary Anne squeezed his arm, "that is my husband-to-be, keeps a journal. He won't show it to me, not even the passages about me."

"Pornographic, probably," our red-haired novice remarked in an uncharacteristic outburst that made everyone laugh.

Both the bride and the groom blushed furiously.

"Doubtless," I said.

"Anyway, to continue my summary . . ." The new admiral seemed quite pleased with himself, as well he might. "Digby embarked on the *Langley* determined to make trouble. He created for himself not merely the most obvious neuroses among the people for whom he was the immediate C.O., he also manipulated various other of his shipmates, most notably, as far as we know, Commander Shorter, who was deeply offended by the changes in the

---

[1] In *Angels of September* and *Happy Are Those Who Mourn*.

navy and some of the members of the so-called patriot study group. Digby also prowled the ship, looking for signs of disciplinary laxity, often using disguises that made him for all practical purposes invisible. As time went on, he became more, ah, deranged. In some instances, he used forged documents, created by Chief Larsen, to prove that he worked for a top-secret government agency concerned about protecting traditional American patriotic values. He received threats that were probably not just imaginary. He felt that to complete his work—and he may well have begun to believe his own forgeries—he had to disappear. He planned his own disappearance with the help of Commander Shorter, who may have had reasons of his own for wanting to cause trouble. With the cooperation of the locksmith, who was part of the patriot group, he obtained keys to his own quarters, which enabled him to do this. He hid in the extra bunk of Shorter's cabin while we searched for him. Then, when he deemed it safe, he returned to his own cabin and continued his now apparently invisible operations. Two of his allies somehow found out that he was still alive and approached him, presumably with offers of help. With more forged documents, he ordered their execution and the necrophiliac rape of Lieutenant Commander Wade, thus binding his allies more closely to him. When he discovered that we had access to his room, he grew more desperate and planned the sabotage of the launch of Megan's plane, again producing documents from Washington ordering such action. When this failed, he tried to kidnap Mary Anne, a desperate action that Bishop Ryan's timely action frustrated."

"Sounds like Bishop Ryan is a character from a Tom Clancy novel," the cardinal mused.

"That's my cousin Jack," I replied.

"Thereupon," the skipper continued resolutely, "he opened fire on us, wounding Lieutenant Larkin, fortunately not seriously, and fell afoul of my six iron wielded by Jack Ryan's cousin. Commander Shorter, apparently aroused by the sound of gunfire, emerged from the next cabin, drew a side arm he was wearing in violation of regulations, and took aim at the fallen Lieutenant Larkin. Yeoman Regan fired first, killing Commander Shorter. Then Chief Larsen appeared with an automatic weapon but was, ah, disarmed by our reenforcements."

Megan blushed. "Poor man, I hit him with your five iron."

"I know that, Megan. . . . What I want to know," the skipper continued, "is why Shorter and Larsen came to his rescue. Even had they succeeded in killing all of us, had they not signed on to a doomed cause?"

"About Glendenning Shorter," I said with my patented sigh, "we can only speculate because of the accuracy of the yeoperson's aim. Perhaps by that time he was already around the bend. Perhaps he wanted to bring down as many of his enemies as he could. By his own admission, Chief Larsen thought he was defending an agent of the real American government. He may still think that."

"And are there still people on the *Langley*," the XO (who would return to the ship after the wedding) asked, "who were on Hoy's side?"

"I wouldn't be surprised if there are. Some of them may believe that he was a good man who was done in by the navy brass or even that he worked for the *real* American government as he claimed. They may always think that. However, after the violence on oh-three level, they are not likely to act on their beliefs."

"That about wraps it up, I guess." The skipper nodded his head.

"It's all crazy," his wife added. "How can there be such people in the world and how can they get such power?"

"Our world is a less-than-perfect place," I offered. "Consider that for a half decade fifty years ago, the two most powerful countries in Europe were dominated by men like Rogers Hoy: Hitler and Stalin. Two bland and dull men whose dementia caused the death of at least a hundred million people. We won this one, at some cost indeed, but order prevailed over chaos, if only just barely. Sometimes 'only just barely' is the best we can do against the mystery of evil."

A grim silence descended on our festive evening. It was too much for the lady leatherneck.

She stood up, cognac glass in hand.

"I propose a toast to Bishop Blackie, who saved the *Langley* from the demons."

Much to my embarrassment, glasses were raised around the table.

"Without whom we would not be here!" Dick Dempsey added.

"Without whom some of us might not be alive," Mary Anne smiled at me.

"Without whom I would never have my fair bride or my admiral's star."

"Best mystery-solving auxiliary bishop in the archdiocese, arguably in the country," Milord Cronin continued the toast.

"Blackie!" they all cried.

There was only one possible answer to such accolades. Like the kid in the Dickens story, I held out my brandy snifter.

"Could I have another glass of Baileys, please?"

Exercising the immemorial right of Irish women to have the last word, Megan concluded, "Me too, Your Eminence!"

The cardinal filled both our glasses.

"I propose a counter toast," I said. "To two institutions of long history and great achievements that are trying to catch up with a changing world and particularly with the changing roles of women, the United States Navy and the Catholic Church. On the basis of my recent observations, the former is making more rapid progress than the latter. Both, I presume, will survive and eventually flourish!"

"Amen," Cardinal Cronin and Captain Monahan replied in unison.

COMING SOON IN HARDCOVER

Robert B. Parker

Family Honor

PUTNAM